HEAVEN'S MATCH

Caroline Ponessa

For Sadie. My first reader, favorite wife and most patient fan.

Prologue

She groans in acknowledgment as I place the pills into her hand. I rub gently on her shoulder, comforting her as she raises them into her mouth.

She swallows down hard and drifts softly into sleep.

PART ONE

Hannah: Week One, Wednesday

I press my right thumbnail into the cuticle of my left, pushing down hard and digging across in an attempt to slice the excess, flirting the thin line before it draws blood. I've never had a manicure in my life, which feels painfully obvious now. As if my slightly unkempt nails are doing an offense to the pure grandeur of it all.

My eyes drift down to the geometric grout lines on the floor. The tiles are hexagonal, a deep reddish brown—the color of a clay flower pot. Very Spanish Mediterranean. I follow the lines across the foyer up and around the curved staircase, the dark wood railing contrasting with eggshell stucco, natural light flooding beautifully through the propped opened doors. They're thick mahogany, floor-to-ceiling. No doubt heavy, no doubt expensive. Whoever built this place thought of all the details. All the things that "add value", as Dad would say. Growing up in a real estate family, it's a switch I can't shut off. Constantly evaluating, appraising, comparing.

I check my watch again, shifting anxiously as I sit on the foyer's solo loveseat. 7:24 a.m. Six minutes to go. A man dressed in dark jeans and a black t-shirt walks in, nodding a brief acknowledgment in my direction as he passes. He's the fifth person to do so since I arrived here ten minutes prior. I put my hand to my mouth to cover a yawn. I used to be a morning person. Up with the birds, seize the day, all that carpe diem stuff. That was back before, well, everything. Now my alarm rings out like a vexation, the curse of another day. But I knew I couldn't hit snooze today. Not on day one.

The commute in hadn't been nearly as nightmarish as the horror stories of Los Angeles traffic had led me to believe, just under an hour from my cousin's apartment in West Hollywood. A gorgeous drive once I reached the foothills of the Palisades, winding my way through summer green trees in my modest Toyota Rav 4, each home more extravagant than the previous, and fewer and farther between—the spaces between reflecting the difference between my own life and the lives of the people who own them. My destination was the final stop on the road, marked only by a gated entrance tucked among an expanse of greenery. The type of place you'd miss if you weren't specifically looking for it. The dial button on the callbox triggered a gruff voice asking me to scan my badge on the receiver. In one too many nervous words, I explained it was my first day so I didn't have one yet. The man on the other end mumbled something I couldn't make out before instructing me to park in the crew lot on the east base of the property. The gate swung open and I continued up the narrow tree-lined driveway about a half mile before veering right at the first fork, marked by a bronze PARKING sign. The trees cleared to reveal a sizable paved lot, eight or so cars scattered throughout about a quarter of the spots. Of course, I immediately sized them up against my own, choosing one next to a slightly rusted white Toyota Camry—the only car with a trade-in value less than my own. As I parked, I took stock of the two-story, three-stall "garage" off the side of the lot. Ivory stucco, Spanish-style, and just slightly smaller than the home I grew up in. If Toto had been in the front seat, I'd have told him we weren't in Minnesota anymore.

The air when I stepped outside was fresh, quiet but for the chirping of birds and rustling of wind through the tall oak trees. I shut the car door and bent down, giving myself one final check in the window. My makeup looked okay-ish. A flash of mascara around my hazel-green eyes, a dab of concealer here and there. Enough to cover a few frustrating acne scars but not to totally cover my freckles. I thumbed at the edges of my embarrassingly split light brown hair, kicking myself for not getting a haircut, the salon small talk something I just couldn't bring myself to stomach. When I took a step back, the curves of the door warped the reflection of my body like a fun house mirror. Admittedly, I wasn't sure how to dress for something like this. Business, business casual? I had no one to ask. I ultimately settled on a slim pair of black slacks and a blousy black button-down to give depth to my rail-thin frame. Very plain, very dull, very unlikely to draw undue attention.

An arrowed sign on the side of the parking lot directed me up a short stairwell behind the garage. It was then that I finally saw it, sprawling across the hilltop in all of its Spanish architectural glory.

The *villa*.

It was a bit surreal. Walking across the brown stone driveway, passing the iconic circular fountain at its center. Descending three steps down to the grand entrance, two pillars supporting the red-tiled overhang and waist-high stone lion statues flanking the open doorway. Stepping inside...

And now, waiting. Gaze down but ready to stand at attention with each passing staff member, most moving through the foyer without so much as a glance in my direction. I keep an eye on my watch, taking a deep breath while watching the numbers flip from 7:29 to 7:30.

As if on cue, a petite woman materializes into the foyer. She's older than the others I've seen thus far—her short pixie hair somewhere between gray and blonde. *Tammy Berg*. Uncle Craig told me she'd be greeting me, but that's about as much as I know. Her online presence is about as nonexistent as it can be in the year 2020. Full name, birth year, a smattering of former residences. Says a lot about a person when all you can find is the digital equivalent of a white pages listing.

"Hannah?"

"Yes!" I spring to my feet and extend my hand. She grabs it and shakes, incredibly firm. I see now just how petite she is, at least four inches shorter than my five-foot-six-inches. Her outfit is practical. Black blazer over a white blouse, straight black pants, sensible black flats. On her nose rests a pair of stylish translucent glasses, lending just a slight flair of personality to an otherwise indistinct look.

"Punctual. I like that. If there's one thing we always seem to be short on around here, it's time." I smile awkwardly at her compliment, happy to not disappoint but unsure of the appropriate way to respond.

"You'll have to bear with me. I don't usually do onboarding tours, but your uncle put in a special request and I just can't say no to Craig." My cheeks flush at his mention. The last thing I want is special treatment, for everyone here to know the only qualification I have for this job is direct lineage to the network's programming director.

A look of impatience grows on Tammy's face as she turns toward the hallway on the left side of the foyer, making it clear she's eager to get on with it.

"I'm not sure how much he prepped you," Tammy moves quickly, projecting her words to the air in front of her as walks, her gait short but purposeful. "I've known Craig for many, many years. Of course, my role now is as Paul's assistant."

I don't know nearly as much about this world as someone in my position should, but I know enough not to have to ask who Paul is. Paul Thomas. Show creator and showrunner. A man often referred to as The Godfather of reality television. He's top of the producer food chain here, the one who ultimately calls all the shots. That I didn't have to Google.

"It's easy to get lost, but you'll get the hang of it." Tammy leads me into a room I instantly recognize. Dark hardwood floors covered in a scattering of Persian rugs, burgundy walls adorned with paintings, long thick drapes covering the windows. Overall a much moodier vibe compared to the brightness of the foyer. In the center of the room are three large taupe couches arranged in a U-shape around a rustic wood coffee table, facing an ornate stone fireplace mantle that holds a well-curated selection of candles and vases. The type of professional staging I've only ever seen when my parents used to drag me to the Parade of Homes. "Family bonding", they called it. For my brother and me, it always just felt like another excuse to work on the weekends.

"This is what we refer to as the 'sitting' room, which probably sounds a bit antiquated but, quite literally, that's what it is. Cameras have access to the entire place, though most of our scheduled programming takes place in here. Contestant conversations, date announcements. You know, you've seen the show. That said, as much as the weather allows, they try to shoot outside. And I think you'll pretty quickly understand why," Tammy says as she pushes open a set of heavy wooden double doors.

I've seen it on television of course, but experiencing the famous courtyard in person dares to take my breath away. I manage to keep it, inhaling the scent of fresh lilacs and ocean air —the deep blue of the limitless Pacific on the horizon. "Wow. This is… insane," I hear myself say as I descend a short staircase to the pool. Tammy chuckles knowingly, remaining beside the door as I take it all in. The water is stunning turquoise, semi-circle shaped with an elevated hot tub butted up to its flat side. Chairs and couches line the deck, lush greenery and flowers making for a beautiful backdrop from any angle. On the very back edge hugging the hillside is a small casita, complete with its own open-air bar. The sight brings me back to a family vacation we took to Mexico when I was in the eighth grade. All-inclusive, a steady diet of sugary virgin daiquiris and poolside nachos. I felt like the luckiest girl in the world. Standing here now, a lot of people's dream job at my fingertips, it still feels hard to imagine ever feeling that way again.

I turn back to Tammy who is now holding open the courtyard's side gate as a cavalry of landscapers in beige overalls carry in overflowing floral arrangements, exorbitant bouquets where their heads should be. As the final passes through, Tammy shuts it securely and gives me a nod, signaling that it's time to head back inside.

The rest of the tour flies by as Tammy power walks me through the remainder of the villa, bustling with more and more scrambling crew members by the minute. She shows me the kitchen, the study, the wine cellar, a handful of other rooms that serve as confessional interview spaces and set storage. We pause slightly longer at the crew break room, which looks surprisingly like what you'd find in any run-of-the-mill office building. Circular white cafe tables, plain black chairs, a long counter with a few microwaves and a fridge. In the corner, two black futon couches face a large mounted flatscreen television. It has none of the extravagances of the previous spaces. Tammy explains that this is where the crew convenes for daily scrum, 9 a.m. sharp.

We move upstairs next, where she shows me the contestant bedrooms. Four twin beds per room, each with its own bathroom and "Four sinks because we all know women don't like to share," Tammy quips. I ask where the lead stays, and she explains that he's kept separately in a private suite on the eastern edge of the property—an area it's "highly unlikely you'll ever be needed." And that's more than fine by me.

As we descend the stairwell back to the foyer where we began, I question whether I'll ever get my bearings in this place. My stomach quivers at the thought. Getting forever lost in this maze of luxury. Maybe it would be better that way.

Tammy's phone dings, interrupting my anxiety. She pulls it out of her pocket and reads the message. "Ah, perfect. Seth's up at the control room, which just so happens to be our last stop," she states. From what I understand, Seth is, for all intents and purposes, my supervisor. A field producer designated to oversee newbie production assistants like myself.

Tammy leads me outside, triggering my confusion. I expected the control room to be inside the villa itself. We head down the side of the driveway and I soon find myself right back where I started—the crew parking lot. It's full of cars now, the doors of the garage wide open as a barrage of men and women in black shirts carry production equipment in and out. I do my best to keep pace with Tammy as she weaves through them, climbs the stairwell and pushes open the door.

What's inside the room floods my brain with sensory overload. A wall of monitors. Rows of tables covered in colorfully flashing buttons. My vision spins at the sight as the imposter syndrome sets in, proactively clenching my stomach to resist the quiver, the subtle little churn, the gremlin making itself known.

"Hannah?" Tammy calls out to me. She's already made her way across to the other side of the room. I feel the heat in my cheeks as I shake myself out of temporary paralysis and hurry over to her. Next to her is a man who I can only presume is Seth. He looks to be in his late twenties, about my age, which I imagine is far older than most of the people he's accustomed to managing. He's dressed in the same black shirt and pants uniform I've noticed on pretty much everyone—only on him, it looks a bit more... shlubby. Maybe it's the patchy beard or the fact that his curly thinning hair looks like it hasn't seen a shower in weeks. Behind him stands a bright-eyed platinum blonde girl beaming at me eagerly as if I'm about to be her new best friend. She, most certainly, does not look my age.

"Hannah, I'm Seth," he abruptly shoves an expectedly clammy hand my way. "And this is Taylor. She's the other first-year PA."

"It's so nice to meet you, Hannah! I'm glad to not be the only newbie on set." Taylor practically bounces as she grabs my hand enthusiastically. I smile politely, wondering if we're even remotely close to the same generation. Tammy wishes me luck with the rest of the day and quickly scampers down the stairs, leaving me alone with this strange little duo.

Seth hands us each an organizational chart. There are so many names and lines that I struggle to make heads or tails of it. For now, I decide my best bet is to focus on the top. Beneath Paul Thomas - Showrunner are two names: Jeremy Rowe and Whitney Erickson. Both Executive Producers. Both people I definitely ought to know.

The next hour is spent running through the production assistant basics. Despite the monotonous droning of Seth's voice, I manage to pay close attention as he describes exactly what we would—and would not—be doing. We are production assistants, not associate producers, and are not permitted to act as such. We are permitted to make coffee runs and assist with any number of random producer requests. These requests may at times seem strange, but we are to perform them no questions asked. On the rare occasion we are permitted to sit in on confessional interviews, we are to do so silently.

I glance at Taylor and wonder if she's at all discouraged by the prospect of repetitive, thankless grunt work. A few years prior, I certainly would have been. But now I find myself quite relieved. Grunt work I can do, my nerves actually calmed by the tedious simplicity of it all. Run when asked. Speak when spoken to. It's shaping up to be just the type of distraction Uncle Craig promised it would be. After all, idle hands are the devil's workshop. And this is much, much better than the alternative.

Tammy: Week One, Wednesday

She struck me as a bit odd. The girl, Hannah. But then again, people have probably said that about me a time or two in my sixty-two years on this earth. I was a bit skeptical when Craig, her uncle, first called. Folks don't take kindly to nepotism around here. But then he explained her situation. All she'd been through. Tough draw for someone her age.

I exhale a sigh as I pass back through the front doors into the pandemonium of the villa. Day one brings a chaotic excitement that can overwhelm even the longest-standing vets. *Keep yourself level, Tamara.* My father's voice rings in my head. Reiterated until I learned how not to let my five older brothers get a rise out of me. I duck under a moving boom mic and step into the break room, setting up shop at one of the tables in the back. A half hour until Paul arrives, I've got just enough time to gather the usual run-of-show intel. Schedule changes, expense updates, notable set guests. Premiere night always comes with an excess of fanfare.

"Morning, Tammy. *Love* that color on you." I hadn't noticed Whitney in the room when I walked in, but the unoriginal jab at my fashion sense instantly alerts me to her presence. I return the greeting with a halfhearted smile, having long since abandoned any effort to like her. I tried in earnest, initially, but everything about her just reeks of arrogance. A scent that's only gotten worse since Paul promoted her to executive producer three seasons ago. Whitney's got on her Sunday best today, a get-up that quite frankly looks pretty damn miserable to me. Skin tight red dress, white blazer, black heels—brand name, couldn't tell you which one if I cared to try. And, of course, that signature glossy dyed blonde hair she probably spent way too much money and time getting professionally blown out on her way in this morning. Lipstick on a pig, isn't that the saying? Feels a bit harsh but, hey, if the stiletto fits the hoof.

Resolve to not waste any more brain power thinking about Whitney, I get back to the multi-tasking at hand. The minutes move fast, but so do I. Behind every strong man is a stronger woman, after all. My focus is lasered on my inbox when I feel a set of hands enthusiastically squeeze my shoulders.

"Game day, Tammy, game day!" I don't have to turn to know who they belong to. There's not a person on set who would dare put their paws on me without the expectation of getting a swift elbow to the ribs in return. I guess I've just got a soft spot for Jeremy.

"Yeah, yeah," I brush him off affably, getting through one final email as the rest of the crew starts to file in for daily scrum. I stow my laptop and move to my preferred spot. Standing at the back of the room means I can make a quick escape to handle anything urgent—and, more importantly, means I can keep an eye on everyone. This includes the new girl, Hannah, who is scrambling to get the morning's spread of bagels, fruit and coffee set out on the counter amidst a barrage of impatient hands. It relieves me to see she's already making herself useful. The only thing worse than a nepotism hire is a nepotism hire without any work ethic.

"One last victory lap?" Paul appears at my side, playfully leaning his weight into me, dressed to impress the big-money advertisers in a navy suit and crisp white shirt.

"Believe it when I see it," I respond. He looks down at me with a wry smile. I just saw him yesterday but, somehow, it seems there are already new lines on his face, more salt overtaking the pepper in his thick side-parted hair. I still remember the first day I met him. A fresh-faced young buck, chest puffed out with big ideas and something to prove. I had my doubts about the shift in assignment, having spent the latter ten years working the desk of a crusty old network executive in the twilight of his career. Paul, on the other hand, was new to this. Not to the industry, but to the high-stakes world of creating your own television show. There was much to learn, and I questioned whether or not I was the right person to guide him through it. Sixteen seasons later, I think we have our answer to that.

But with every day that goes by, the spark dims more and more in his pale blue eyes. Perhaps more than anyone, I know how the last few years have worn on him. The increasing pressure of declining ratings, long conversations with the network to convince them it's only temporary, that things will turn back around. Generally speaking, early fifties is young to be contemplating retirement in this business. But, all things considered, I can't say I blame him. Better that than be shown the door. At least then he would leave with his pride intact.

There's no sign of that now, though, as Paul cheerily jaunts to the front of the room, singing "it's the most wonderful time of the year." The chatter in the room subsides as the crew directs their attention toward their fearless commander-in-chief. Jeremy and Whitney assume their positions at his right. Seeing the two men side by side, the resemblance is striking. About fifteen years his junior, Jeremy is just as long, lean and handsome—a carbon copy in a khaki suit.

"Good morning, beautiful people!" Paul's voice booms. "I can't tell you how happy I am to be back here, back *home* with all of you... There are lots of favorite familiar faces in this room, but I'd also like to extend a warm welcome to all the new ones. And, with that, extend a reminder for the rest of you... be nice to the first-year PAs. Even when they get your coffee order wrong. That said, mine's a triple Americano and don't you forget it." A laugh reverberates throughout the room, a different version of essentially the same joke he tells every year. My eyes find Hannah again, nervously smiling from where she sits in the corner of the room. The other new PA is beside her—peppy blonde with curled hair pulled back into a bright pink scrunchie. Will be quite interesting to see how the two of them will get along. This environment has a tendency to breed competition, but something about Hannah's aura makes it hard for me to believe she's that type.

"I'd also like to start with a thank you. I know a lot of work has already gone into making this season a success," Paul continues. "More than ever, I'm excited for what we have in store. Patrick is unlike any lead we've had..."

"Blonde?" interrupts a wisecrack from the crew.

"No—nice." The room again fills with laughter at Paul's quick rebuttal. "But in all sincerity, I couldn't be more thrilled to be joining Patrick on this journey. I think everyone in this room can agree that if anyone deserves to find their soulmate, it's a genuine kid like him." I nod along. Though the "nice guy" line was said in jest, there's certainly truth to it. Especially when you consider the size of the egos on most of our past leads. There's an irony in there somewhere about the "safe choice" being the most unsafe of all. A show like this could eat a boy like Patrick alive.

"Now, it's no secret that the ratings have been a thorn in our side the last few seasons. I will take ownership for that. Admittedly, this old dog has been reluctant to learn new tricks." As Paul speaks, Jeremy looks on at him earnestly, hanging on his every word. Whitney's gaze, conversely, lords over the rest of us, scanning the room like a Rottweiler in a choke collar. "But after some convincing from my youthful sidekicks here," Paul's words linger momentarily as he gestures to the two of them, "I can promise you, this season will feel different."

It's far from the first time Paul's uttered those words at a season kick-off. But, for the first time in sixteen seasons, knowing full well the pressure he's up against, it's the first time I actually believe them.

Patrick: Week One, Wednesday

I pinch my fingers around the knot, straightening my tie in the mirror. I'm still not entirely sold on the tiny flowers, another ultra-skinny tie with a trendy micro print. Normally a more traditional solids guy, the wardrobe department insisted it was just the touch I needed to "add a little personality." Kind of a dagger, right? I wish they'd just lied and told me it would make the blue in my eyes pop.

Offense aside, they did knock it out of the park. Deep blue slim fit suit, crisp white shirt, freshly shined brown loafers. I could have never put this together on my own. I look and feel like myself, only better. My hand runs through my hair, pushing the blonde bangs up off my forehead, tucking them casually in place behind my right ear. A nervous habit I didn't know I had until last season's fans gave it a life of its own. And I mean that literally—a fan actually created an account called @PatrickOlsensHair. All it is is pictures of me cropped at the eyebrows.

"Ready, Pat?" A familiar voice calls out from the hall. It's Isaiah, my assigned producer for the season. I exhale deeply, give my hair another run and say goodbye to life as I know it.

Isaiah's leaning in the open door frame, clipboard in hand, his short black afro grazing the top of the frame. Ridiculous as it sounds, he was one of my conditions for agreeing to this whole thing. If a producer was going to be coordinating my schedule down to the second—when I eat, when I sleep, when I take a piss—it had to be someone I like. And rarer yet, after getting to know him last season, Isiah's someone I actually trust. As paid friendships go, he's as good as it gets.

"Last chance to turn back," he raises an eyebrow, looking down at me. At six-foot-one, I'm moderately tall, but Isaiah is massive. Six-six, big and broad, a former college basketball player who keeps up the physique. Sports are the common ground that bonded the two of us to begin with. I was never quite good enough to play anything at the college level like he was, but that certainly didn't stop my passion. Basketball, football, baseball, you name it, Isaiah and I BS about it all. It's a refreshing change of conversation from what you get with a lot of these wannabe-highbrow LA types.

"Really?" I play along with the bit. "Awesome. I'll just sneak out the side."

"Hell no. You're stuck now." He laughs loudly at his own joke. Isaiah's one of those people, the kind that are amused by just about everything. He laughs too much, too loud and at inappropriate times. But it's so dang infectious and genuine that you can't possibly hold it against him. As his laughter comes down, he gestures with his clipboard down the hall in an "after you" type of motion. A flush of anxiety washes over my entire body. It's finally time.

The lead suite, where I stay, is a long walk from the other side of the villa, something that's going to take a little getting used to. Last season I was right in the thick of it. Bunking with all the other guys, a revolving door of production crew members milling about. Don't get me wrong—the setup in the suite is absolutely unreal. It's double the size of my apartment with all the luxury of a hotel I can't afford. But being so far away from the action is a bit, well, isolating, I guess.

"You feeling ready for this?" Isaiah asks earnestly as we make our way down the hall.

"I'm feeling like we're not even outside yet and I'm already sweating through my suit," I reply, eliciting another of his laughs.

"Hey, man, that's normal." Isaiah's laughter subsides and he takes a more serious tone. "I won't lie to you, tonight is going to be the toughest. Live TV is a gauntlet." He says it as if I don't already know. As if the live premiere isn't what's kept me up at night for the last three weeks. "Once you've got night one under your belt, it's smooth sailing."

Somehow, I doubt that. I never quite got over the jitters last season and I was just a contestant. The lead bears an entirely different level of pressure. Cameras on you constantly. Week after week of live eliminations. Breaking up with women over and over again with an audience of millions.

Isaiah stops in his tracks. My silence has not gone unnoticed. He puts a reassuring hand on my shoulder. "Come on, man. Have a little faith in yourself. You got this." He pulls his phone from his back pocket and his brown eyes lock with mine. "If you tell anyone I showed you this, I'll deny it. And then I'll kill you."

He pulls open his social feed and types @PatrickOlsen into the search bar, prompting an eyebrow raise from me. As protocol goes, I'm supposed to be completely quarantined from any outside media, so this is a big no-no. Isaiah must really think I need it.

Preparing my heart for two straight months of @PatrickOlsen on my TV

Season hasn't even started yet and @PatrickOlsen is already my favorite lead

@PatrickOlsen is fine as hell and you won't convince me otherwise

Seriously though, what's a girl gotta do to meet a guy like @PatrickOlsen?

@PatrickOlsen is almost too pure. WBN must protect him at all costs.

Convinced my husband to style his hair like @PatrickOlsen for premiere night. It's... not the same.

"See, Pat? You've got absolutely nothing to worry about. America loves you," Isaiah states.

Having just broken code to put my mind at ease, I don't have the heart to tell him it only made the pressure worse.

—

It's early evening in the courtyard but the California heat is showing no sign of letting up, the breeze off the Pacific granting little reprieve for the sucker in the dark suit.

"I always knew you were cute, but I'll be damned if you're not downright studly!" Jeremy sidesteps a group of producers, grasping my shoulder with one hand and extending his other. I grab it, my sweaty palm betraying any illusion of confidence. "How you settling in, bud? Liking the new digs?" I'm about to respond when Whitney appears, as if a middle schooler at a sleepover just chanted Bloody Mary three times in a bathroom mirror.

"Save the flirting for later, boys," she snides, eyes shifting with impatience. "Can someone get Patrick mic'd already? Reg is on his way." Before I can blink, a producer's cold hands are up my shirt, winding a microphone cord from my waist to my collar. I thank the young woman awkwardly as Whitney stands by, up downing me judgmentally as though I've already managed to do something wrong in the mere thirty seconds I've been here. It's the type of treatment I've come to expect from her. Isaiah told me not to take it personally, that she's like that to everyone. But there's obviously something more. She's not just in the camp that I'm not rugged, sexy or interesting enough to be the lead, she founded it and sold t-shirts.

"It's good to be home!" A voice booms from the side gate of the courtyard as Reg, the show's longtime host, bursts through with his usual fanfare. Thick head of silver hair, dressed to the nines in a light gray three-piece suit. He looks the same as always, as if they keep him preserved on ice until it's time to thaw him out for a new season. Everyone loves him, of course. He and his late wife were the first marriage to come out of one of those match game television dating shows back in the sixties. Personally, I'm not sold. Something about the way he hangs around set, passing glances and questionable lines at just about every woman who walks by. It's like he gets off on it, knowing he's untouchable, knowing the network will forever brush it off like it's no big deal. "He's just from a different time." You know, the same old excuse everyone gives their Grandpa. And you can't fire Grandpa.

"Patrick, my boy," Reg saunters over and puts his reptilian hands on my shoulders, as if he's trying to remind me who's in control. "It's *so* wonderful to see you again."

"It's good to see you too, Reg," I lie.

"Five minutes!" A shout rings over the scrambling crew. A producer signals for Reg and I to take our seats. The interview is set up poolside, him in the chair, me opposite in the white loveseat. The set lights blind me when I sit down. I blink hard, seeing stars in the backs of my eyelids, the high-frequency buzz of the cameras ringing in my ears. There's a soft padding on my forehead and I open my eyes to a crew member swiftly blotting away my sweat. I run a hand through my hair, self-conscious of the sweat pooling in my armpits and my low back. Meanwhile, Reg sits completely relaxed, one leg crossed over the other as if he's enjoying Sunday brunch at the stuffy country club he undoubtedly belongs to. His smug sense of calm has the opposite effect on my nerves, so I turn my focus to the feed monitor off to the side of the cameras. I study the quadrants, an angle of us from each camera with the fourth quadrant displaying the live network feed. A front-row seat to my unease.

"Take a breath, Pat." I hear Isaiah's voice and search a sea of crew faces until I find his. We lock eyes and he lowers his hand, mouthing "relax." I hear Reg chuckling at the interaction, dripping with condescension to the rookie on his left. My fist clenches. Surely I can't be the only lead in the history of *Heaven's Match* who's had to actively resist the urge to punch an old man squarely in the jaw.

"One minute!" Another time call. I press down on my knee firmly to stop the shake, forcing my heel flat to the ground. I stop my sweaty hand before it gets to my hair, opting instead to briefly close my eyes and take Isaiah's advice of a slow deep breath.

"Live in three... two... one..."

"Good evening, America. And welcome to the live season premiere of *Heaven's Match*. As always, I'm your host, Reginald Simpson," fifteen years of introductions snake effortlessly off his tongue.

"For the next two months, we'll join America's boy next door, Patrick Olsen, for a once-in-a-lifetime opportunity to find his perfect match." I bristle at the extra emphasis he puts on "once-in-a-lifetime." A subtle reminder from the network about how grateful I should feel to have been chosen above their many other options.

"As every lead before Patrick has learned, it won't be easy. Each Wednesday, we'll share in all the emotional highs and lows of his journey, culminating in a weekly live elimination where he'll choose which ladies he'd like to continue exploring a relationship with and which to send home broken-hearted... But we can't move forward without first reflecting back. Let's take a look at how we got here..."

The director mutters something into his headset and the live feed flips over to a montage of clips from my appearance on last season's show. I keep my eyes locked on the monitor as Reg calmly sips his water beside me, reliving the most vulnerable experience of my life with no sound.

If it were up to me, I never would have even applied to be a contestant. My over-involved sister-in-law took care of that for me. You can imagine my surprise when I received an email in the middle of the work day to schedule a casting interview. My first thought was "no way, no how." I had never watched the show but knew enough women who did to assume it wasn't really my thing. Dating shows like this were for the loud, overly confident types. Peacocks ostentatiously fanning their proverbial feathers in exchange for fifteen minutes of fame. But the more the email burned a hole in my inbox, the more I thought "what do I have to lose?" I was a twenty-eight-year-old financial advisor living with three college buddies in a subpar apartment in Minneapolis. Everyone around me was getting into serious relationships but, hard as I tried, I just couldn't make the dating scene work. Nearly thirty years old and I'd never once been in love. Or anything even close to it, really.

The shouting of the countdown brings me back to the couch, the courtyard, the villa. One year but a million lifetimes from that world I once knew. Crazy how fast things change.

"Wow." Reg turns to me and I feel my heart rate rise again as we transition back to live coverage. "Seeing all of that, the raw emotion, the drama. What made you want to do all of this again?"

"You know, I wasn't really sure if I did," I laugh nervously, feeling the eyes of the producers on me. "I didn't expect to get the call. There were so many great guys last season. Guys who deserved another chance. And even though I made top three, I kind of just figured it would go to one of them instead." I hear Isaiah's voice in my head instructing me to take a breath—a persistent reminding that began last season to keep me from fumbling over my words. "But WBN was persistent and, well, those emotions last year were real. I was definitely starting to fall in love... I experienced first-hand that this process actually can work. So I guess I just took the same attitude as I did the first time around. Like, well, why not?"

Reg laughs boisterously and I awkwardly smile, not entirely sure which part of what I said was funny. "'Why not, America?'" he repeats my line. "I absolutely love it. A worthy philosophy for all of us, I think... And, with that, we're going to take a break, but don't go anywhere! We've got plenty more in store with Patrick here, including something never before seen on this show. It all happens next on the live season premiere of *Heaven's Match*." Reg's second to last sentence catches in my brain and I question whether or not I heard him correctly, confused eyes finding Isaiah's. He looks at me apologetically while walking toward me, water bottle in hand. Never before seen? Surely they wouldn't blindside me with anything on week one... Would they?

"You're doing great, man. Just one more segment here then the focus will shift to the women for the introduction reel," Isaiah holds the bottle out to me but I don't take it.

"What the hell is he talking about?" I steamroll over his reassurance, fixated on *never before seen*.

"I, uh, it's..." Isaiah pauses, the words catching in his throat. "I just need you to trust me, okay? It's nothing you can't

handle."
The pounding in my chest says otherwise.

Whitney: Week One, Wednesday

"You sure about this?" Jeremy whispers quietly, exuding doubt directly into my eardrum. His breath is icy, and smells of fresh wintergreen gum. I wave my hand, brushing him off, keeping my eyes locked on Patrick, his eyes staring laser beams through the large envelope that one of my producers just placed into Reg's hand.

"And we're live in three... two... one..."

"Welcome back to the live season premiere of *Heaven's Match*," Reg begins. "Patrick here is but mere moments from embarking on a two-month journey to find the love of his life... But before we officially get underway, we have a little surprise. A new twist, if you will." Reg gives the words space to breathe, expertly building the suspense for our viewers—and for Patrick. I can practically see the wheels turning in his simple little brain. A better person might feel bad but, when the network pushes a lead this vanilla, what choice did I have? Someone has to manufacture a little excitement, God knows we're not going to get it from him.

"Normally on night one, our lucky lead would meet and welcome all fourteen of the women into the villa. Initial connections would be made, everyone getting equal opportunity to spend time with Patrick ahead of the first elimination." Reg explains, every word out of his mouth drawing more white out of Patrick's clenched knuckles. "But this season, we're switching things up. Inside this envelope are photos of the fourteen angels of *Heaven's Match* Season Seventeen." The relic of a reference from the early seasons never ceases to make me cringe. Fucking *angels*. Fucking *Reg*. "Armed with these photos alone, we will put the theory of love at first sight to the test... Tonight, we will ask Patrick to send one woman through to week two based solely on her appearance."

Patrick's expression softens slightly in relief and his hand goes to his hair, almost as if we cued him. The corners of my mouth curl ever so slightly up as Reg passes him the envelope and he runs his point finger through the seal.

"That's not all, though," Reg's words slow Patrick's movement to a stop. "As the journey giveth, it also taketh away. With the same stack of photos, Patrick will select two women for which the journey will end before they ever step foot in the villa."

He pauses and I can practically see Patrick's stomach drop. "How's that for opening night?!" Reg cheerily directs the question to the camera, leaving another pause for America's rhetorical answer before turning back to the ghastly white face beside him. "What do you say, Patrick? Shall we have a little fun?"

There's not a muscle in Patrick's body that moves. Not a single twitch as he stares down at the envelope vice-gripped in his own fingertips. A second passes, then another, then another. We're at about six seconds when I start racking my brain on if there's some live television protocol for this. A bead of sweat drips down his forehead and I feel the crew's eyes turn on me. The eighth second might as well be a minute. For the love of Christ, kid, enough already. *Say* something. *Do* something.

I feel Jeremy's presence leering behind me. "Dammit, Whitney, if you don't cut it, I will. He's fucking catatonic." Jeremy hisses, his breath hotter now. I hold up a finger. Not. Yet.

The envelope fumbles in Patrick's hand. A sign of life.

"Ah, um, wow, yeah. That's, well, ah, that's a lot, Reg." A collective exhale releases from the crew, a moment of relief I'll never admit to a soul that I shared.

But hey, you know what they say... pressure makes diamonds. And I'm going to force this kid to fucking shine.

—

"I've got to hand it to you, I had my doubts." Paul relaxes back on the futon and flips on the crew room TV. A rare moment, only the two of us. Jeremy is taking lead on move-in while the women's pre-recorded introduction videos air. The lucky twelve ladies who survived the premiere night twist.

"You should know by now never to doubt me." I pull a Diet Coke from the fridge and crack it open, the sweet taste of cold aspartame fizzing down my throat as adrenaline courses through my veins. It wasn't just good, it was a fucking masterpiece. The look of sheer nausea on his face when good boy Patrick was forced to do something less than noble. Nice guys can't finish last if there are no nice guys left.

When I initially pitched it, no one was having it. But "good enough" is exactly the type of crap that got us into this ratings slide to begin with. By the end of last season, the critiques were as stale as the show. And I wasn't about to let another big idea die on the brainstorming table. I'm not a sheep, I'm a goddamn wolf.

But I'm also not new to this. I know the ratings remains to be seen. Some critics will see it as cheap, low-brow. An overly sensational grab at suspense. No doubt there are already droves of mouth-breathing cat ladies barraging our social media mentions with accusations of being shallow and superficial. The type of losers who don't watch the show but feel the need to heave their agro-feminist bullshit at us from the bowels of the internet. I'll be sure to think about how much I don't care when I'm counting my end-of-year ratings bonus. How's that for women's empowerment?

I turn my attention to the TV monitor as the introduction videos begin to roll. Patrick's pick, Sarah, a twenty-five-year-old dental assistant, airs first. Anyone who isn't legally blind could understand why she stood out above the rest. She's Rita Hayworth incarnate. Flowing auburn hair, long legs, great tits and ass. The girl you hated in high school for no reason other than all the boys liked her more than you. And to make matters worse, she actually seems nice. The type that doesn't want the attention but gets it anyhow. The other women would have been jealous of the poor girl even if Patrick hadn't singled her out. That was a Whitney Erickson special, a gift from her to me. You're welcome, America.

"Sheesh," Paul mutters. "If my wife knew I got my teeth cleaned by a woman who looked like that, I'd be finding a new dentist."

I set down my Coke and walk to the futon, scanning the room though I already know we're alone. Draping my hand across his chest, I bend down, feeling Paul's heart begin to race through his shirt as my lips brush the back of his ear, shocking a wave of goosebumps across his neck. "I think there are a lot worse things your wife could find out about."

The door handle flips behind us and Paul coughs, promptly sitting up. My eyes dart to the door as it opens. It's a younger woman, one I don't immediately recognize. But as I stare into her stunned eyes, it hits me.

The new PA. Craig Burnside's niece.

Fuck.

Tammy: Week Two, Thursday

I'm not used to having company in the office at 6 a.m. Not used to it, and I don't like it. In nearly thirty years at the network, I've made a habit of getting in a good hour before anyone else arrives. Allows me to set myself up for the day without any distractions. Distractions like Whitney and Jeremy's frantic whispers as they stand waiting outside Paul's locked office door this morning. On a good day, Jeremy will bring me a white chocolate raspberry scone from my favorite bakery—a West Hollywood staple I used to frequent before I moved out to Redondo Beach. But today is not a good day. I know that because of the text that came through from Paul just before 4 a.m.

Overnight ratings in. Cancel all of my meetings today.

The elevator dings down the hall, silencing Jeremy and Whitney, both of them standing stiff straight as if strings were yanked on their backs. Punch and Judy, two little puppets. Up until this point, I wasn't sure Whitney was capable of expressing anxiousness. The uncomfortable shifting of her weight from heel to heel is foreign, another thing this morning I'm not used to. Only this I do like.

I keep my gaze straight ahead, locked on my desktop monitor as the hollow clomp of Paul's leather dress shoes on the carpet draws closer and closer. I don't have to see his face to know it's not a look I want to be on the receiving end of. No words are exchanged as he passes the two of them and turns his key in the lock, pushing the door open. They hesitate momentarily before filing in behind him. Jeremy pulls the door shut, but not far enough that it clicks closed completely. Not far enough that I can't keep an ear on things.

It remains quiet in the room and I paint myself a picture of the scene. The bright LA morning sun lighting up the room through the floor-to-ceiling windows of Paul's corner office. He's sitting behind his massive mahogany desk, photos of his wife and kids smiling back at him in golden frames. Jeremy and Whitney, not so much—their eyes cast down at the floor, looking like a couple of puppies that just peed on the carpet.

"It was just the first night," Jeremy's stammer carries through the crack in the door, breaking the silence.

"Oh, save it. You know as well as anyone that it wasn't *just* the first night. It was premiere night," Whitney replies, ever the glass half-empty ying to Jeremy's half-full yang. They're quite the foil, those two. Almost like siblings. I'm not sure how Paul does it most days.

"Not sure you're one to be giving me attitude." Jeremy's insinuation makes me smirk. Usually he doesn't stoop to her level, but I'm happy to hear he's not putting up with her shit today.

"What the hell is that supposed to mean?" Whitney snaps.

"Enough." Paul's voice interrupts, a rogue knight cutting the two duelers off at the knees. I hear his chair roll back from the desk, followed by the pad of footsteps and the closing of the blinds. "We all knew the risk last night. We all decided it was worth trying. And, now, we all have to pay up for it... We're going to lose advertisers. It's no longer a matter of if, it's a matter of when. We're in damage control mode." When is now, I think, looking at all of the blinking lights on the answering machine, messages left for Paul between last night and this morning. I struggle to understand how they didn't see this coming, pulling a cheap stunt like that. Desperation can make people do crazy things, and Whitney reeks of it.

"What's the protocol on switching to a new lead after the

premiere?" Whitney asks. Her lack of enthusiasm for Patrick is no secret. She lobbied hard for last year's runner-up, Kaleb, to be selected as lead instead. He was one of those beefy All-American asshole types. Never missed an opportunity to flirt with her, to stroke her ego. All things Patrick would never do.

"Give it up already, Whit. It's not Patrick." Jeremy comes to Patrick's defense and I catch myself giving a little fist pump to no one. "Whether you think he's deserving or not, the audience does. And so do the rest of us."

"I said, *enough*." Paul's tone is even sharper than last time, going for the jugular now. It's very rare that his anger gets away from him, and hearing it makes me worry. His blood pressure is high enough as it is. "Patrick isn't going anywhere. But the same can't be said for the rest of us unless we figure out how the hell we're going to turn this around. And we most certainly won't if you two keep at each other's throats like this." Jeremy and Whitney remain silent. Reminds me of childhood, being scolded by my mother in the back of the station wagon. "You guys are my A-team and I need you both working together on this." Paul's tone softens. "The critics at the Times were right. The show is getting tired." The sadness as his voice trails off sends a pang through my heart. People like to joke around here that *Heaven's Match* is Paul's firstborn. That he loves it with a passion the rest of us will never fully understand. For most of us, it's only a television program, a job. For Paul, it's his life's work, his legacy. He's the only person here whose name will be forever immortalized as CREATOR in the credits. And he'll protect that with everything he's got.

"Changing the perception is going to take a lot more thoughtfulness than what we pulled last night," he continues. "We've got to think bigger. We've got to figure out how we can really raise the stakes."

A momentary silence precedes the sound of Paul's footsteps again, louder as they move in my direction. I look up from my desk to the door, fully at attention, anticipating his instruction.

Averting his eyes, he shuts it.

Hannah: Week Two, Friday

It's been two agonizingly long days since I learned my lesson about opening closed doors. A lesson that awakened the gut gremlin with a vengeance, spurring a state of nausea I haven't experienced since moving to LA. I don't know what it is I saw between Whitney Erickson and Paul Thomas, but I know for certain I wish I hadn't seen it. And that it hadn't seen me.

Needless to say, I've done my best to avoid Whitney since. Unfortunately, the same can't be said for her. I much prefer she not know I exist to the uncharacteristically cheerful "Hi, Hannah!" I get every time I see her. It feels like a threat veiled in kindness. Like keeping your friends close and your enemies closer.

The same enthusiasm can't be said for Seth, who greets me this morning with the usual monotone as I wipe away crumbs using coffee-stained napkins left scattered around the break room after crew scrum. My reply is cut off by Taylor, the other new PA, who immediately unloads a barrage of small talk at him. I often wonder what it's like to lack social embarrassment. I imagine pretty nice, considering even the thought of someone rolling their eyes at something I've said makes me want to crawl into a small dark hole never to be seen again.

"Where do you want me to start today?" I ask Seth, finding an opening while Taylor's attention is temporarily diverted by another unlucky passerby. "I already finished unboxing all the candles that came in yesterday." All the candles being thirty cases worth. The box cutter might as well be an extension of my wrist at this point. Even my blisters have blisters.

Seth grunts without looking up from his phone, as if making a deliberate point to appear unimpressed. "In that case, Whitney requested you be allowed to sit in on Kate's confessionals today." The gremlin perks up when her name leaves his mouth. *Whitney.*

"Oh… Whitney asked that? Are you sure that's okay with you? I know there's a lot to get done around here." I hate myself for deflecting an opportunity to spend the next few hours doing something other than ordering lunches, but I can't shake the feeling that this doesn't come with tangles of attached strings. Whitney doesn't strike me as the type to hand out goodwill gestures. Plus, how would it look to the rest of the crew? Network hotshot's niece getting preferential treatment. If only they knew that it isn't who I know, it's what.

"Not really up to me," Seth replies. "Anyway, CR 3. Find me whenever you're done."

"CR 3?" I ask to no one, Seth's back already turned as he trudges on to the next task on his list. Thankfully, a kind cameraman overhears my question and points me in the direction of the confessional room in the far corner of the villa. I smile graciously and head on my way.

For all the people in this place, the walk is eerily solitary, the commotion gradually fading as I get further from the main living area. Up to this point, my interaction with the contestants has been virtually nonexistent. Any familiarity pertaining almost exclusively to placing grocery orders based on their various—and numerous—dietary requirements. My search history is filled with questions like "What is lectin?" Followed by, "Will soy sauce kill someone with an intolerance to it?" The answer is *probably* not, if you're wondering. I don't intend to test that theory.

I reach the end of the hall and find the doorway slightly open. Through it I can see Kate, who I've been instructed to meet. She's a senior field producer, reports directly to Jeremy and

Whitney. I know this only because of the hour I spent studying the organizational chart the first night. Kate is sitting on a backless barstool in the corner, nibbling on the end of a pen as her eyes scan her clipboard, thick tortoise glasses sliding down the bridge of her nose. Her face is one you might describe as mousy—big brown eyes, petite button nose, her lips both small and thin. Like most of the crew, she's dressed in all black, her dark brown hair loosely thrown up into a messy bun. The slight wrinkles around her eyes tell me she's probably older than me, but not by much, five-six years, maybe. She's definitely more physically fit—and notedly taller considering the toes of her ballet flats are grazing the floor.

I can't help but wonder if she's been told I'm coming. Or if she knows who I am at all.

"Kate?" I push open the door and her blank stare immediately answers my question. "Ah, excuse me, sorry. I'm Hannah," I stumble, "Seth sent me to sit in with you this morning? On Whitney's request?"

"Oh!" Her face twists from confusion to kindness. "Yes, of course. Come on in." I can tell she's lying, but I appreciate the attempt to make me feel like less of an idiot. She sets her clipboard down on her lap and turns toward me, removing her glasses. "Hannah... You're Craig's niece, right?" The question makes my cheeks burn.

"Afraid so," I laugh uncomfortably at the end of my response, a horrible habit I can't seem to kick. It was one of Ellie's pet peeves, drove her crazy when I did that. "Stop being so awkward. Be confident," she'd tell me. Easy for her to say. She could strike up a conversation with anyone, anywhere, anytime. One time, en route to a vacation with my family in Florida, she got to chatting with the older gentlemen next to us on the plane about God knows what. Before I knew it, we had an invitation to join him and his wife for dinner on his sailboat. At the time, it embarrassed me. How she *always* needed to talk to the stranger next to us. Now I'd do anything to see her do it one more time.

"How have things been going so far?" Kate's question breaks me out of my memory. It's the first time a producer has asked me something that isn't a request. The first time anyone but chatterbox Taylor has asked something about *me*.

"Oh, it's been great. Busy, but great," I reply, rubbing the box cutter blister bubbling on my thumb.

"You can say it sucks. I won't tell anyone," Kate's remark elicits another of my awkward laughs. "My first PA gig was here, too. I once spent four hours bedazzling a horse-drawn carriage only to find out the lead had severe equinophobia."

"Equinophobia?" I ask.

"Fear of horses. Sent her into absolute hysterics," Kate laughs at the recollection. "It's all worth it, though, I promise you that. Tons of people out there would kill to be on this crew. Tough as it gets sometimes, there's not a day I don't wake up grateful to be on this show."

"Yeah," I nod, "It's definitely a great opportunity." One I don't have any reason to deserve. Any reason, except, well, *that*.

I shimmy awkwardly to the side as two large men—members of the camera crew—push through the door, attempting to finagle tripods and boom poles into the ten-foot room. I wish I could say I recognized them, but they all have somewhat of the same homogenous look. Big, burly, bearded. You could tell me every camera guy was related and I wouldn't think twice.

"Did Seth give you any type of overview?" Kate asks, followed by a brief pause. "Who am I kidding, of course he didn't." She removes a stack of papers from her clipboard and hands them to me. "Each field producer gets assigned a group of contestants. Mine are tagged with the purple tabs. Now, I've been here long enough so, for lack of a better term, I get assigned to the 'good' girls. Flagged by casting as story setters, most likely to dominate screen time. The girls you see in the episode teasers week after week. For the most part, anyone not in my group is just filler." Kate's honesty surprises me. I mean, I always kind of assumed there were designated frontrunners, but it takes me a bit aback to hear it referenced so casually, like it's protocol. I page through their headshots. A flip book of symmetrical faces and blemish-free skin. Each woman as gorgeous, if not more so, than the last. If seventy-five percent of them are fillers, I can't even imagine how they'd classify me.

"These confessional interviews can be a bit of a toss-up. Usually they're fun, but occasionally it's like pulling teeth. All depends on the mood you get. And each producer takes a different approach. Some will do just about anything to get the soundbite they're looking for. Wear the contestants down, make them feel like they can't leave until they get that one golden line. It's what I call emotional waterboarding. Certainly a tactic, but not my style. I'd rather make them feel comfortable. Ease in with small talk, maybe offer them a drink. Don't get me wrong, there's still a job to be done, but I've found people are much more likely to open up when they feel like they're talking to a friend."

"Reagan's up first this morning," Kate directs to the cameramen before turning back to me. "If we get nothing else today, this one will be worth the price of admission alone." I'm about to ask what she means by that when a petite blonde comes barreling into the room like she's been shot out of a cannon.

"Kate, *girl*, why is there not already a mimosa in your hand?" Reagan overlooks me entirely as she bounds over to the beverage cart in the corner and effortlessly flicks the cap off a bottle of vodka. Her form-fitting red leggings and matching crop top leave little to the imagination, showing off all of her perky curves. It's the type of body that requires an excess of cardio and a deficit of carbohydrates. I've never had the discipline for that, though the idea of having my appearance scrutinized on television for two months straight would be pretty good motivation. I watch in awe as Reagan pours herself an incredibly stiff drink, adding just a splash of orange juice to the top.

"Mimosas are champagne… That's a screwdriver," Kate laughs.

"Even better," she shrugs. "What about you, mystery girl in the corner?" It takes me a moment to realize her question is directed at me. I glance to Kate for approval and find her again preoccupied with her notes. I'm pretty sure I shouldn't drink on the job but, by the blank stare on Reagan's face, I'm more afraid of what will happen if I tell her no.

"I'm Reagan." She extends me the glass in her hand and starts pouring another. "It's Irish for 'little ruler.'" I stifle a laugh at the nonchalance of her introduction, a line that's clearly rolled off her tongue a hundred times before. Reagan doesn't care what my name is. I know this because she turns around and heads back to the stool before I can start to get it out.

Kate nods a signal to the bearded brothers, a notice to turn the cameras on. She starts the interview with simple questions. Asking about Reagan's morning, how she's been enjoying the villa thus far. She gets through them about as quickly as the first cocktail, shaking the empty at me when she hits the bottom. I take it and make her another without thinking twice.

As if the second drink is the cue she needed, Kate advances to the next level of questioning—getting more into house dynamics and how Reagan's been getting along with the other women.

"I mean, it's whatever. I can pretty much get along with anyone. Not sure the same can be said about everyone, though..." she tails off dramatically, an obvious ploy to bait Kate's interest.

"What do you mean by that? Are some of the women not getting along?" Kate plays dumb, a question she obviously knows the answer to considering the entire villa is bugged with cameras recording their every interaction.

"I mean, there's *definitely* some jealousy going on."

"Jealousy? Of who?" Kate asks, again with the clueless act.

"Sarah, duh," Reagan replies as my mind places a face to the name. Sarah, yes, the unbelievably stunning redhead singled out by Patrick on premiere night. The woman who unfathomably stood out amidst a group of standouts.

Kate scribbles a note at the response. "Why would they be jealous of Sarah?"

"Are you blind, Kate? She's friggen hot. I've never munched a rug or anything but, you know, if I had to..." Reagan's response makes me choke on my screwdriver, Kate's 'worth the price of admission' preface becoming more and more clear with every one-liner.

"Are you jealous of Sarah?" Kate digs further.

"Me? Please. Why would *I* be jealous? She might be an eleven, but the girl's got a personality as exciting as dry toast. I'm not worried."

"Fair enough," Kate laughs. "Let's go back to the other women then. How can you tell they're jealous? Do they talk about her?"

"Do they *talk* about her? Girl. She's *all* they talk about. It's like they're obsessed."

"What do they say?"

"All the usual mean girl stuff. 'She thinks she's better than us... she's not even that pretty... he must just like redheads...' She'll try to talk to them and they'll either brush her off or fake like they're interested. Laughing about the things she says as soon as she leaves. They nitpick literally everything she does. Don't get it twisted, I've got nothing against a healthy dose of bullying, builds character. But they're not even good at it. Be original at least, right?" As Reagan speaks, I look down at the stack of bios in my hand, thinking of all the mean girls I knew in high school. Most of whom grew up to look a lot like this.

"Honestly, you should have seen the looks on their faces when Reg announced she was also getting the first solo date with Patrick. I mean, she's already safe through the week, and then she gets even more time with him?" Reagan drains what's left of her second cocktail and twirls a wrist casually through her blonde ponytail. "It was almost like they wanted her dead."

Patrick: Week Two, Wednesday

Genavié, Reagan, Olivia, Kya, Anna, Mallory, Imani, Jade, Sloane.
   Genavié, Reagan, Olivia, Kya, Anna, Mallory, Imani, Jade, Sloane.
   Genavié, Reagan, Olivia, Kya, Anna, Mallory, Imani, Jade, Sloane.

I repeat the names out loud as I flip through the nine headshots, a strongly recommended exercise by the producers to make sure I don't botch any of the women's names on live TV. Honestly, the whole thing feels a bit like cramming for a middle school vocabulary test, which is totally killing the bourbon buzz I was hoping would calm the first elimination nerves. They say it gets easier. I'll believe it when I see it.

I've been in my current holding cell, the "study", for about a half hour now. It's got a dramatically moody vibe, filled with dark wood and heavy leather furniture. Something straight out of Sherlock Holmes. A backdrop that's much better suited to writing the next great American novel than playing this strange high-stakes version of the memory game.

Genavié, Reagan, Olivia, Kya, Anna, Mallory, Imani, Jade, Sloane.

Nine names, nine women. And then, of course, Sarah, already safe for the week. Not that I'd overlook her even if she wasn't. But as I learned on our date, there's a lot more to her than just a pretty face.

I should have known the producers would pull out all the stops for the first solo date of the season. Private yacht. Five-star chef. The whole nine yards. Because being on a date with the most beautiful woman I'd ever met wasn't already enough to make me feel completely out of my league.

Sarah was incredibly shy at first, a saving grace for me to know I wasn't alone in my nerves. I could tell the producers weren't digging it though. Awkward smiles and nervous laughter don't make for great TV. But, somewhere during the cut between the champagne toast and dinner, someone pulled her aside and said something that completely turned our date on its head. We'd hardly gotten through the appetizers by the time she completely unloaded on me. Only child, born to junkie parents. Spent most of her childhood bouncing in and out of foster care, never really feeling like she belonged anywhere or to anyone. I can only assume the producers pulled the usual tactic—scaring her into thinking if she didn't release her skeletons she would fall behind. It's unfair, but effective. And doubly effective in making me question if I'm really ready for all this. I held her hand tightly as she shared her pain, at a complete loss for what to say. After all, what the hell did I know about struggle? Upper middle-class kid who grew up with two loving parents and a golden retriever in the backyard. I had this overwhelming desire to rescue her, to protect her from ever suffering again. But fighting against that was an equally strong doubt that I could ever be man enough for the task. Here's this stunningly beautiful but broken girl who's been put through the absolute ringer, and she put a pause on her life to date *me*?

Genavié, Reagan, Olivia, Kya, Anna, Mallory, Imani, Jade, Sloane.

I remind myself that Sarah's already safe and redirect my focus to the task at hand. When it comes to depth of conversation, this week's group date with the rest of the women delivered decidedly less. Zip lining was the activity. Tons of fun but not exactly conducive to building connections with eleven women at once. Attempting to converse between jumps from canopy to canopy was basically just speed dating with an adrenaline rush. But hey, whatever's good for the teaser.

Genavié, Reagan, Olivia, Kya, Anna, Mallory, Imani, Jade, Sloane.

Their faces blend more and more in my head the longer I sit here waiting. Tonight's pre-elimination social hour was exhausting, a two-hour revolving door of desperation. And I mean that with no offense to the women, it's just how this process works. I've been in their shoes. Convinced that a single sentence can make someone fall instantly in or out of love with you. I feel like a jerk admitting that it didn't change a thing. It's not that the two women I'm sending home don't seem great, but you either feel it or you don't. And when I compare them to the others, there's just nothing there. No interest, no potential. Is it okay to feel that way? Is it normal? You can seek advice from as many former *Heaven's Match* leads as you want, but you can never fully understand what it's like to date so many people at once until you're actually doing it.

Genavié, Reagan, Olivia, Kya, Anna, Mallory, Imani, Jade, Sloane.
Genavié, Reagan, Olivia, Kya, Anna, Mallory, Imani, Jade, Sloane.
Genavié, Reagan, Olivia, Kya, Anna, Mallory, Imani, Jade, Sloane.

I look down at my wrist to check the time. I'm not normally a watch guy but, when Rolex is one of the show sponsors, you become a watch guy. It takes my brain a few seconds to register the 7:44 showing back at me. I jump to my feet as panic rises in my chest. Live elimination always starts at 7:40 sharp. Why hasn't Isaiah come to get me yet? I disregard the instruction to stay put and head impatiently to the courtyard. I push through the door and see all of the women lined up beside the pool. The scene stops me dead in my tracks. "Wow..." I hardly realize I've said it out loud, stunned at how beautiful they all look in their gowns. Stunned at my own life. That they're all standing there waiting on *me*.

"Patrick!" Isaiah hustles over and puts a hand on my shoulder, steering me away from them. "Hey man, am I crazy or did we tell you to wait in the study?" I turn my head to face the crew, huddled nearby, putting off an altogether panicked vibe that does very little to settle my rising nerves.

"It's 7:45," I say, "What's going on?"

"Ah, so, here's the thing," Isaiah stalls. "Not a huge deal, but, we're down a woman."

"What? Which one?" I spin back to the women, urgently scanning their faces.

Genavié, Reagan, Olivia, Kya, Anna, Mallory, Imani, Jade, Sloane.

All nine on my list accounted for, plus two others. Eleven total. Is that right? No. It can't be. There's twelve. There should be twelve.

Sarah.

"Where is she?" I demand, the protective instinct barreling through all my other anxieties. I told myself I wouldn't get swept up in the gossip, but that doesn't mean I haven't heard it. I'm not stupid. I know what the other women have been saying about her. Jealousy rearing its ugly head already. It was bad enough when I was on the show with twelve other men, with women it must be tenfold.

"It's nothing major," Isaiah lowers his voice to a hushed whisper. "Sounds like she just may have been a bit... over-served."

"Over-served? How do you even let that happen? She was fine when I saw her an hour ago," I reply without matching his discretion. My question was rhetorical. I know exactly how they let it happen. Another reckless production tactic. "Can I go check on her?"

"No time," Whitney interjects from the collective mass of the crew. "We've stalled long enough."

"Whit's right, we've got to keep this thing moving." Jeremy chimes in. "She's safe through next week anyway."

"Thank God, I'm freezing my tits off," one of the women, Reagan, shouts from behind us. Her comment is followed by a chorus of laughter from the group. I don't join in, instead letting my hand run nervously through my hair, the general lack of concern not sitting well with me in the slightest.

"She's fine, Pat," Isaiah tries to reassure me. "We've all been there, right? She just needs to sleep it off." I reluctantly concede a nod. I'm far from convinced, but I know it's not a battle I'm not going to win. Isaiah leads me over to Reg and the women. They all smile widely at me as I scan their faces, hyper-aware of the one that's missing. Isaiah's words take the place of the nine names in my head as I desperately will myself to believe they're true.

She's fine, Pat.
She's fine, Pat.
She's fine, Pat...

Hannah: Week Three, Wednesday

Hour three of paying homage to the porcelain throne. I've gotten used to the gremlin, ways to manage it, tactics to force it down. But food poisoning goes beyond that—food poisoning answers to no one. I curse the leftovers I found in the back of the crew fridge as I wipe the inside of the toilet bowl, ashamed to have had to request a night off work already. Most people can't hold their liquor. New girl can't hold her pad thai.

Lying on the expensive white marble tile for the last hour has only enhanced my appreciation to Uncle Craig for letting me stay in his daughter, my cousin, Lindsay's apartment while she's off building schools for the children of Uganda for the next four months. I insisted they charge me rent but, based on the rates listed on the building's website, I'm getting far better than the friends and family discount on a one-bedroom off the Sunset Strip. Renting for a month here would run more than double our monthly mortgage. Well, what used to be our mortgage, I guess.

Our house was *nothing* like this. Pretty much the opposite of turn key. Windows that stuck, tacky popcorn ceilings, an infuriating drip from the bathroom sink if you didn't turn the handle off just right. There was no shortage of upgrades to be made, but it was a home. And it was ours.

I managed to scrape myself up off Lindsay's fancy floors long enough to catch most of tonight's episode, watching with a drastically different perspective than I had prior to my time on set—back when I was green enough to believe drama happened a bit more serendipitously. Now, after only a few days, it was almost too obvious which storylines the producers were setting up. Sarah, the gorgeously misunderstood frontrunner with a tragic past. Her uphill battle against the jealousy of the other women. I will say, the mysterious disappearance just as the live eviction was about to start threw me a bit. I was tempted to text Taylor to see if it was scripted or not, but I already have an unopened message from her asking how I'm feeling and I'm not quite prepared to open the floodgates into "text friends" yet. Outside of Sarah's absence, everything went as I predicted. Two "filler" contestants went home—leaving all four of Kate's frontrunners still intact. I'm happy for that. I genuinely like all of them from what little I've observed over the past week. There's Kya, the badass female coder with more cool in one braid of hair than I have in my entire body. Olivia, the stereotypically sweet nurse. Genavié, the glamorous French Canadian with the annoyingly sexy accent. Even Reagan who, for some odd reason, seems to actually like me.

I upend what I hope is the last of rice noodles and fish sauce and relocate to the living room couch, cozying up under a blanket and doing what every reasonable twenty-eight-year-old does when they're sick—call Mom. I've been feeling guilty about how little I've checked in with her and Dad. I know the short texts here and there don't do much to put her mind at ease. She worries more than I think is healthy—for her and for me. Knowing that, I've been dodging her. Cutting conversations short because I'm busy with work or running off to happy hour with my new LA friends—only one of which is ever true. But tonight, I caved. I guess sometimes you just really need your Mom.

I can practically see the dimples lining her round and rosy cheeks based on how cheerily she answers the phone. It's a feature I wish I'd inherited, along with her warm complexion and soft heart-shaped face. I got Dad's high cheekbones and harshly sharp jawline instead.

Mom tells me they're in the middle of dinner and, though I

try to say I'll call back later, she insists we stay on the phone, laughing that she can "eat a boring old tuna casserole with Dad any night of the week."

It doesn't take long for her to dive into all sorts of questions about the show, about life in LA. I do my best to keep the conversation surface-level. No mention of the Paul-Whitney encounter, or how I haven't "cooked" anything but cereal. Most importantly, I don't tell her I haven't made any new friends. Being alone was her biggest fear with me moving out here. Losing the support system I had leaned on so much in the past ten months. Leaned on too much, if you ask me.

I keep her distracted for twenty minutes or so with stories about bizarre production requests, which she responds to with cackling laughter at the ridiculousness of Hollywood. She can hardly wait to share with all the ladies at church, "Oh Hannah, they'll just *die*."

"So, have you met Patrick yet?" Mom asks, a jarring transition that kills the lighthearted mood and stirs the gremlin in its slumber. It's the one question I've been most avoiding, the one I know she's been desperate to ask since she answered the phone. The one ever-burning question that's kept me from calling in the first place.

Mom's tone is delicate, an attempt to come off unassuming, to not strike a nerve by coming across overly concerned. I read right through it. It kills her not to know.

"No, I barely ever see him. They keep the lead pretty separated," I deflect with a partial truth. Obviously I've seen him, he's the show lead. But as far as I'm aware, he hasn't seen me back—and I'd prefer to keep it that way.

"Oh, okay," she replies. I wait through the silence for the more I know is coming. "I was just wondering, you know. You keep telling me everything will be fine, but that doesn't keep me from worrying. You don't think he'd ever say anything, do you?"

"Mom, stop. I keep saying everything will be fine because it will." The words snap from my mouth and I immediately regret their harshness. I try to remind myself that she's only asking because she cares. "I'm sorry, I just don't want you to worry so much about me," I trail off and, through the pause, I hear her sigh. "I gotta go, okay?"

"Okay. Goodbye honey, I love you. Please call again soon."

"I love you, too."

I hang up just in time to make it to the bathroom and throw up all over again.

—

I arrive at the villa an hour earlier than usual in effort to make up for the time I missed last night. I feel mostly better, taking on the day cautiously optimistic that at least the foodborne bacteria has been successfully exorcised from my system. I won't speak for the rest of it.

Without any dates today, it should be a relatively quiet morning—contestants and cast sleeping off the hangover of the first live eviction. I push the front door open slowly to reveal nothing of the sort.

Everything inside is complete and utter chaos. Crew members scrambling up and down the halls, ducking in and out of doorways. Oh God, am I late for something important? What email did I miss?

I step down the left corridor and spot Tammy, her short legs shuffling swiftly out of the sitting room. I call out to her and she whirls around to face me. Her graying hair is disheveled and her eyes are sunken, as though she hasn't slept in days. "What's going on?" I ask as her gaze lingers on me momentarily, shifting from surprise to sympathy. But then the phone in her hand rings and she's gone as quickly as she appeared. I follow slowly behind her, the volume of pandemonium increasing as I approach the sitting room, peering inside before I fully commit myself to whatever is going on here. Through the open doorway, I see a group of contestants and producers huddled together on the couch. One of the filler contestants sits at the center with another beside her, rubbing her back gently. Flanking them are two others, both crying. What the hell happened?

I turn on my heels at the sound of heavy boots and rolling wheels behind me. I see the police officers first. Then, the medics. Then, the gurney. Its pace painfully familiar. Slow, somber, a telltale sign that there's no longer life underneath. My legs wobble and I stumble backward, bracing myself against the wall to keep myself out of their path as the gremlin reclaims its hold in my stomach. *Please God, no. Not here, not now.* With everything inside me, I know I should look away. Close my eyes, plug my ears and let the moment—and the body, whoever's it is—pass. But I don't. It's as if my eyes are magnetized to it, desperate to see, desperate to know, desperate to suffer. And then I see it, ever so slightly peeking out from beneath the sheet.

A single strand of auburn hair.

PART TWO

Whitney: Week Four, Thursday

Notify the court, the verdict is in. The universe is out to fucking get me.

About an hour after they wheeled out Sarah's lifeless body, Paul showed up and sent the crew home until "further notice." Time to process, time to grieve. Time to figure out how the fuck we're ever going to recover from this. Most went to Isaiah's apartment to drown their sorrows, sing kumbaya and just "be together." If I'm being honest, and I always am, nothing sounds fucking worse.

I uncork a bottle of wine and lean my back against the hard ledge of the cold marble countertop. Like any other evening, I take in the floor-to-ceiling view of Los Angeles while downing the first of many swigs. This is one of those no-glass, straight-from-the-source nights. Hell, I'd inject merlot directly into my bloodstream if I had a hypodermic needle. Given how fucked things could become, I should probably start doing the math on how much longer I'll be able to stay in this place. Can only afford the dream apartment if you're still living the dream. And right now, I'm living a nightmare.

I carry the bottle to the couch and curl up under an egregiously chunky white knit blanket—last fall's trendy impulse buy, purchased courtesy of the five glasses of chardonnay in my system at 2 a.m.. It's so heavy that if I pull it over my head, maybe I'll be lucky enough to suffocate and die.

Normally, I'd unwind by watching rich housewives debate whose plastic surgeon gives the best facelifts, but the remote remains untouched on the glass coffee table tonight. There's no point in even trying. There's not a thing in the world that could distract me from this morning. From Sarah. Gorgeous. Sweet. Young. *Dead*.

You wouldn't believe the crocodile tears on some of these women. We're talking professional mourner-worthy. Like they hadn't spent the entire week bad-mouthing Sarah behind her back. On a long list of things I can't stand, sympathy suckers are definitely up there. Like, remember when Prince died? You couldn't scroll for more than five seconds without some no-name loser lamenting on how *profoundly* he had impacted them. The dead deserve better than that. Which is exactly why Sarah won't get a single tear from me. Oh, wouldn't mother be so proud? Those four words: "Why are you crying?" She'd asked it as casually as if I had fallen off the monkey bars and scraped my knee. As if my father hadn't just taken his last breath right in front of my eyes. No, Mom's tears dried up long before that. Before he was bedridden. Before he lost control of his bodily functions. As if he chose to let cancer turn him into a fragile paper mache shell of a man. As if he chose to die.

If anything, Dad's passing was a relief for her. One less mouth to feed. Of course, by then, my sister and I had already picked up part-time jobs at Albertsons to help pay the bills. Cara, sixteen, me only twelve—lying to the manager about my age, cursing early puberty for curves that enabled me to be subjected to child labor. I should have been stealing slushies from the 7-Eleven with other kids my age. Instead, I was getting preyed on by creepy old men in the grocery checkout line.

Keep moving forward. That was Mom's M.O. Either adopt it or get left behind. And for the better part of my existence, I've done exactly that. This thing with Sarah though, it feels… unmovable. Like the inevitable end of my career—and my life—as I know it. None of us "forced" her to drink all that alcohol, but it's not like we cut her off either. Wouldn't be too much of a stretch for someone to claim negligence, to claim that this twenty-eight-year-old girl's blood is on our hands.

I take another big gulp of wine as my phone begins to ring. I flip it over, *Jeremy Rowe* flashing across the screen. I send it to voicemail and it immediately rings again. I send it, again, flip the volume off and toss my phone to the other end of the couch. Whatever he has to tell me will have to wait until at least bottle number two.

Across the couch, a text message buzzes. Then another. And another two after that. Jesus Christ, Jeremy, fine. I reach over and unlock my phone.

Just talked to police.

Overdose.

Prescribed sleeping meds.

It wasn't our fault.

—

The bright sun blaring through the floor-to-ceiling windows of the boardroom only makes my head pound harder. Jeremy's text was a huge relief, but not enough to prevent me from putting down two more bottles of merlot. Shutting the shade would require standing, so that option's off the table. I tell you, nothing humbles you quite like than the increasing brutality of a hangover. I used to be able to rip shots until 4 a.m., power nap for three hours in my car and still show up ten minutes early for my gig as a PA. Here I am now at age thirty-six contemplating putting sunglasses on indoors.

The energy in the room matches how I feel. I'd ask "who died?" but, well, you know. I might be a bitch at heart but I still have one. Paul requested only the senior production team for this morning's meeting, a core group to discuss where we go given the information from the police. We relocated Patrick and the contestants to a nearby hotel during the investigation. Not a bad spot, but it's definitely not the Four Seasons. But, contractually, we can only keep them holed up over there for so long.

No sign of Paul yet. I keep my eyes down on my phone, preferring a thousand unread emails to all of the solemn faces around me.

Five minutes pass before the boardroom door clicks and in walks Paul, Jeremy closely on his heels. It hardly feels happenstance, and jealousy twitches through my entire body as he takes a seat flanking the head of the table. Paul remains standing beside him, as forlorn of an expression across his face as the rest of the sad sacks around me.

"Morning, everyone. Thank you for coming in." Paul looks down at the floor, a momentary pause to reset his composure. "I know waking up wasn't easy for any of us, and this office is probably the last place you want to be." Paul's always had a surprisingly sensitive side for a man of his position. Normally I consider it to be a weakness, but I'll give him a pass today.

"There's no easy way to have this conversation," he continues. "What occurred at the villa was a complete and utter tragedy. Sarah O'Brien was a sweet, sweet girl in the prime of her life. She deserves to be properly grieved." There's another pause before he cuts the silence with a clear of his throat. "We're doing our best not to be insensitive but, as you all know, decisions need to be made. We've got a hotel full of folks waiting in limbo on what we're going to do next.

"Jeremy has been cooperating with law enforcement on our behalf. Copious amounts of zolpidem were found in Sarah's system. Zolpidem is the active sedative in Ambien, a medication she had a valid prescription for. There was *also* alcohol. Alcohol *we* provided, but I've been assured multiple times it was not a factor in her death… To be very clear, I'm not telling you this to diminish any bit of what happened. This still occurred on our watch. But I need all of you to understand that no one in this room is to blame." The crew remains completely silent through every word that leaves his mouth. It's a first for a group who could find a way to form an opinion about exit signs if you asked them.

"Kate, were you able to get in touch with Sarah's family?" Paul turns his attention to Kate—Sarah's producer and the closest of any of us to her. She looks particularly disheveled, tangled hair falling out of her bun, dressed in the same clothes she was wearing yesterday. I've been there many a time—a clear sign of a sleepless night.

"Ah, sort of. She doesn't really...," Kate trails off, as if choosing her next words carefully. "She doesn't really have any. It's been a bit of a runaround, you could say... I did find someone, a distant cousin, but he hasn't spoken to her in almost fifteen years. Passed along his condolences but that was it." A murmur spreads throughout the room.

"Hmm...," Paul echoes it. "What about friends? Coworkers?"

"I can try to dig up more there today. Her social media accounts aren't giving me much to work with. She really only posts photos of herself." Christ, how depressing. No wonder the poor girl offed herself. I guess if there's any consolation, it's that we won't have an angry mob of relatives coming after us. Remind me not to say that out loud.

Jeremy starts to speak and stops, pensively putting a hand to his chin for dramatic effect. A collective expression of intrigue passes throughout the room—idiotic plankton predictably eager to take the bait.

"Did you have something, Jeremy?" Paul asks. Yes, please, Jeremy. Do share with the rest of the class.

"Well, I was just thinking, you know, mental health is such a huge issue right now. Rather than crawl under a rock and hide until next season, maybe we can put ourselves out there and have those tough conversations. We could raise awareness, make a donation, promote the hotlines. Use our massive platform to make a real impact." I scan the crew to gauge their reactions. A few nods, a couple raised eyebrows. Personally I hate it, but it's only because I didn't think of it first.

"I don't think we should get ahead of ourselves," Isaiah speaks up, releasing air from Jeremy's proverbial balloon. "This whole thing has Pat pretty shook. Getting him to agree to anything besides a flight home will be nothing short of a miracle."

"I can talk to him," Jeremy persists. "And the women, too. If anyone still wants to leave, we'll respect it."

"Might be best if I talk to the women," I interject, "You know, woman's touch."

"No, Whitney, that's okay. Let's leave this to Jeremy. We can use your skills better elsewhere." Paul's words land like a sucker punch. *We can use your skills better elsewhere?* What the fuck is that supposed to mean? I'd hardly describe myself as delicate, but I damn well know how to crank the right dials when a job needs to be done.

Honestly, what a couple of bastards. Conspiring up a plan and performing it for the rest of us like a Broadway fucking show. It all but confirms my suspicion that Paul is putting the training wheels on Jeremy, prepping him for showrunner succession. I mean, fuck me, right? Literally though—Paul did. For eight years. And now I've got absolutely nothing to show for it.

I'm so deep in my rage spiral that I don't even realize the meeting is over until everyone starts pushing in their chairs and filing out. I remain seated, pretending to do work on my phone as I wait for Paul to give a consolatory hug or shoulder pat to everyone who walks out of the room. Jeremy leaves last and the lingering handshake between them boils my blood even more. As the door clicks shut behind Jeremy, Paul looks to me longingly, pathetic sympathy in his feeble blue eyes. Part of me wonders what it would be like to finally let it break me. To run to him and let his arms support the weight of every emotion I've suppressed since I was 12 years old.

I shut that curiosity down with authority.

"What the actual fuck was that, Paul? Didn't think you guys should clue me in?"

"I know, Whit, I'm sorry." He runs a hand anxiously across the back of his neck. "I know how all of that looked. But this has nothing to do with Jeremy, I promise. We just… dammit, this is hard… we need to talk about some things."

"So talk then," I bite back, preparing myself for the political corporate bullshit. *You're a great producer, Whitney, just not the right fit for showrunner.* Fucking spare me the rerun, I've seen this episode before. Destined to be another female footnote in a man's biography.

"Sarah's death caused me to rethink a lot of things," he pauses, breaking eye contact. "This thing between us, it has to end."

The words trigger such an immense wave of relief that I literally laugh out loud.

"Jesus, Paul is that all?" The nonchalance of my reaction twists his expression from confusion into hurt. Admittedly, it's a blow to my ego. Being rejected always stings a little bit, especially when you know you're the superior catch. But I made a vow a long time ago to never let a man see me in pain, and I don't plan on breaking it over Paul fucking Thomas.

"Oh come on. Don't be like that, Whitney."

I flash him a soft smile as I stand and calmly push in my chair. I walk to the door without looking back, my smile twisting into a smirk. Here I was thinking my dream was dead in the water. Thinking I'd have to choose between my pride and my WBN career. But it's going to take a lot more hell and high water than this to keep me from running this show.

Patrick: Week Four, Friday

I've been sequestered in room 317 long enough that I'm starting to resent Tom Hanks.

As hotels go, this one is as painfully average as it gets. King bed, lifeless pillows, stiff pullout couch, oil-painting prints of Los Angeles tourist attractions on off-white walls and an unobstructed view of the parking lot. Guess the network only pulls out the stops when the cameras are rolling.

At least at the villa there were distractions. Activities to do, people to interact with. Here, there's nothing. Zero contact with the outside world. No phone, no cable or network TV. Isaiah had the nerve to make me feel like I should be eternally grateful for the permission to order pay-per-view movies. I'm sure the front desk is perplexed if not concerned about my eighth purchase of Forrest Gump. It's a comfort thing. From the time I was eight-years-old, it's the one movie that always makes me feel better—whether I've had a bad day at work or I'm laid-up sick with a bowl of chicken noodle soup and a can of 7Up. Or at least it used to, back before I killed Sarah O'Brien.

See, if it weren't for me, Sarah would never have been here. Her unforgettable twelve words, forever burned into my psyche: "If they had chosen any other lead, I wouldn't have signed up." Because of me, Sarah O'Brien was here instead of off somewhere getting the help she clearly needed. And to think I ever believed for a single second that I could save her.

Isaiah told me I can't think that way. Whatever was going on with Sarah was between her and God. Sounds exactly like something Mom would say. I wouldn't know though because they won't let me talk to her. If I hear the words "contractual obligations" one more time, I'll put my fist through this cheap drywall.

I'm so disoriented in here I hardly even know what day of the week it is. Friday, I think? That's Little League night back home. My brother, Mac, coaches his son's team—my nephew, Frankie. God, I love that kid. More than I ever thought I could, and he's not even mine. First grandkid, Mom and Dad never miss a game. She'll sit in the stands cheering loudly with my sister-in-law and three-year-old niece while Dad watches from behind the backstop, slinging hot dogs to hungry parents at the concessions table like he's done since I was four. It's those family nights that make me miss living in Minnesota most.

I never thought I'd want to move away. I love being from the midwest. Everything about it is unassuming. Just a quiet pocket of the country where nothing tries too hard. It's content just being exactly what it is. The people are nice, the seasons are fine and there's plenty of room for your dog in the backyard. But when I came back home after last season, I realized quickly that nothing would ever be the same. People I'd known my entire life started treating me like a stranger and strangers started treating me like they'd known me my entire life. My ability to blend in was gone, forever branded the "big shot" from that TV show. I shouldn't complain, I know. I signed up for it. A lot of former contestants move to LA, try to eke out a few more minutes of fame. But that wasn't it for me. I'm still a heartland guy, partial to cold winters and the Great Lakes. Chicago was a good compromise, more my speed. One of my closest friends from last season had recently made the move and I knew a few college buddies living there. When work said they could easily transfer me, I just went for it.

Forrest is mowing the football field again when he's interrupted by a firm knock at the door. I mute the TV and lazily swing my legs around from the bed to the floor, in no rush to go vertical for only the second time today. I make the mistake of glimpsing myself in the mirror on the way to the door. Oof. I pause and run a hand through my blonde hair, cringing at the oily texture. My palm moves down to my chin and I rub gently over the scratchiness of patchy stubble. I look like I feel—which is absolute shit. Admittedly, showering has been pretty low on my priority list. Low meaning it hasn't been on my list at all. I'm still wearing the same faded maroon University of Minnesota shirt and basketball shorts I was in when Isaiah woke me up two days ago with the bad news about Sarah.

I expect that to be him again now, the only human contact I've had besides the nasally teenager who drops off room service and fresh towels. You can imagine my surprise when I open the door to find Jeremy instead.

"Hiya, Pat. Mind if I come in?" His tone is friendly, unassuming. I step back and wave my arm without regard, an invitation into my mess of empty soda bottles, chip bags and unmade bed sheets.

"Sorry, haven't really picked up," I mutter, making no attempt to conceal how much I really do not care at all.

"No, no, don't apologize." Jeremy awkwardly relocates a pizza box from the couch to the coffee table and sits down in its place. I take a seat on the floor across from him, legs out, my back uncomfortably pressed into the knobs of the cheaply made dresser.

"Big Dodgers fan?" I ask flatly, making note of his matching Los Angeles hat and t-shirt. I like Jeremy, genuinely, but it's about as much enthusiasm as I can feign for his presence today.

"Oh gosh." Jeremy's face turns red as he looks down at his chest. "Yeah, embarrassingly so. Big game today. Lucky shirt. Guess I'm a little superstitious."

"You from here? Or is that a bandwagon thing?"

"Portland. Dad was a huge fan. No baseball in Oregon, so it was this or the Mariners."

"Yeah, I guess," I reply, doubling down on apathy as I fiddle with the knotted waistband string on my shorts.

"Well, anyway, listen, man. I'm really sorry about all this. We just, you know, we have to keep with protocol."

"There's protocol for this?" I question. "Must have missed that part in the handbook."

"No, no, of course not. Sorry, that's not what I meant." It's odd to see Jeremy fumble over his words like this. He's typically more polished, more confident. I stare at him blankly through the silence. It's a gap I have no interest in filling.

"That's actually why I'm here, though. I wanted to talk to you about our options."

"Options?" I laugh in disbelief. "Jeremy, all due respect, I know you have a job here, but a woman is dead. *Sarah* is dead. The only option I'm entertaining is packing up my shit and getting the hell out of here... As soon as you'll release me, that is." I hold my wrists up in front of me as though they're bound by invisible handcuffs.

Jeremy sighs and nods understandingly. If I didn't know the network better, I'd think I was about to get off easy.

"Listen, Pat," Jeremy's tone softens as he leans toward me, resting his elbows on his knees and clasping his hands together like he's hosting an after-school special. "I know it's really hard for you to imagine a scenario where this works out. Where all of this turns into something good... Hell, maybe even something great."

I meet his words with more silence. He meets my silence with a sigh.

"It sounds like your mind is mostly made up. And I understand that. But will you please do me one final favor and just hear me out?"

I begrudgingly nod in agreement, but he's wasting his breath.

On my life, there's not a single thing in this world that could convince me to stay.

Tammy: Week Four, Friday

I reach under the passenger seat and slide the case out from beneath it, the smooth plastic handle thick and heavy in my palm. The parking lot is much emptier than when I'm usually here in the evening. It was the only place I could think to go after Paul sent me home early again. Today he told me he was just meeting with Jeremy and Whitney, no need for me to wait. Paul hasn't sent me home before 4 p.m. in sixteen years. He's done it twice in the last two days. Combine that with hushed phone conversations and meetings I didn't schedule, something's off. And I'll be damned if I'm not going to find out exactly what it is.

The familiar shopkeeper bell chimes when I push through the door. Al momentarily looks up from his newspaper and gives me a nod from behind the counter. An old buddy of my brother, Joe, Al's never charged me a membership fee. I just make a sizable donation at the annual Wounded Warrior fundraiser and we call it even. I'm a regular now, like Joe used to be. Joe's best friend, Russell, and I started coming here after he passed. It wasn't easy at first, being here, listening to all the condolences and fond memories of him. But keeping up with the things and people Joe loved felt like the best way to preserve his legacy. Russell and I showed up together every week for those first six years. Then, when Russell met Ada and they had the kids, he started coming less and less until he eventually wasn't coming at all. Russell's life naturally went on. But I guess mine didn't.

I pass by Al at the counter and head toward the back. There's not much to it, white walls and cement floors. It's got a T-shape layout from the door, five divided stalls on each side. I've got my choice of the place, but I still go to my usual spot—fourth stall down on the left. The latches on the case open with a satisfying snap and my eyes linger on it, the nine-millimeter Smith & Wesson, paying a momentary respect before picking it up. It's cold but familiar in my hand.

I go through the routine on autopilot. Check the safety. Pull the slide back gently. Double-check that the chamber's empty. Set the pistol down. Remove the magazine from the case. Load ten rounds in the clip, pressing down firmly with my thumb to make sure they're fully sealed. Pick the pistol up with my right hand. Slam the magazine into place with my left. Pull the slide back. Flip the safety off. Point. Aim. Fire.

The scent of gunpowder sets off a Pavlovian echo of my father. *Don't carry a gun unless you're prepared to take a life.* A lesson I learned the hard way at only ten years old.

It was our annual trip to visit my father's cousins on the family farm in North Dakota. An unseasonably cool day for late August, my father took my brothers and I out to the hunting land—the "big land", as they called it. It was the first time I'd been allowed to come, and wow, how big it was. Wide open fields of tall wispy grass. The freshest air I'd ever filtered through my nose. I couldn't begin to comprehend the boundlessness of the horizon, endless in every direction. It was nothing like the suburgatory we lived in at home in Sacramento.

My father had gifted me a gun for Christmas that year. A 20-gauge Remington shotgun, much to my mother's chagrin. She didn't think it was proper for a woman to know how to use a gun, much less own one. But, as with everything, my father was adamant. Male or female, there would be no weak links in his lineage.

The homemade shooting range was off the open field, tucked into the first cut of trees. It looked like a mix between a junkyard and a garage sale. Empty soda cans, beer bottles, magazine covers. I was appalled to find that even my poor old stuffed teddy was a target for their ammunition. As usual, my brothers were relentless in their teasing. Never mind that my adrenaline was already high enough without them pushing my buttons. To this day, I can't for the life of me remember what Joe said. All I know is it was something bad enough to make me turn the gun on him and threaten him to say it again.

Before I knew it, my father had snatched the rifle from my hand and pinned me to the ground. The weight of his body was so heavy I thought I would suffocate right then and there. My father didn't often lose his temper, but I did something in that moment that unleashed a fresh hell inside of him. He stood up and yanked me from the ground by my arm, screaming at me for my carelessness. Tears in my eyes, I watched in fear as he removed his belt in one swift motion.

"Turn around," my father instructed.

"Daddy, I'm sorry! I won't do it again!" I wailed.

"God damn it, Tamara. Turn around!" he shouted, ignoring my desperation.

"No, Daddy, please!" I cried as I ran toward him with my arms outstretched. I had seen him put a beating on my brothers, but surely he wouldn't do it to me. Not to his one and only little girl.

My father side-stepped me and turned to my brothers. "Boys, hold her arms." My two oldest brothers, Dan and John, nodded sullenly and walked toward me, each grabbing an arm. I kicked and screamed for the cows to hear as they carried me toward a fallen tree, coercing me down to my knees, holding me so firmly against the bark I could feel the bruises forming beneath my skin. I was still screaming as the first crack of leather came down hard and fast against my bottom. Over, and over, and over again. By the sixth or seventh whip, I was crying so hard I could barely breathe.

"Stop it, please!" I finally heard Joe plead for him to stop.

"You shut your mouth or you'll be next," my father retorted sharply and continued to strike me ten more times.

Not one of us ever spoke word of it to my mother. And, to this day, every time the sulfuric smell of gunpowder hits my brain, I'm back there. Red backside, dirt-caked knees. It's a bit masochistic, perhaps, but it forces me to respect the sheer power of what's in my hand.

I continue to shoot for about an hour. Mindless, but never reckless—all of my shots peppered in a four-inch radius of the target's center. When the stalls begin to fill up next to me, I take my cue to leave. I give a quick wave to Al before I walk out the front door, shopkeeper bell chiming another farewell as I pull my phone from my back pocket. Three missed calls—all from Paul. I dial him back and he answers before it even rings.

"Great news, Tammy. We're back on."

Hannah: Week Four, Monday

For an introvert like me, it's hard not to be overwhelmed in settings like this. Packed together like sardines with everyone in the sitting room. And I mean *everyone*—Reg, Patrick, the women, the entire crew. I do my best to avoid eye contact, instead tracking up and down the exposed wood beams of the ceiling, counting all eleven over and over using inhales and exhales. I tried to hang back on the wall, but Kate spotted me immediately and insisted I sit front and center on the open couch spot beside her. I'm really not sure why she's taken such a liking to me, but whatever the reason has put me smack dab in Patrick Olsen's direct line of sight.

So focused on not drawing attention to myself, I didn't even notice Paul standing at the front of the room. He's scrolling through his phone, elbow leaned against the mahogany mantle for support. He looks as though he's aged six years in as many days. Whitney and Jeremy stand poised beside him, conversing casually as they lord over the room.

Paul stuffs his phone in his pocket and takes a step forward, a signal to the group that it's time to quiet down. Whitney and Jeremy abdicate their posts and retreat to the open spots along the wall.

"It's good to see everyone together," Paul addresses the room. "Patrick, ladies—I know you've all already had very difficult and lengthy conversations with your producers. I want to personally reiterate that the decision to move forward with this process was not taken lightly—nor was it made without the utmost respect for Sarah and her family.

"I also want to express my gratitude to each and every one of you. None of this is possible without the collective buy-in of this group. And, with that said, I want to be clear that the network and I hold no judgment or hard feelings toward those who ultimately did not feel comfortable moving forward with us." Paul's reference confirms the rumors I'd overheard this morning. A few crew members and one contestant, Imani, opted not to return for the rest of the season. Part of me wonders if I should have done the same. After I told Mom about Sarah's death, she was adamant I pack it up and come home. Staying couldn't possibly be good for me. It was still too soon, too fresh. I have a strong suspicion she was the catalyst for Uncle Craig's call, the one where he reassured me the show would have no issue at all finding a new production assistant. But what they all don't understand—what they'll never understand—is how badly I need to see this through. No matter the circumstance, I won't go back to where I was. I can't. Not for anything.

"Now, as I share our plan to move forward, please do not hesitate to speak up with any questions or conce-"

"You're not going to make us sleep in that room, right?" A voice pipes in from the opposite couch. It's Reagan, of course, wasting no time in opening up the floor.

"No, of course not," Paul replies. "In fact, a lock has been put on the third bedroom. Those who were staying in that room previously will be moved." The answer seems to satisfy Reagan as she settles back into her spot on the couch. "Any other questions right away?" Paul pauses but the room remains silent. "Alright then, onto logistics. Much of our production will go on as previously planned. The exception to that will be this week. We will still air the episode live on Wednesday, but there will be no elimination. To be clear, no one will be sent home." A physical wave of relief spreads through Patrick and the women, as though a very real weight has just been lifted from all of their shoulders. "We will instead use time at the beginning of the hour to open with a candid conversation about mental health. We've already lined up one of the nation's leading docs to Q & A with Reg on the importance of destigmatizing mental illness. Now, obviously, there's no perfect way to handle this. But this feels like our best path forward." As Paul speaks, I tip a mental cap to the public relations team. It's not that I don't believe the network is coming from a good place, but it's hard not to wonder if there's an ulterior motive—one that involves exploiting a poor girl's suicide to boost declining ratings. But, really, who am I to judge? Sitting here nodding along just as spinelessly as the rest of them.

"Any final questions?" Paul's ask is met with silence, which he returns with a clap of his hands. "Okay then. Let's get back to it."

As everyone starts to disperse, there's a noticeable shift in the energy of the villa. Scenes to be set, tasks to be completed. A return to natural chaotic order. I'm standing to join it when I spot Reagan power walking in my direction. My eyes widen and my heart rate rises, unsure as to what drama she could possibly be bringing my way.

"We've got a big problem," she states, voice flooded with worry. I'm about to stammer a response when I realize, to both my relief and embarrassment, she is not looking at me, but at Kate—who I'd completely forgotten was standing right beside me.

"What's wrong?" Kate asks. The look of distress on Reagan's face intensifies as she lets out an anxious sigh.

"My leave-in conditioner is locked in that bedroom."

"Jesus Christ, Reagan. Read the room." Kate's concern deflates with an eye roll. "Did you check your stuff? The police cleaned everything out during the investigation."

"Only like a million times. I had stashed it in an opening under the sink so the other girls wouldn't steal any of it."

"We'll get you another one," Kate replies.

"It's Oribe Aprè Color. They don't even make it anymore. Can you pretty pretty please just go see if it's still under there? It's the only one that works for me. And America will outrage if they have to see my split ends in 1080p."

"Would you mind?" Kate turns to me, an illusion that I have a choice in the matter.

"No, not at all," I say with a smile that hides how much I do mind. If only she could fathom how desperately I do not want to go into that locked room.

"Yay!" Reagan perks up. "You're the best!"

"Thanks, girl," Kate says, "Eric can get you the key."

The two of them walk away together, leaving me by myself in the middle of the room as my stomach begins to turn—a reminder from the gremlin that I'm never fully alone. My eyes catch Patrick's as I quickly sidestep in front of the couch. His gaze lingers a bit too long for my liking, the soft blue of his irises piercing the hazel of my own. I quicken my step, deftly escaping before my paranoia regurgitates with this morning's cereal. I grab the key from Eric, one of the set producers, and head for the bedrooms on the second level.

There's an inverse correlation between the pace of my legs and the beating of my heart as I reach the foyer. I reluctantly climb the stairs as the sound of conversation—and life—fades below me with every step, quieter and quieter until there's nothing but silence. I make a left at the top, passing the wide open doors of the first two identical bedrooms. They're brightly lit, four twin beds lining the walls, all freshly made up with crisp white sheets and fluffy white faux fur pillows, a scene out of princess summer camp.

My pulse starts to thud in my wrists as I reach my destination. The only closed door. The third bedroom. I breathe in slowly as I slide the key into the lock, secretly wishing it won't turn. My stomach pangs when it clicks. Losing a battle against my own will, I slowly turn the handle and push it forward.

Inside is the same setup as the other rooms, save for one barren mattress. No crisp white sheets, no fluffy white faux fur. Stripped of everything but death.

The gremlin shoots bile from my stomach to my throat and I swallow it back down, the sour taste coating my esophagus. My mind fights but the gravitational pull of the bed is too strong for my body. I run my hand softly across the smooth cool frame. I know full well I'm about to go back there and there's not a therapy trick in the book I can do to stop it.

The memory arrives visceral as ever. Dark brown hair cascading over the pillow. The beautiful olive of Ellie's skin draining before my very eyes. Her lifeless body. In our house— our *home*. The one we had just closed on, not three weeks until the wedding. Our entire future right there in front of us, fading into gray along with her.

"Please, no..." I plead out loud now the same as I pleaded out loud then. I plead with God. I plead with the devil. I plead with anyone and anything to bring her back to me. I plead so hard that I throw up, vomit dripping from my chin to my shirt. I crumple to the floor when the exhaustion hits, paralyzed by the weight of grief as it presses down upon me like a concrete bodysuit.

"Hello?" A voice cuts through the ringing in my ears. Warm, gentle. I wonder if it could be death, finally come to rid me of my misery.

Through heavy eyes, I see her. Long brown hair, smooth olive skin, mystifyingly dark eyes. She's walking slowly toward me but I'm unable to move, the heat of trepidation rising more and more in my body with her every step. She kneels next to me and places a soft hand on my shoulder, her touch not at all cold as I expected.

I blink hard, existing momentarily in the blacks of my eyelids. When I open them, my breath suspends in my acid-wretched throat as her features come into clarity.

Patrick: Week Four, Tuesday

"You sure you don't just want to hit the weight room instead?"

I hear Isaiah before I see him, catching a glimpse of his lumbering body through the crook of my arm, bent over as I pull tightly on my shoelaces. A five-mile run isn't quite the same hair of the dog I defaulted to when I was twenty-one but, like it or not, I know fresh air and a good sweat are just what I need today. Running is something I've had to learn to love, having been my least favorite part of playing sports growing up. That disinterest certainly didn't stop anyone from telling me I was built for it though. Tall and thin, a "slow-twitch" muscle kind of guy. Seemed to me like it was just a backhanded way to imply I didn't have the strength or coordination to excel in all the sports I tried so desperately to be good at.

If Isaiah's lack of enthusiasm for cardio wasn't a clear enough indication, he's here because he has to be. Upon coming to the villa last year, I quickly realized a bonus of running is that it's one of the only ways to get a little breathing room from the cameras. But that bonus, like everything else, comes with a catch —Isaiah has to chaperone me. Unlike me, he is decidedly not "built for it."

"You didn't have to come, you know. I know the route," I laugh as I observe his running attire right side up. Sweatband, tight muscle shirt, thick quads on full display in shorts that fall well above the knee. He looks more like he's about to play pick up with Magic Johnson than run through the woods with a lanky white boy.

"Trust me, if there was a way for me to get out of this, I'd have figured it out by now. Let's just get it over with already," he replies, alternating between quad stretches. I laugh again as I swing my arms widely around my body, twisting through my trunk to loosen up my torso—the final step in my warm-up routine. I give him a nod and we set off down the driveway, passing a handful of crew members on the way. Some are carrying boxes, others are directing trucks. No doubt pertaining to whatever surprises await me on my next date.

We reach the end of the driveway and take a left down the road, towering trees surrounding us, the freshness of the pines invigorating my senses and reminding me of home. There are no words exchanged, only the sound of light breeze through the branches, birds chirping and our feet padding on the pavement.

"I'm sorry, man, but I'm going to need some form of distraction to take my mind off this hell you've put me in," Isaiah breaks the silence, making it glaringly obvious that we are not sharing the same transcendental experience. "Tell me more about how you're feeling after last night. Worth the hangover at least?"

"Ha," I begin, still piecing together the evening in my brain. "It was a good time, we had a lot of fun." No point wasting breath on details I'll undoubtedly have to repeat to him on camera later.

Isaiah lets out a booming laugh that echoes through the trees. "Tell me something I don't know."

The comment makes me cringe. I really hope I didn't make too much of an ass of myself to my date, Genavié—or to all of America, for that matter. I blame the first date back for firing up my nerves. Nerves I apparently decided the best way to calm was with copious amounts of white wine—which I don't even like all that much, by the way. But after cashing a handful of bottles in front of a dinner we never actually ate, Genavié and I were singing Celine Dion and recreating the "I'm Flying" *Titanic* scene on the front of a stranger's docked boat. I mean, seriously, what kind of insensitive shit do I have to be to respond to one woman's death by getting piss drunk with another?

"So you think you'll keep Genavié around?" Isaiah asks between increasingly heavy breaths.

"Ah, yeah, I think so," I pause before correcting myself. "I guess I'm still just waiting to feel that spark." It's not like there isn't plenty to like about Genavié. She's intelligent, well-traveled, sexy in that mysterious type of way. She's an art curator, which gives her an eye for beauty that I'll never understand. The idea that she's the opposite of my usual type is why I picked her for the date in the first place. It's out of my character to go after something new. But even though Genavié is an amazing woman, the experiment only reinforced my inclination.

"I know it sounds contradictory when we only give you two months to find your wife, but give it some time," Isaiah replies. "Not everything is love at first sight. Sometimes feelings pop up when you least expect them to."

I nod but don't respond, allowing myself a few moments to consider Isaiah's advice. Giving anything time seems nearly impossible with the speed of this process. Especially now, with the heightened emotion of continuing on after losing Sarah. I know we only went on one date, but I felt something with her. Something deeper, something real. I was hoping I might find that feeling with Genavié. Then again, I probably drank too much to even give myself a chance.

I'm jarred from my thoughts as a black BMW coupe rips up from behind us, wheels spitting out gravel as they skid over the pavement's edge while taking the sharp corner in front of us. I halt, adrenaline pumping as I brace my hands on my sides to catch my breath.

"Fuckin' Whitney." Isaiah says before hawking a loogie onto the road. "She's been on one lately." The sound of another vehicle comes from behind us and we step further to the side as a Jeep passes, slowing to take the turn much more carefully. I recognize the driver as Paul Thomas' assistant. Tammy I think is her name? Isaiah gives her a quick wave as I walk up to the corner and peer over the edge. It's a steep drop, fifteen or so feet of thick brush before it levels out into a patch of thick tree trunks. Certainly enough to warrant a guardrail.

"Jesus. That's a widow maker," I say as I turn back to Isaiah.

"Ha," Isaiah laughs. "No widows for Whit. Unless you count Paul."

My brow furrows in response. "Paul? Like, Paul Thomas Paul?"

"Worst kept secret on set," he replies. "Neither of them thinks anyone has any idea. Truth is, we're all just too afraid to admit we know."

"Damn. He's married, right?" I ask.

"Sure is. Man, if I were Jeremy, I'd tell everyone. The way she's always ragging on him, I'd shut that down real quick. Let the media jackals have at them and take the showrunner spot for myself. Guess Jeremy's a much better guy than me."

"You think Jeremy's next in line?"

"I sure hope so. He might not be the flashy choice, but he's better for the overall stability of the crew. Whitney's just reckless —obviously," Isaiah gestures toward the curve she almost ran us down on.

It's weird to think about the drama that goes on off camera, within the crew. I'm so used to everyone in the villa being hyper-focused on me that it's easy to forget they have their own lives. And complicated ones, at that.

"You want to head back?" I ask even though I know he'll have no objection. "I lost momentum when we almost got killed."

"Awh, bummer. Here I was so close to hitting that elusive runner's high!" Isaiah says with another laugh that dares to reach the treetops.

Our conversation returns to the usual banter as we make our way back to the villa. Things like whether baseball should really be America's pastime, if LeBron James is better than Michael Jordan. Both of us arguing the same points as always with neither willing to concede.

Isaiah badges in at the security gate and we slow to a walk, catching our breath as we wind up the drive.

"Ooh, if we take the shortcut, I can show you my new ride!" Isaiah says enthusiastically. He just pulled the trigger on a Land Rover, and he's been talking my ear off about it ever since.

I laugh and follow Isaiah past the bronze PARKING sign toward the crew lot. "Ah, this reminds me, I've been meaning to ask you… there's a few new girls on the crew that weren't here last season. Interns maybe? You know anything about them?"

"Oh, yeah. Not interns, but close. Those are the PAs. Production assistants. Blonde one is super friendly. And cute as hell. Your boy might just have to shoot his shot before the summer's over."

I laugh. Funny, but not quite the insight I was looking for. "What about the brown-haired one? I'm almost positive I know her from somewhere, but, for the life of me, I can't place her. It's driving me crazy."

"Hmm, yeah she's pretty quiet. All I really know about her is that she's Craig Burnside's niece." Isaiah speaks casually as if it's a name I should know.

"Craig Burnside?"

"Yeah, programming director for the network." Isaiah rubs his fingers together in a big money type of motion. "Dude calls a lot of shots."

"Interesting." I want to ask more, but I let the conversation die there as we reach the lot. It's a mixed bag when it comes to vehicles. Some high-end, some missing hub cabs. Isaiah is hooting and hollering in excitement at his own when I see it. Not the Land Rover, but a Toyota RAV4. Minnesota license plate, U of M sticker on the back windshield.

And suddenly, everything clicks.

Whitney: Week Four, Tuesday

It takes a second for my eyes to adjust as I step inside. Long burgundy curtains trap the dimly lit and cooly air-conditioned sushi bar into a seemingly different world than the bright sunshine of LA. But for the small sign stickered on the door, you might not even know it's here. Tucked away next to a shuttered insurance agency in a one-story building on a sleepy street corner. There are plenty of spots in this town where I go when I want to be seen. Niji is one I go to when I don't.

I wave off the hostess and find my usual seat at the far end of the bar. My favorite bartender is here. A cute Japanese kid who minds his own business, doesn't ask anyone anything besides if they'd like another. If only more people were like him. I rap my fingertips aimlessly on the black granite bar top as he uncorks a bottle of my usual. I'm not sure what to expect out of tonight but, if nothing comes from it other than a spicy tuna roll and a heavy pour of Chardonnay, it'll still be time well spent.

"Evening, Whitney." The voice comes from behind me. "I actually already grabbed a table."

"I'm good here," I respond without turning, taking a long sip from the stemmed glass the bartender just placed in front of me.

"Of course you are," she laughs in a way that's somewhat sarcastic, somewhat genuine. *Classic* Whitney, as if we're old friends. "I'll flag down my server and have her move my tab." I give her an up-down as she steps away. Hot pink power suit.

76

Louboutin stilettos with the red soles. Lisa *fucking* Perez. The saucy little Latina who hustled herself to head of programming at NTV. I respect the hell out of her, whether I can trust her is another story.

I turn my gaze back to the bar as I wait for Lisa to return. It's the usual happy hour scene. Corporate hacks in loosened ties, unwinding with two-for-one sashimi and half-price sake bombs. I've got my eye on a cube farm douche canoe failing to flirt with a much younger colleague when the front door pushes open behind his receding hairline—through it walking an unmistakable spike of neglected gray roots in a clearance rack blazer. Fucking *Tammy*. On a list of the last people I typically want to see, she's got a stronghold on number one. She's been passive-aggressively bitchy to me from the moment I met her. Jealousy, of course. I'll always be younger and hotter and more successful than she could ever dream. All high and mighty because she makes Paul's doctor appointments. I can't tell if she wants to fuck him or be his mom. Weird, either way.

I keep a close eye on her as she asks for her takeout order. The taut-faced young hostess checks for the ticket and lets her know it will be at least fifteen minutes. *Great.* Tammy nods with annoying understanding and grabs a spot at the other end of the bar. There's no indication that she's spotted me yet, but I shift my body to the side for good measure.

"I was starting to think you'd never agree to meet with me." Lisa sets her martini on the bar and pulls out the stool next to me. "Don't suppose your change of heart has anything to do with the shitshow I hear you've been dealing with over there."

"Oh come on, am I that obvious?" I steal a glance down the bar as the bartender slides Tammy a lowball glass of dark liquor on ice. Shitty rail whiskey, if I had to guess. She graciously takes it and shifts her attention to her phone. The bartender heads our way next and asks if we're ready to order. I go spicy tuna and Lisa declines, citing a lack of time.

"You know I'm not the type to beat around the bush, and I know you aren't either. Which is exactly why I think you'd make a great fit for us. I'm running a no-bullshit ship over at NTV.

And you already know I'll do whatever we can to get you on deck. Money, your pick of the shows. I mean it, Whitney. Name your price and I'll make it happen."

The maritime references make me cringe, but the offer is hardly anything to balk at. NTV has already offered nearly forty percent more than my current salary and I don't doubt I could talk her up even more. They don't exactly have a history of strong programming, but Lisa's been steadily changing that. Her recently refreshed lineup is showing solid potential in the ratings. Problem is, it's still no WBN. I don't want to be showrunner for any show. I want to be showrunner for *Heaven's Match*, the highest-grossing reality show in television history. It's the top of the mountain—and Lisa knows that as well as anyone. I was far less inclined before but, she's spot on now. Given everything that's happened lately, I'd be a foolish woman to not give it more serious consideration. The thought of sitting around and waiting only to be publicly humiliated if Paul passes the castle keys to Jeremy? I'd rather die.

My eyes shift back to Tammy as the bartender hands her a takeout bag across the bar. I'm still watching her as she spins around on her stool, eyes locking with mine before she glances at Lisa with an expression of smug acknowledgment. She toasts her glass in my direction and downs the rest in a single gulp.

—

I speed home a little faster from Niji tonight, scanning guardrail to guardrail for cops, pressing my foot to the floorboard when it's clear, hands obsessively ringing around the baby soft leather of the steering wheel. The faster I drive, the easier it is to distract myself from the colossal life decision I have in front of me.

God, I love this car. I'll never forget the first time I got behind the wheel of a BMW, moonlighting as a valet at Gordy's Steakhouse in West Hollywood. Not even the creepy owner patting me on the ass could ruin that experience. Dripping in luxury, I swore to myself then and there that someday I would have one of my own. The moment I signed the title on this 8-series coupe, I had officially made it.

I flash my parking transponder out the window before

peeling down the ramp to my reserved spot, in good company with the other Beamers and Bentleys. My apartment charges more for an extra-wide air-conditioned spot and I pay it gladly —it's not like I'm just going to park this car anywhere. A delivery notification came through earlier today, so I take the elevator to the main level first. My hectic work schedule prevents me from frequenting Rodeo Drive as much as I'd like, but I've remedied that by making sure my personal stylist ships me the latest trends on the regular. Some days I feel like she knows me better than anyone.

"Evening, Ms. Erickson." Neil, the sweet older bellman, tips his cap from behind the lobby desk, revealing his thinning white hair smoothly parted beneath. Along with the BMW, moving into an apartment with a bellman was another big made-it moment. If only Mom could see me now.

"Neil, you're looking dapper tonight as always."

"You flatter me, ma'am," he replies with a blush and rolls his chair over to package intake. "Would appear you have a suitor." Neil returns carrying an elaborate bouquet—a dozen cream roses wrapped in black craft paper.

Oh for Christ's sake.

"They're lovely. No tag, though. Who do you reckon they're from?" Neil asks in earnest.

"No one important," I reply. "Thank you, Neil. Have a good evening." I pick them up with a half smile and head for the elevator. Cream roses can only mean one person... Paul. He gifted me red once for Valentine's Day and I laughed in his face at the cliché. Told him to bring them home to his wife instead. When I reach my apartment, I consider throwing them directly into the trash. Beautiful as they might be, romantic gestures trigger my gag reflex.

My opposing instinct ultimately wins out and I climb precariously onto the kitchen counter to reach the top shelf of the cabinet. There's one vase in this apartment, buried in the back behind all the shot glasses from the phase when I apparently didn't think it was tacky to bring back mementos from every beach vacation. I really ought to throw them out. Or donate them. Nothing says goodwill offering like *I Got Plastered in Playa.*

I fill the vase with water and clip the stems before tossing the roses in without fuss. Giving them life is about all I have energy left for tonight, so I grab a hydrating mask from the fridge and head straight for the bedroom. I scroll mindlessly on my phone until my eyes become heavy. Just as I'm about to drift to sleep, the most haunting image pops in my head…

Tammy and her smug face, toasting me from across the bar.

Tammy: Week Four, Wednesday

I awake in a sweat, pajama shirt damp, an uncomfortable stickiness between my back and the bed sheets. My heart is pounding. That damn dream again.

It's the same as ever. I'm sitting at the kitchen table in my parents' house, the modest little split-level we moved into when I was thirteen. It's Christmastime, I can tell by the magnificent Scotch Pine tucked in the corner of the living room. My father always brought home such a beautiful tree, and my mother always defaced it with mismatched ornaments and popcorn garland. My brother Joe sits opposite me, strong square jawline freshly shaven, the same tight crew cut hairstyle he's worn since he was a boy. Handsome as ever at thirty-one, about five years removed from service, no longer training but still at the peak of his health. His broad brick-house shoulders are evident even under his loose gray Vietnam Vet crewneck sweatshirt. It's almost comical how tiny the cribbage cards look in his massive hands. He's looking at them and laughing, both of us well aware of how close I am to skunking him. It's a short-lived moment of joy before the inevitable... when Joe's laughter turns into that horrible hacking cough and I watch his body deteriorate before my very eyes, unable to look away. The cards drop from his hands and he reaches for me desperately as the paralysis spreads from his arms to his face. Only I'm paralyzed too. Unable to touch him, to grab his hand and comfort him.

Abandoning him when he needs me most. Joe's mouth opens wide in a silent scream, cheeks caving, bright baby blue eyes fading to dull gray. The last air in his lungs escapes with a gasp and an exhale. And then, like clockwork, I awake.

Even though it's still dark outside my bedroom window, I can sense dawn isn't far off. 5:15, if I had to guess. I turn to the analog clock on my nightstand. 5:12. Damn. Close but no cigar. I'm wide awake as usual following that dream, resolve to start the day slightly earlier than usual. Thanks for that, Joe.

I swing my legs out from under the sheets and tuck my feet snugly into the hard-soled slippers set routinely by the bedside. My knees pop as I stand and stretch my arms toward the ceiling, tilting my neck delicately from side to side, awakening each vertebra. A still sleeper, it's quick work to make the bed, only having to tidy the right side while the left remains tightly made, unslept in by anyone but me since I bought it those many years ago.

I align the final accent pillow into its proper place and head for the closet, thumbing through tops and sweatshirts. I pause when I get to Joe's Vietnam sweatshirt and run my hand gently across the front, the cheap screen print catching ever so slightly on the pads of my fingers. "I'll see you again soon, Joe."

I swap my pajamas for a pair of plain gray sweatpants and a navy zip-up sweatshirt before heading to the kitchen—my favorite stop of the morning. I open the cupboard and pull out a bag of Guatemalan coffee beans, a gift brought back specially by my niece from her stint in the Peace Corps. I slide out the kitchen scale and hit the tare function, zeroing the weight of the small white ramekin. Two full tablespoons. 8.99 grams. I remove three beans. 8.42. Just right. Coffee snobs will tell you the perfect cup is not an ounce over 8.3. And maybe that's so—but strong always beats perfect if you ask me.

Fresh filter, pour in the beans, add water, press start. I wipe away yesterday's stains from the single mug in the drying rack as I wait for the puttering dribble of today's final drops.

The bitter black coffee scalds the tip of my tongue. It's a lesson I'll never learn, too impatient for the first hit of caffeine to let it cool longer than a few seconds. The unsightly stack of unopened mail mocks me from the edge of the counter. It's another reminder of free moments I've yet to find. No time like the present, I guess. I rifle through it with indifference. Clothing catalogs I didn't subscribe to, local pizza delivery coupons, another reminder to sign up for an AARP card. At this point, it's starting to feel like a personal attack. I toss everything aside but the utility bill and balance my cheater glasses on the tip of my nose. "It's time to switch to paperless billing!", the bill scolds when I unfold it. As I struggle to recall which bag my checkbook is in, I wonder if it's time to succumb to that AARP membership after all.

I've still got about an hour before I need to head to the office, so I take advantage of a rare opportunity to enjoy my coffee on the back patio. I open the sliding glass door and the sun hits my skin with the soft warmth you only get at this time of the morning before the LA summer heat smokes you out. It's a modest little backyard, but any green space is appreciated after spending so many years in cramped apartments. You can only grow so many plants on a five-foot balcony but, now, my garden is flourishing. Hearty tomatoes, vibrant peppers, fragrant herbs, fresh lavender. And roses, of course, my favorite. I've got them in practically every color. As I wander toward them, one stands out among the rest. Red but withering, it's amazing how a single dying rose can tarnish the beauty of an entire garden. I reach for it and it bites me, a single pesky thorn pricking just below the knuckle on my pointer finger. The small cut elicits one slow drop of blood that I swiftly wipe away with the pad of my thumb.

I leave it for now and return to the patio. The wicker chair creaks through quiet air as I take a seat. I rest my feet on the ottoman, taking long slow sips of my now-cooler coffee. It doesn't take long for the incessant buzzing of my phone to kill the tranquility of the morning—a reminder that nothing in my world is ever truly sacred. I sigh and click into my email to see what all the fuss is about.

To: allhm@wbn.com

From: paul.thomas@wbn.com
Subject: Hollywood Post Article
-Message sent with high importance-
I'm sure most of you have seen this by now. If anyone reaches out to you from the post or otherwise, do not engage. We are handling it.
hollywoodpost.com/heavens-match-suicide-scandal
- PT

So much for that peaceful start to my day. I click into the article expecting the worst. Hollywood Post is the entertainment industry's most shameless gossip tabloid, and an article by them rarely yields anything but trouble. They only get it right about thirty percent of the time but, by the time anything gets corrected, the damage is usually done.

"I WOULDN'T PUT ANYTHING PAST THEM" - FORMER HEAVEN'S MATCH PRODUCER SPEAKS OUT

Beneath the article's headline is a haunting black and white photo of the villa's exterior. Sarah O'Brien's death had already made us the nation's biggest fascination, and the network's decision to continue filming fueled all sorts of conspiracies. But unfounded theories sprouted in dark corners of the internet are very different than allegations made by a former employee. The heat in my body rises more and more with every word, mind reeling at who could possibly betray us like this. I have my moments same as anyone, but *Heaven's Match* is still my family. And family is always worth protecting.

I exit out of the article and navigate to my contacts, scrolling until I get to a number I haven't dialed in years. I tap it without hesitation.

"Hi, it's Tammy. I need your help."

Hannah: Week Four, Wednesday

I scroll through the directory and begrudgingly dial the number. It was only a half-mile walk from my cousin's apartment to Taylor's, a detail I have zero intention of divulging lest she get any ideas about us carpooling to work every day. Up until now, I had successfully dodged all of Taylor's invitations. After-work drinks, weekend brunch and—you can't make it up—a double date with a set of identical twins. I feel a little badly about all the excuses I've made up, but not bad enough to stop making them. Unfortunately, there wasn't a fake obligation in the world that could have helped me avoid this one. Seth pulled us aside this morning and assigned us to live monitor and catalog social media feedback during tonight's episode. When Taylor cited the villa's spotty wifi connection as a reason for us to do it at her apartment instead, I knew I was trapped. And with an apathetic "yeah, sure, whatever," Seth sealed my Wednesday evening fate.

It's not that I don't like Taylor. Genuinely. She's a sweet girl. We're just… different. Monogrammed accessories, spiced lattes, woo-ing it up for bottomless mimosas at drag show brunch. Taylor, God bless her, is the type of girl who shares a three-bedroom apartment with four other girls and thinks it's *fun*.

The apartment in question is exactly what I expected. One of those trendy new builds with an expensive look but cheap construction. Landlords who target naive first-time renters, churning and burning recent college grads in and out before they start paying enough attention to realize it's all just lipstick on a pig. Twenty-two-year-old me probably would have lived in one myself had Dad not ingrained it in me. Old bones are good bones.

I check the time as the elevator rises up to the fourth floor. 7:52. Only eight minutes for socialization, perfect timing.

"Hannah! I'm so excited you're *finally* here!" Taylor exclaims as she swings open the door, greeting me with a hug as if it's been two years instead of two hours.

"Yes, thanks so much for having me," I do my best to sound gracious, arms pinned against my sides as she squeezes. If there was any doubt about my apartment theory, the kitchen quickly dispels it. White cabinetry, gold-painted fixtures, laminate counters made to look like marble. I give it five years max before it all starts falling apart.

"Ugh. I so wish my roommates were here to meet you. I've told them so much about you!" she says, contorting her lower lip into a little baby pout.

"Bummer, maybe next time," I respond, hoping there won't be a next time.

"Definitely! Eeek, it's almost time! I need to grab my laptop. Help yourself to charcutes and wine!" I wince at the way she says "charcutes" while she skips out of the kitchen.

The spread is nothing if not impressive. All sorts of expensive meats, cheeses, nuts and jams aesthetically arranged on a slab of reclaimed wood. I'm completely unfazed by the cliché—it's exactly the type of thing girls like Taylor excel at. I load up a paper plate that reads "Sweet Dreams Are Made of Cheese" and pour some pinot grigio into a glass that says "I only drink on days that end in Y."

"Can you believe we get paid to do this?" Taylor exclaims as she sprawls her laptop and work binder across the glass coffee table and sits cross-legged on the floor behind it. Mint condition when Seth gave them to us, hers is now a stickered billboard for cities she's traveled to and yoga studios she's taken classes at.

"Mhmm, crazy," I mumble through a perfectly balanced mouthful of crackers, hot honey and brie. I scan the room for somewhere to sit and decide to make home in the light pink faux fur chair in the corner. When in Rome, right? I settle into the polyester and focus my attention on logging in to the various feeds, absently nodding along as Taylor catches me up on her current dating app prospects. To her disappointment, there are "so many cute guys in LA" but "none that want to get serious." Her innocence makes me feel bad for her. To have such genuine surprise over something that's seemingly so obvious in a town like this. I don't inquire further, but I do find myself hoping it wasn't too hard of a learned lesson.

"Ohmigod, okay, here we go!" Taylor squeals as the TV screen goes black. The show typically begins with a dramatically narrated title sequence, but tonight they're going cold open—no introduction, no "tonight on *Heaven's Match*" teaser. It's just Reg, sitting in his usual chair beside the pool, one leg crossed over the other. Opposite him is an attractive and scholarly-looking brunette in a modest cap-sleeved black dress. The neckline is high, showing no cleavage, bottom hem hitting right at her knee. Reg is wearing a dark grey suit with a black tie and white shirt, far more subdued than his usual flashy ensemble. Clearly, the network wanted no distractions tonight.

"I am *so* glad we're doing this," Taylor speaks over Reg's introduction. "My cousin's best friend OD'd once. *So* friggen sad."

"Yeah, very," I trail off as the woman on the screen's name and affiliation flashes below her. *Dr. Francine Feldman. National Institute for Mental Health.* The social feeds go wild as Reg begins detailing the tragedy, at least fifteen new posts materializing by the second.

Mental health is real, y'all.

Sarah seemed so kind. Rest In Peace, beautiful girl.

Monetizing suicide? This is a new low, even for reality TV.

I don't care what anyone says. This conversation is important. Good on you, WBN.

"I can barely keep up!" Taylor says breathlessly over the alternating sound of fingers scrolling the trackpad and hammering the keys. "It's like the whole world is talking about us."

"Yeah, it's... something," I say, anxiety rising. I thought I'd be able to handle it, but each "overdose" reference that pops up onto the screen has me fighting harder and harder against the urge to upend a block of manchego onto her peel-and-stick vinyl flooring. The last thing I need is loose-lips Taylor finding out how triggered this whole thing makes me.

I hold my breath in waves as I monitor the onslaught of reactions to the interview between Reg and Dr. Feldman—equal parts support and criticism. As always, the heated debate between the strongest opinions is drowning out the reasonable middle. The interview concludes and the episode moves inside to the sitting room. We see Patrick and the women for the first time, gathered on the couches for a more casual discussion.

My cheeks flare red hot as the camera pans past Olivia. As the days have passed, I've only become more mortified about our encounter in Sarah's bedroom earlier this week. Me, lying on the ground like a woman deranged, terrified as I mistook her for the ghost of my very dead ex-fiancé. I'm just lucky she handled it so well. Even made a joke about violating HIPAA after I shamefully asked if she would please keep it between us. I guess as the list of people you'd want to find you in a catatonic state goes, a nurse ranks pretty high.

My breathwork continues its battle against the gremlin as the women compete similarly for air time, each trying to garner more sympathy than the last with tearful accounts of the effect Sarah's death has had on them. The conversation presents disingenuously through the screen, causing the sentiment on social media to shift for the worst. A deluge of harsh judgments cast by strangers on far away sectionals.

Cry me a river, they barely even knew this woman.

I'm sorry but this whole thing just seems SO staged.

This is pathetic, they should go back to the Doctor. At least she has brain cells.

If WBN doesn't want people to believe the @hollywoodpost article, they're not doing a very good job.

A contestant dies of a sleeping pill overdose the same year this woman gets hired? Coincidence or…? bit.ly/3sbT5

I click into the link and immediately slam the laptop shut as my face appears on the screen.

Patrick: Week Five, Friday

"I look fucking ridiculous."

"Come on, man, it's not that bad," Isaiah replies with a grin, doing a horrible job of stifling his laughter.

"I look like I'm going to the Sadie Hawkins Dance," I say, recalling the not-so-fond memory of pretending it didn't complete obliterate my confidence to stand by awkwardly while my best friend slow danced across the gym with my junior high crush. Isaiah doesn't even try to hide his laughter this time, letting it fly for the entire villa to hear. Not that I blame him. I'm dressed like a total square, standing here in a denim pearl snap shirt, snakeskin cowboy boots and—wait for it—a literal bolo tie. A real cowboy would knock me in the teeth.

"I refuse to wear this, though." I shove the straw hat toward him, determined to draw the line somewhere.

"Fine, you big baby," Isaiah grins and presses it down onto his afro, tipping the brim toward me. "How do I look?"

"Like a black Garth Brooks," I respond with a laugh.

"Wee, doggy! Saddle up, partner!" he does the best Southern accent he can muster as our black SUV pulls into the drive.

It takes about an hour to get to our destination, weaving out of the hills into traffic on the 405. We're not far from the Hollywood sign, well into the tourist trap part of the city, when the driver parks outside of the Coyote Ugly bar. I've never seen the movie but, based on what I've heard, it's a lot of women dancing in Daisy Duke shorts—giving me a pretty decent guess on what today's group date has in store.

"Hope you brought your dancin' boots!" Jeremy greets us with bravado as we walk in, confirming my suspicion. It's weird to see a bar so brightly lit, the crew deploying twice as many rigs as usual to compensate for the lack of windows. They've cleaned out most of the tables and chairs, clearing ample room in front of the long wooden bar on the back wall. Above the liquor shelf is a lighted marquee spelling out COYOTE UGLY in three-foot block letters.

"So tell me, Pat, you do any two-steppin' up there in Minnesota?" Jeremy slaps me playfully on the shoulder. I laugh anxiously and run a hand through my hair.

"Oh, sure, big pastime." Rhythm isn't exactly something you're born with as a lanky Scandinavian kid. At a wedding, you'd much sooner find me chatting up the groom's overly handsy aunt than embarrassing myself out on the dance floor. Though the thought of both still makes my palms sweat.

"Don't worry, no one's going to be making you get up on the bar," Jeremy replies. "Or anyone, for that matter."

"Damn," Isaiah interjects lightheartedly and I can't help but wonder if that was a change made because of recent events. Last season they didn't think twice before making the men strip down to our boxers for numerous group date challenges, critics be damned.

The saloon door at the back of the bar swings open and Reg steps through. It amuses me to see production has forced him to wear an equally stupid get-up to my own, looking like a fish out of water in bad bootcut jeans. I give him nothing more than a half-smile greeting and he responds with the same. If there's one thing we align on, it's that we're both beyond pleasantries at this point. He's here to do his job and so am I. Simple as that.

I hear through a nearby crew radio that the women are arriving and the director follows up with the two-minute time call. Isaiah escorts me to my mark, a small X made with electrical tape in front of the bar. There are two cameras pointed at me and another toward the door, situated to capture the arrival of the women. I have a wicked case of imposter syndrome as I try to play it cool, leaning my elbow casually against the bar top. I've got a feeling I look more like Howdy Doody than John Wayne.

The director's count reaches zero and the front door flings open with gusto, all eight women bounding toward me in tight tank tops and cut-off jean shorts, leaving little to the imagination. The wolf whistle feels a bit skeezy but I do it anyway for the sake of the producers. Reagan leads the pack and jumps into my arms, wrapping her legs so tightly around my waist that I find it hard to inhale. It's a classic dating show cliché—one that I know will have the other women staring daggers, so I give Reagan a quick courtesy spin and set her back down with the rest of the group.

"Ladies, Patrick, welcome to the world-famous Coyote Ugly," Reg begins, waving an arm to the marquee behind the bar as the women clap enthusiastically. "I take it some of you have seen the film?" A loud cheer rings out in response. Must have been mandatory viewing for the women while I was preoccupied with Forrest Gump.

"Fantastic!" Reg continues. "Guiding you all on today's adventure is my good friend Shayna. She will be your instructor as you learn how to line dance with the best of 'em."

The group lets out another collective "woo" as a woman, presumably Shayna, skips peppily into the shot. She's short and curvy with unnaturally died red hair, no shortage of cleavage spilling out the front of her skin-tight Coyote Ugly-emblazoned tank top. "Well for heaven's sake, there is nothing ugly about all ya'll!" Shayna lays on the southern accent extra thick. If I were a betting man, I'd say it's just one of many she's picked up as an aspiring actress in LA. She's probably from somewhere like Connecticut or Washington—nowhere near the Mason-Dixon Line. Seems to be the way it goes around here more often than not. No one's who they say they are.

The cameras continue to roll as we follow Shayna to the dance floor to begin the lesson. They've elected to dumb it down for us, swapping a simple line dance in place of what we're told is the far more challenging "Devil Went Down To Georgia" routine from the movie. Shayna asks us to form two rows and a few of the women passive-aggressively jockey for front and center—an awkward routine that inevitably happens on every group date. Mallory, another of this season's confidently spunky blondes, ultimately prevails, loudly touting the skills she picked up while attending multiple Nashville bachelorette parties. Some guys would probably be flattered by her effort but, if I'm being honest, the whole thing is a turnoff for me. I hardly envision my future wife being someone willing to literally throw elbows for the spotlight.

Shayna starts the lesson and, while I want to be focusing on the women, all I can fixate on is how detached my legs feel from the rest of my body. America's most eligible bachelor? More like the village idiot, stumbling around, tripping over my snakeskin boots. The only saving grace is that the women seem more focused on one-upping each other than watching me. I'm basically a viral video waiting to happen.

"Wow, I'm impressed. Clearly, you've done this before." I look up from my frustratingly uncoordinated feet and see Kya, who follows her sarcasm with the cutest little shit-eating grin.

"Is it that obvious?" I laugh, feeling tension release from my shoulders. Kya is the definition of a natural beauty. Skin like smooth caramel with a smattering of barely-there freckles beneath gold-specked green eyes. She looks far more comfortable in today's attire than when she was all dressed up for last week's elimination, her tight black braids pulled loosely into a ponytail that falls casually down her back.

"Just relax," Kya lays a hand gently on my forearm. "You played sports, right?" I nod, enjoying the reassurance of her touch. "Okay, so, did you ever do the grapevine as, like, a warm-up exercise?" I respond to the question with a blank stare, which elicits a laugh from her. "Or, ah, shoot. What do they sometimes call it... carioca?" Kya steps back and slowly crosses her feet. Over in front, step behind, over in front, step behind. I instantly recognize it from my high school sports days. I replicate her and, while it's still not pretty, it's far better than whatever I was doing before.

"See? Not that hard," she says with nonchalance.

"Guess I just needed the right teacher. Next you'll have to show me how to code websites like you. Then I'll really be dangerous." I lean in and nudge her playfully with my elbow. She grabs my bicep firmly and pats it. "One thing at a time, cowboy."

The urge to kiss her builds and, for what might be the first time in my life, I don't fight it—turning gently to meet her lips with my own. It's a soft sweet kiss that I break much earlier than I'd like, solely out of respect for the other women in the room. I've got a flutter in my stomach as I pull away, energized by the newfound connection. Besides Kya, I've only kissed Genavié— and that was more a product of the alcohol than anything. I wanted desperately to kiss Sarah on our first date, but I chickened out. This moment with Kya gave me that same kind of rush. It's exciting to feel excited again.

I'm still lost in Kya's eyes when the director calls for a ten-minute reset. They use the break to relocate all the camera equipment around a big semi-circle corner booth. I make a quick trip to the bathroom before cramming into it with the women, me in the middle with Reagan and Mallory beside me. I'd rather be next to Kya, but she hung back and let the others battle it out —yet another reason to like her.

The director signals we're rolling again and Shayna appears through the saloon doors, sliding two pitchers of light beer and a stack of plastic cups across the worn wooden table. I grin at the familiarity as I start filling and passing, observing a mix of reactions from the women. It's not exactly the five-star experience most of them applied for but, personally, I couldn't feel more at home.

"We having fun yet or what?" Reg saunters over and leans smarmily against the edge of the booth. I raise my cup and the women elicit another synchronized "woo" of approval. "Now, I know you're all eager to spend more time with Patrick but, unfortunately for seven of you, the bartender is issuing last call." The leather of the booth squeaks as the women nervously shift in their seats at the mention of the date's competition. I run a hand through my hair and prepare myself for the secondhand embarrassment I'm about to feel on their behalf. "We asked Shayna and the marvelous team here at Coyote Ugly to come up with a fun way to determine which lucky lady will get to stay after hours with Patrick... With that said, who's ready to turn up the heat?" Reg smirks as Shayna returns, balancing two trays filled with red checker-lined plastic baskets.

"Hope ya'll are hungry!" Shayna drops the trays down on the table and begins dispersing the eight baskets, one for each of the women. Their eyes widen as they see the contents—five bone-in chicken wings generously slathered in a reddish-orange sauce, the heat enough to assault my senses from two feet away. "These little suckers here are our Pit Wings, and they're hotter than a two-dollar pistol!

"The rules are simple, be the first lass to take down all five wings and win yourself extra time with the prize pig." Shayna winks at me as Reagan's hand moves its way from my quad to my thigh and up to the intersection of my hip flexor. I laugh awkwardly and quickly relocate it back toward my knee.

"Gross. Obviously I'm out," Sloane, the season's token vegan, dramatically shoves her basket to the middle of the table. "Do you realize how many chickens are inhumanely mutilated each year just so we can douse them in buffalo sauce?"

"Not enough if you ask me," Reagan responds as she tucks a napkin into her shirt. "Remind me, Sloane, what animal was sacrificed for that leather clutch you were showing off the other day?" A few of the women laugh out loud and I have to bite my lip to prevent myself from joining them.

"Oh my God, it was faux leather!" Sloane's defense goes unheard as the group readies themselves for the challenge at hand. It's a challenge I'm grateful to not partake in, my northern nose running from even being in the vicinity.

The women, as it turns out, are decidedly tougher. Or crazier, at least. Shayna's countdown reaches zero and the whole thing is over in all of three minutes—a whirlwind of saucy fingers, groans, coughs and curse words. It ends so quickly I'm not even certain who won until Shayna congratulates the winner. A name I didn't expect to hear...

Whitney: Week Five, Sunday

I pull up to Bar Blanca at 7:22 and take ten minutes longer than I need to touch up my makeup in the visor mirror. I was supposed to meet Paul at seven, so twenty-two minutes late puts me pretty right on schedule. You should always make a man sweat it out a little, but especially when that man is a grade-A bastard.

I drop my keys with the handsome young valet. He's got a face that reminds me of a young Brad Pitt—a throwback to all the *Tiger Beat* posters my sister and I had pinned onto the walls of our childhood bedroom. I slip him a fifty and a wink, which makes his cheeks flush bright pink. And who says men can't be objectified?

The other less genetically gifted teenage valet opens the front door and I step inside. Low lighting and expensive clientele, Bar Blanca is your quintessential don't-ask-don't-tell spot. Seems I'm spending a lot of time in places like this these days.

"Mr. Thomas is downstairs," a stuffy maître d' in an all-black suit directs me before I even have a chance to give him my name. Cigar smoke infiltrates my nostrils as I take the staircase down to the speakeasy in the basement, even more poorly lit than the main floor. The tobacco smell reminds me of my grandfather, but significantly more expensive. God, I hated him.

Hushed whispers crawl from the corners to the ceiling—their owners obscured in a haze of smoke. I don't have to see their faces to know most are old, fat and white. Paul whistles sharply out to me from the shadows. He's sitting in the corner on a grandiose tufted leather chair, one leg crossed over the other, a lit cigar resting gently between the fingers of his right hand. If you weren't me, you'd probably get the impression that he was a strong and powerful man. Thankfully, I know better.

Paul smiles softly when our eyes meet, standing as I approach.

"There she is, not a minute too soon." Paul smirks and reaches out for an embrace.

"Ha. Not on your life." I sidestep the contact and settle into the chair beside him, his cheeks flushing as though I've made a scene. A waitress in a pin-neat black vest and tie appears not seconds later and hands me a glass of merlot.

"I'm more into cabs lately," I lie. I'd rather drink a subpar wine than let Paul feel like he has the upper hand.

"My apologies, Annalise, I'll take it." Paul grabs the glass from the waitress. "A glass of the Harlan Estate cabernet for the lady?" He insecurely lobs the question my way and I give a silent half nod of approval.

"Aren't you going to offer me one of those?" I gesture to the cigar in his hand.

"I, ah, sorry. Do you want one? I thought you hated cigars," he fumbles.

"And yet, you invited me here." I gesture to the room, my words hanging momentarily in the smoky air.

"Mr. Thomas, your table is ready." The maître d' appears out of nowhere and cuts the tension, presumably to Paul's great relief.

"Wonderful. Thank you, Nico," Paul says with haste as he stands and waves an arm out in front of us. "After you."

"Nico" leads us back up the stairs to a secluded booth in the back corner of the restaurant. The tuxedo'd pianist gives a familiar nod to Paul as we pass. There's not an empty table in the place, most of them occupied by breathing liver spots spoiling their much younger dirty little secrets. Not worth the payout if you ask me but, hey, more power to you, ladies. I slide into the buttery leather booth and a new waitress, who looks eerily identical to the one from downstairs, sets an empty glass in front of me and fills it with what I only assume is a very expensive cabernet. Paul does have great taste in wine, I'll give him that.

"Considering we're not fucking anymore, what was so important that you just had to waste my evening over it?" Paul winces at my indiscretion and glances around with visible unease. No one's paying attention, everyone in here is hiding enough of their own skeletons to be concerning themselves with ours.

"Do you actually not care at all?" He asks, hushed. The sadness in his tone matches his eyes as he casts them down at the table. I sit back defiantly and take a sip of wine, determined not to let his dejection break me. "I hate myself for what I did to you, Whitney. These past few weeks have put me absolutely out of my head. It's like I can't focus on anything else when I see you. But you're so tough, Whit. And maybe you really are completely unfazed by this whole thing. I hope that's true. Because I- we can't afford to lose you on set Whit. Not with all that's happened, with everything we know." Paul's leg involuntarily shakes the table as I remain quiet, processing. It's all bullshit, of course, a ruse for a read. He knows about Lisa Perez, about NTV. He has to. Paul would never baselessly suspect I'd quit over the inevitable demise of a tired affair. This has Tammy's spying nose written all over it.

"Please, Whit. For the sake of my own sanity, I just need to know that we're good."

I stop spinning my wine and look straight at him, at the tiny drops of sweat forming on his brow. I take another sip and set down my glass, maintaining eye contact as I flash him a thin smile.

"We're good, Paul."

—

The lunch order is short five sandwiches, three soups and, most importantly, chicken salad. Not just any chicken salad—the holy grail of goddamn delicatessen delights. Made fresh daily, the perfect ratio of mayo to dijon, just enough celery to give it that refreshing snap. But nope, no refreshment today. Taking up its sacred space on the counter is an unsightly trough of tuna instead. Which not only makes a severely subpar replacement, but creates a sure source of stank in the crew room for the rest of the week. I've got too much pride to stomach a ham and cheese, so I settle for a bag of barbecue chips and a Diet Coke to wash down the bitter taste of the chicken salad I should be enjoying instead.

"What gives? Cecil's never gets our order wrong," I sit down in the empty chair next to Jeremy, who's busy unwrapping a turkey on rye.

"Error was on our end. One of the new PAs placed it." He subtly nods to the young blonde in the corner, buzzing anxiously around the counter like a fruit fly, apologizing profusely to anyone who lingers a moment too long. Taylor, is it? Who knows, who cares. I might have cared in another life. A life where I had walked away with a mound of chicken salad. Guess now we'll never know.

"Why didn't Tammy place it?" I ask. Putting aside every resentment I feel about the woman, she knows how to place a damn good lunch order.

"Paul told me she took the day off." *Paul told me*, the childish voice in my head mocks Jeremy's response as I crunch down on a chip.

"Interesting," I reply. "Didn't know Tammy took days off." Much to my chronic disappointment, she hasn't missed more than a handful of work days since I've known her. Convenient that today is the one I wish she hadn't.

"Good work with Foster, buddy." Isaiah walks behind us, slapping Jeremy on the back.

"Yeah, A-plus, Jeremy," a crew member whose name I've forgotten fires a thumbs up from across the table.

"Foster? As in Rosalie Foster?" I ask defensively. Rosalie Foster is the chief editor of the Hollywood Post, the poor excuse for a tabloid that seems dead set on running us into the ground.

"Shit, my bad, Whit. Did I not tell you that? I thought you

knew." Jeremy responds through a grotesque mouthful of turkey. "The article must have just gone live."

"What happened to 'we're not commenting on it'?" I ask. After the Post's last hit piece quoting the "anonymous" former producer, Paul's instructions not to engage with these jackals seemed very clear.

Jeremy swallows his bite. "We weren't but, the more I sat with it, the more it bothered me. Just because everyone knows they're a shameless gossip tabloid, we're supposed to let them bash us like that? Let them imply we're all sick enough to literally kill a girl for the sake of ratings? It's insanity. The industry gets a bad enough rap as it is. Someone had to stand up for us."

"And Paul just let you do it?"

"Ah, well," Jeremy runs a hand along the back of his neck. "I actually didn't tell him. I mean, he knows now, obviously. But I didn't come clean until after I met with her. You know what a tinder box M can be. The whole thing easily could have backfired."

"Exactly," I reply, "That's why I'm wondering how in the hell you managed to pull it off."

"Come on, Whit, one flash of this smile and I had her eating out of the palm of my hand." He puts a hand cheekily to his chin and beams his stupidly white teeth, eliciting an eye roll from me in response. "Kidding, of course." Jeremy's voice softens. "I don't know how, still trying to figure it out for myself, honestly. I just went to her in earnest and, for some reason, she took it to heart."

Of course she did. Much to my annoyance, everyone who meets Jeremy loves him. It's always been that way. Even when he was the scrawny mid-twenties guy with the horrible wire-rim rectangle glasses, pleated khakis and a never-ending rotation of J Crew gingham shirts. He used to lacquer so much gel into his hair that it doubled as cologne. Things were different back then between us. Just two young field producers against the world. We formed a special bond over the shared experience of scraping paycheck to paycheck, living off eating crew meal leftovers in cramped apartments filled with wannabe actors and models. We'd stay out late drinking piss-yellow light beer in greasy dive bars, taking bets on which contestant would be the first to cry that week. The Jeremy I knew then is hardly recognizable now, what with his effortlessly flowing black hair, trendy tailored shirts and an "in" with the Hollywood Post. It's like he's all but morphed into Paul entirely.

And I hate him for that.

Hannah: Week Five, Tuesday

A contestant dies of a sleeping pill overdose the same year this woman gets hired? Coincidence or…? bit.ly/3sbT5

I'm staring at the social media post again. The one that came through during last week's episode, leaving me shell-shocked in Taylor's apartment. It's now day six of torturing myself with it, no amount of busy work enough to distract me from its siren song. It loops through my brain on repeat, urging me to check for new likes and responses at every free moment—paranoia over who else has seen it completely consuming me.

The post creator's page is cryptically nondescript. A username of abc382923 and a stock avatar photo, it's the definition of a burner account. Someone created this for the sole purpose of exposing my past. And there's a pretty short list of who that might be.

I drag my thumb down and refresh the screen again. Still only three replies. I breathe a sigh of relief and hope by now it's been buried by other content, lost in the ether.

I read the first one again: *Craig Burnside is her uncle… bet that's how she landed the job.*

Then the reply: *Who is Craig Burnside?*

And finally: *I feel a true crime podcast coming on…*

I scroll back up to the post and, like an addict seeking one more self-destructive hit, I click into the article.

FAMILY FILES WRONGFUL DEATH LAWSUIT AGAINST

DAUGHTER'S FORMER FIANCE

Northfield, Minn. (December 18, 2020) - A local family filed a wrongful death lawsuit against their daughter's former fiancé following her suicide in September.

The lawsuit claims the family's daughter, Ellie Russo, took her own life as a result of being subject to "extreme control" and "gaslighting" by Hannah Baker.

Russo's death on September 15 was ruled a suicidal overdose after copious amounts of sleeping medication were discovered in her system. Russo and Baker were living together in St. Paul with plans to be married in October.

Russo's family maintains that their daughter, a heterosexual woman, was manipulated by Baker into believing she was attracted to and had desires to marry her. Russo's mother, Michelle, likened Russo's state at the time of her death to "Stockholm Syndrome"—the psychological phenomenon in which a hostage develops a positive association to his or her captor.

"Long before Ellie lost her life, she had been taken from us. Our daughter was a God-fearing Christian woman when she met Hannah Baker. She would have never willingly entered into such a relationship without extreme manipulation," Russo's mother said. "We did everything we could to save Ellie and are devastated it was not enough. Our focus now is to preserve her memory as we once knew her and make sure such a tragedy is not allowed to happen to someone else."

Baker and her attorney declined to comment. Baker has no previous criminal record.

—

"No matter what they throw at us, we are not going to respond." My attorney's voice echoes in my head like it was yesterday. Every memory I have from those few weeks is like that... Visceral. Grating. Eternal.

I was sitting motionless in the kitchen of my parents' house, staring holes into the dilapidated wood grain of their dining room table, a time capsule of my formative years. A fork mark from when I got angry with my brother for asking my best friend to prom, pen stains from the multiple letters I drafted and scrapped before finally coming out to my parents at twenty-three.

That particular afternoon, Mom was in the chair next to me while Dad stood behind her, back leaned against the outdated granite countertop of the kitchen island. For a man who makes his living selling houses, Dad's never been all that interested in making any major updates to our own. Says it feels too much like "bringing work home." He kept his arms crossed so long that day I remember wondering if they would become permanently stuck that way, the subtle back and forth of his jaw betraying the concern he thought he was doing well to hide. Tom, my attorney, sat directly across the table. Thirty-five years of experience showed in the lines on his face and the white in his thinning hair. He was the best defense we could find—and afford. Dad claimed he was nowhere near ready to retire anyway, but I'm not oblivious. I know the financial toll I took on my parent's plans.

Tom did his best to show us we were more than just a paycheck. Intense but kind, he showed genuine compassion for the hell we were going through.

"This case is going to get thrown out," he spoke directly and with confidence, focusing his gaze on me, much as I'd prefer he not. "It's honestly pretty preposterous an attorney even took it. There's a total lack of evidence. Anything for the right price, I guess." We learned shortly after that the attorney in question previously had a stint representing the Minnesota Archdiocese in a string of money laundering and embezzlement scandals. "The Crooked Crusader", as Mom would go on to call him.

"And what if it doesn't? Get thrown out," Dad asked. He handled nearly all of the communication with Tom by this point. Mom tended to get too emotional and me, well, I was stuck in a perpetual state of shock and denial.

"It will," Tom doubled down.

"Just play it out for me here, will you Tom? What happens if, for whatever reason, it doesn't get thrown out?" Dad asked again, his impatience growing. I was just getting to know the gremlin then, and questions like this made it stir. None of us wanted to think about worst-case scenarios but, ever the realist,

Dad knew we had to. I ran my fingers anxiously across the fork holes in the table as I waited for Tom to reply, wishing my brother was here with us instead of holding down things at the agency for Dad. Ryan's calm demeanor had always anchored our family, and this was a moment when we needed him most.

"Ah, it's hard to say," Tom finally replied. "There's no precedent for this in Kent County. More than likely it would result in a settlement of some sort. Damages paid to the family, that type of thing. But, again, it won't come to that."

"We're not giving a dime to those horrendous people!" Mom shouted, bursting into tears. Dad stepped forward and rubbed his hands gently on her shoulders. She took a few deep breaths and softened her voice to almost a whisper, "I just won't. Not after what they did to Ellie. What they're doing to our Hannah now…"

—

"Helloooo, earth to Hannah." Kate's voice snaps me out of the past. She's standing in the doorway of the crew room, clipboard resting at her hip. "You ready?"

"Yes, sorry. Must have been dozing off," I reply, shaking myself out of it with a shudder.

"With your eyes open?" she laughs and I smile awkwardly as I push myself back from the table. I've been invited to sit in on Kate's confessionals again today, a small reward for all the busy work I've been distracting myself with over the past week. "I was starting to think Seth was never going to give you up. He must really like you."

"Hah, yeah," I laugh absentmindedly as I follow her down the hall to the confessional rooms, too drowsy from the emotional memory to consider whether that could even be remotely true.

"You okay?" Kate asks. It's impossible not to wonder if she or anyone else on the crew has seen the post and the article. If they have, they're not saying. And the not knowing is almost worse.

"Yeah, sorry, I'm good. Just been a crazy few days," I follow up. "Thank you for this, by the way. I could use the break."

"Don't mention it. I do it because I wish someone had done it for me. Simple as that." I nod and smile in response, finding it very hard to feel like I deserve Kate's kindness.

As she finishes finalizing details with the camera crew, I realize I don't even know who we're interviewing. I'm about to ask when the answer walks in.

"Morning!" Olivia says cheerfully with a charmingly slight Southern twang, as if the "g" in "morning" is silent. She's wearing black joggers and a grey University of Kentucky v-neck t-shirt.

After our mortifying first encounter, I was determined to learn everything I could about Olivia—my online stalking driven by equal parts paranoia and admiration for the beautiful stranger who showed extreme kindness in an incredibly unsettling situation. A Kentucky native and graduate of UK, Olivia moved out to Seattle for nursing school and still lives there now. Based on all the photos of her enthusiastically smiling beside mountain summit signs, I gathered that she's fully embraced the Pacific Northwest lifestyle. Her captions were all simple. Short and sweet descriptions of family and friends, the occasional Bible verse sprinkled in about expressing gratitude or choosing joy. Everything fit the mold of the ideal dating show contestant.

"Have you two met yet?" Kate looks from Olivia to me and my entire body tenses.

"I don't think we have! Not officially, at least," Olivia walks over to me and extends her hand. "I'm Olivia."

"Hannah." I do my best to show gratitude for her discretion with only my eyes. My stomach does a flip when she smiles softly in return, finding a momentary comfort in her doe brown eyes.

"Hannah's one of our new production assistants. She sits in on these from time to time—when she's not filling portable hot tubs in the middle of the desert, that is." Olivia giggles at Kate's joke, a nod to the five hours I spent setting up for Patrick's date yesterday with Sloane, another "filler" contestant. In a crazy turn of events, my effort turned out to be all in vain. Patrick went rogue and sent her home before they even popped the champagne. The producers obviously weren't thrilled, but it's not exactly something that can be rewound once the words leave his mouth. He just kept saying, "When you know, you know." Suppose it's hard to fault the guy for that.

Olivia grabs a sparkling water from the fridge and takes her seat in front of the cameras. I find myself fixated on her every move, in awe of the effortless grace she has about her, as if she's never felt awkward or uncomfortable in her life. It's something I can't relate to in the slightest.

"So, Olivia, seems like this was a pretty good week for you?" Kate opens up the conversation casually. "You made that hot wing eating challenge look easy."

"Oh my goodness," Olivia laughs and puts her hands up to cover her face. "I'm actually so embarrassed about that. Honestly, I just love hot wings. Getting the time with Patrick was just an added bonus." I hold my breath to stifle a laugh, trying not to throw off the audio, again struck by how charming and infectious she is.

"And how was that extra time? We just talked last week about how you really haven't had many opportunities with Patrick yet, so I'm sure you were excited to finally set yourself apart from the rest of the women."

"Right, I mean, as I said before, it felt like everything up until that point had been so chaotic. Four weeks in and I wasn't sure where I stood with him or, even more so, how I felt about him in return." Olivia takes a breath and smiles. "But, after Friday night, it's really obvious to me that there is something special there. Patrick is so different than the guys I've dated in the past."

"Oh yeah? What do you mean by that?" Kate prompts.

"He's just… well, there's something very calming about him, very sweet. The opposite of an asshole, basically." I smile as Olivia laughs out loud again. "He just made me feel so comfortable. I thought I had my guard up but, there I was, spilling my spicy hot wing guts to this guy."

"Is there a reason you had your guard up?" Kate asks.

"The reason is men," Olivia laughs. "Particularly the cheating kind. The most serious relationship I've had ended when I came home to him in bed with my roommate. That really messed me up, you know. This person is your whole entire world and, in a matter of seconds, you realize you're basically worth nothing to them. It's not easy to come back from that."

If I had been watching Olivia's interview from my couch as a viewer, I'd probably have eye rolled. Another woe-is-me sob story from a beauty queen who could easily find someone equally attractive to help her get over it. But there's just something different about being in the room here with Olivia, listening to her heartbreaking story firsthand. It's a reminder that we've all got our gremlins... no one makes it through this life unscathed.

Patrick: Week Five, Wednesday

"Well, at least tonight will be a little easier with one less woman to contend with."

Five hours until tonight's live elimination, Isaiah and I are out on the private patio of my villa suite, looking out over the boundless blue Pacific Ocean in the distance. I'm feeling pretty relaxed, all things considered, kicked back in a chair with my feet up on the table. Isaiah sits next to me, loudly crunching on a bag of Cheetos.

"Ha, ha," he replies sarcastically. "Still a little too soon to be making that joke around here."

"What can I say? When you know, you know," I repeat the line again, my go-to defense for sending Sloane home not even a half-hour into this week's solo date. I wouldn't be joking about it if I thought she actually cared. No tears, hardly even acted upset. Seems obvious that Sloane wasn't into me any more than I wasn't into her.

"You know that's not the point." Isaiah pops a handful of bright orange puffs into his mouth.

"I just don't see the big deal. And anyway, isn't that what you guys want? Whatever happened to 'drama drives ratings'?"

"It only drives ratings if you loop us in on it first. No one hates a surprise more than the network." The unfamiliar sharpness in Isaiah's voice takes me aback. There are very few times I've seen him take this tone, and it's never been directed at me. "Listen man, you like me, right? Might even go so far as to say that we're friends?"

"Yeah, of course," I reply, backing off the banter to show I'm taking the conversation more seriously now.

"And you're a good guy. The type of guy that wants what's best for his friends. Like, gainful employment, for example?" He asks as I start to get a better sense of his direction.

"Yeah, I'd say that's accurate."

"Your apartment in Chicago, it got a guest room?"

"Ah, no?"

"Well if you don't want me sleeping on your couch for the next year, you better never pull anything like that again. You are my responsibility here. When shit like that blows up, I'm the one who has to answer for it. And I've seen people get fired for far less. I might not be so lucky next time."

"Alright, alright, I'm sorry." I pause, my hand going through my hair. "It's just harder to go through the motions now that I'm actually starting to make real connections."

"Connections being Olivia." The corners of my mouth instinctively turn up at sound of her name. Isaiah's words are not a question, they're a confirmation—and I can tell by the stern look on his face that I'm not quite out of the woods yet.

"No, there's more than just Olivia. I'm into Kya, too." My response isn't a lie. I am into Kya. She's beautiful and smart and funny and so many other things that would make me a damn lucky guy to end up with her. When I kissed her at Coyote Ugly, there's no denying that I felt something. But when I got time alone with Olivia after the hot wing challenge, the whole game changed. I've never experienced anything like it, I can't get her out of my head. All of the outrageously hopeless romantic feelings you hear people describe on this show but never believe could possibly be true. Here I am now, living breathing proof—a reality TV sucker without a damn to give about what the skeptics think.

With Olivia, two hours felt like two minutes. I couldn't believe how much we had in common—faith, family, sports. I mean, the girl might actually be a bigger college basketball fan than I am. At one point, we started up a fierce debate over whether Kentucky, her alma mater, or Michigan State, my childhood favorite, had a more historic program. She was right by a landslide, of course, but I was having way too much fun watching how riled up it made her to admit that. It was like someone trapped boisterous ESPN analyst Stephen A. Smith in an adorable little five-foot-three woman's body. She made me laugh so hard I thought I'd never stop, all the way through the point when I finally kissed her, the heat of those stupid Pit Wings still on her lips—which, then, we laughed about too. Even with the lingering burn, the moment was perfect. So, yeah, I guess you could say I really like this girl. Sue me.

"I've seen some crazy shit happen on this show, Pat. Watched sure things go up in flames over one conversation. I mean, you remember what happened with Nicole's season, don't you?" I grimace in understanding. It wasn't watching the show back then, but you had to be living under a rock to not have heard about it. The season's clear favorite, a real Prince Charming, slips up, calls Nicole by his ex-girlfriend's name. Except it turns out she's not technically an ex, and he confesses he's very much still in love with her. So Nicole sends him home and suddenly she's left with two guys she hardly knew. Marries one of them anyway and they're divorced before the next season begins.

"All I'm saying is, don't write the other ladies off just yet," Isaiah continues. "Give the process, and I mean the *whole* process, as it was *designed*, a chance. If Olivia's really the one, so be it. She'll still be the one at the end. No more of this going off-book stuff," Isaiah finishes his point and crunches down on his last Cheeto, crumpling up the empty bag and tossing it toward the trash bin in the corner of the patio. The slight breeze holds it up and it deflects off the side. Normally I'd razz him for missing, but I think better of it today.

A low rumble sounds in the distance and I assume it's a plane. When I hear it the second time, I crane my neck around at the sky behind us. A wall of thick dark clouds looms to the east.

"Huh," I say, watching as they slowly roll our direction. "I didn't think it ever stormed here."

Isaiah stands and brushes orange Cheeto dust off his shorts. A crack of lightning rips across the horizon. "Storms everywhere, sooner or later."

PART THREE

Hannah: Week Six, Thursday

Word around the villa is dead on impact. Missed the corner entirely, shot straight through the gravel before plummeting down into the thick tree trunks at the bottom of the embankment.

That's the word, at least.

No one is really sure when it even happened. Could have been days ago. Roads were slick after that nasty storm rolled through.

It's somber at the villa today, about twenty percent crew capacity between those who took the dismissal no questions asked and those who stuck around to speculate about it. Why I'm still here, I'm not sure. It's like I can't will my legs to stand up and leave—paralyzed by this feeling that death is following wherever I go.

I can't imagine how hard Uncle Craig is taking this. The thought that I ought to check in on him is what ultimately gets me up and out of the crew room. That gives my body the motivation it needs to carry me all the way out to the car.

I get three rings before I'm sent to voicemail. I'm not much for phone conversations, so there's always a wave of relief that washes over me when someone doesn't answer. It's stupid, really—only delays the awkwardness for another time. With the accident top of mind, I'm highly alert as I wind my Rav 4 down the lush greenery of the hillside, slowing to a stop as I come upon the scene. A police SUV is parked on the gravel just before the corner, but no officer in site. They've set up barricades along the right half of the road, leaving space for only one car to pass through at a time. I peer under one and try to make out tire tracks, but any indication has been washed out by the unusual amount of rain that's fallen over the last few days. I have the urge to get out and look over the edge, but the thought of an officer being down there—and having to converse with said officer—keeps me inside my car. I wonder how many other crew members passed through and contemplated the same thing.

There's a ringing through my speakers and Uncle Craig's name flashes across the console. I click accept and shift the car back into drive. "Hey, Uncle Craig. I'm so sorry."

"Thank you, Hannah, for calling," he stammers, sounding absolutely exhausted. As if losing someone you care about isn't enough, I can't even imagine the logistical nightmare he's facing at the network. "It just, it doesn't make any sense. Everyone knows how dangerous that road can be. We've all driven it a million times." The road in question rolls smoothly underneath my tires, an unapologetic killer right below my floorboards. Goosebumps crawl up my arms and I release my foot slightly off the gas.

"What will happen with the show now?" The thought over whether my subject change might be insensitive comes too late, the words having already left my mouth.

"Ah, well," he hesitates and loudly sighs, further solidifying my regret. "It's tough to say for sure… It's not the first time a WBN show has had a crew member pass mid-season. There's precedent for pushing through. Sounds like the network is ultimately going to put that decision on the production team. They're the ones closest to it." I squeeze the wheel a bit tighter, the gremlin lurching at another uncertainty over what lies ahead.

"Listen, kiddo, I have to run. But thank you again for calling."

"Take care of yourself, Uncle Craig."

"You too, Hannah… Please."

—

The exhaustion of the day hits the moment I twist my key in the lock and push open the door. My eyelids feel like they're being weighed down with rolls of quarters and, for a moment, I contemplate collapsing right there in the entryway. Like a scene straight out of a sitcom, only everything is the opposite of funny.

I hate myself for how disheveled the apartment looks. A half-drank water glass creating a ring on the counter, pillows and blankets strewn out of place. I kick off my shoes in the middle of the kitchen, succumbing to the mess, a problem for tomorrow. Or the next day. Or maybe even the one after that.

I drop my backpack beside the couch and let my body sink into it, lazily kicking the blanket at my feet up to my hands. My fingers fumble their way through my backpack's zippered compartment until I find the catalyst to tonight's fever dream...

I'm out quickly, transported from the couch to a local county fair. Not the fair from my childhood, but the random small town one Ellie and I stopped at years ago. It was her idea, of course, a spontaneous detour en route to Northfield, her hometown. It was my first and only visit, moving the last of her things while her parents were away for the weekend. She never did tell them that I came with her. That I slept there, in their home, cuddled closely next to Ellie beneath one of her mother's many hand-sewn quilts. I was there and gone without a trace. If only it had stayed that simple.

The dream fair is as quaint and charming as the real one was. My shoes kick up dust on the trodden dirt path as I meander through, the sweet smell of mini donuts wafting through the air, carnival games dinging over the slow steady cranking of the Ferris wheel. Only this time, there's no Ellie. This time, I'm alone.

A carnival barker jumps out onto the path in front of me. He's dressed in old-timey attire—red pinstripe vest, velvet arm bands, blonde hair whisping out from beneath a black top hat. My brow furrows as I squint to recognize him. *Patrick?* I smile curtly and pick up my pace, hoping to dodge any interaction. My efforts are in vain as he moves to meet me, blocking my path. He puts a hand firmly onto the small of my back and guides me with a gentle force toward the fun house. I look up in fear as he pushes me closer and closer to the entrance, which I now recognize is a giant open mouth—*Reg's* giant open mouth. I turn back in panic as Patrick flashes a Cheshire cat smile and shepherds me inside.

There's a loud cranking of gears as Reg's mouth closes behind me and engulfs me in total darkness. I spin around, but Patrick is gone, leaving me alone in the black. I frantically run my hands on the cool metal backside of the entrance, looking for something, anything I can grab that might allow me to force it back open. But there's nothing. Only a smooth seamless wall. A short clicking noise begins, followed by a dull whir. I turn back to the fun house, the spinning peppermint walkway now lit up in front of me. Nowhere to go but through, I step onto the spiral precariously, maintaining my balance by locking my eyes on the only fixed point I can find—a neon "Lover's Lane" sign flashing in the darkness beyond the end of the tunnel. I'm jarred off balance when my feet return to solid ground, the startle you get as a kid at the playground jumping off the merry-go-round. An arrow below the sign directs me to the right and I follow it. As I turn the corner, a burning vehicle comes into view. A green SUV, smashed nose-end into a rotting tree trunk. A couple sits in the front seats, clearly the "lovers", their heads huddled closely as they exchange intimate whispers and kisses. I get a better look inside as I pass, discovering that it's Paul and Whitney, their blistered skin illuminated by the flames. The blood drains from my face at the ghastly sight of them. Lost in each other's glassy eyes, neither seems to notice as I quickly sneak by into the next passageway.

I release the breath I'd been holding as I come to the other side, finding myself on the villa patio, the lights of the pool exposing a deep and murky red cloud billowing through the water. Flanking the pool deck are fourteen women—this season's contestants. They're all dressed for the elimination ceremony in blindingly sparkly gowns, grinning ear to ear with perfect beauty pageant smiles. All of them except for Sarah, whose head holds nothing—literally. Only a horrifying blank stretch of skin where her face should be.

My stomach begins to retch but I can't bring myself to look away from her. I'm startled as someone gently takes my hand in theirs. I recoil, turning in shock to see Olivia, a literal glow exuding from her ruby-red dress. I try to pull back, but she holds firm as a grainy gramophone recording plays the familiar Wizard Of Oz line, "There's no place like home, there's no place like home."

Olivia pulls me forward to the next room, the house of mirrors, where I'm assaulted with twenty reflections of my own terror. I'm wearing a freshly ironed white dress shirt tucked snugly into a knee-length pencil skirt. I know it well, it's the outfit I wore to the court hearing. My eyes shift to Olivia's reflection next, only it isn't Olivia anymore. Same red dress but her face has changed into Ellie's. Stricken white, eyes sunken deeply into protruding sockets, blue veins spiderwebbed all over her chest and arms. The sight drops me to my knees, the taste of bile rising in my throat. I reach out to her and she mirrors the movement, her hand flowing seamlessly through the glass. Her fingers are cold and rigid as they intertwine with mine. She clasps down hard and yanks me forward.

The sensation of falling jars me awake. My heart is beating so fast it feels as though it might actually explode through my sternum. I jump to my feet and stumble to the bathroom, flipping the toilet lid just in time to empty what little was in my stomach. I stand, still shaky, and splash cold water on my face. It provides a jolt but not enough to quell the aftershock—my body needs something much stronger. I don't even bother to strip off my clothes before stepping into the shower, hastily twisting the valve and letting the icy water penetrate me to my core. I stand beneath the stream for nearly thirty seconds before cranking it back 180 degrees, the stark contrast of the heat delivering the shock I was looking for. I twist the valve back to a comfortable warmth and stay there, standing still as a statue for ten minutes until the water soothes my prickled skin and lowers my rapid heart rate.

With my hair wrapped in one towel and my body in another, I

return to the living room in search of my phone. I unearth it from the depths beneath the couch cushion and the armrest to find a "high importance" email notification displaying brightly across the screen.

To: allhm@wbn.com
From: paul.thomas@wbn.com
Subject: Update
-Message sent with high importance-
Team,

In my sixteen years on this crew, never before has an email been as difficult to send as this one. As you are all very aware, we lost a member of our HM family this week. Tammy Berg was a beloved daughter, sister, aunt and friend. On many occasions, she was also a hell of a stand-in mother to all of the members of this crew. Hard as I try to make sense of her tragically unexpected passing, I regret to tell you I simply do not have the words.

As I grapple with this loss, I want to let you all know that I have made the painstakingly difficult decision to step away for the remainder of the season. I am simply not in the right headspace to provide the thoughtful and informed leadership you all deserve as we push this through to the finish line.

Both Jeremy and Whitney have proved themselves more than capable of taking on showrunner responsibilities in my absence, and I have full confidence in their ability to navigate the ship through any other unforeseen storms. I suspect they might even show us that two is much better than one.

Please know that the entire network, as well as Jeremy, Whitney and I, understand that this will impact each of you differently. If there is anything you need to help you process and grieve, do not hesitate to ask.

Good luck, be well, and I'll see you on the other side.
-PT

Whitney: Week Six, Monday

The only place I hate more than hospitals is churches. And since my Dad died twenty-two years ago, I've successfully managed to avoid both. Judging by the state of the one I'm currently standing in, they clearly haven't changed much since then. Is dusting a cardinal sin? Or is the permanent scent of must all part of the effect? I'm not even sure what type of church this is. Catholic? Lutheran? Protestant? As if it makes a difference. It's all just a different dressing on the same lie. The one parents tell kids so they grow up believing all of this actually means something. So when their Dad wastes away before their eyes, they can point to a reason other than the truth—that the world is just a randomly cruel and unforgiving place.

If there had been some way for me to get out of this without coming across badly to the network, I'd have taken it. Tammy Berg doesn't want me at her funeral any more than I want to be here. I'd put my own life on that.

"Here, accidentally grabbed two," Isaiah says as he hands me a program. I didn't intend to pick one up, but what choice do I have now? I flip it over and Tammy smiles at me from her permanent resting place atop a cheap piece of recycled paper.

In Loving Memory of Tamara Elizabeth Berg
June 18, 1960 to August 1, 2021
Tamara "Tammy" Elizabeth Berg was a beloved sister, aunt and friend. She left this world tragically on August 1, 2021 at sixty-one

years old.

Tammy was born to Vernon and Delores Berg on June 18, 1960 in Key West, Florida where her father was stationed with the U.S. Marine Corps. She was one of six children, and the only girl.

Tammy enjoyed gardening, hobby shooting and, most of all, spending time with her many nieces and nephews. She also found great fulfillment in her long career at the television network, WBN. She often referred to her Heaven's Match colleagues as a second family.

The Berg family finds some solace that, in death, Tammy will be reunited with her beloved brother (Joseph), father (Vernon) and mother (Delores). In lieu of flowers, they have requested that donations be made to the Wounded Warrior Foundation.

I look up from the program to see Paul with his wife, Kelly, and two kids in tow, the entire family color-coordinated in a sad little quadrant of dark grey dresswear. His son and daughter should be about elementary-aged now, I think. I've never been good at guessing kids' ages, probably a result of doing whatever I can to spend as little time around them as possible. It strikes me how much Paul's son, Danny, is starting to look just like him. Tall and angular with a mop of thick wavy brown hair that hangs past his eyebrows. His daughter, Kennedy, is largely hidden from my view, the young girl gripping tightly to the dress that hangs loosely on her mother's board-flat frame. Kelly's brown hair is cropped at her shoulders in the exact same boring style she's worn I first met her all those years ago. It was a retirement party for some old network executive, a few months after things had started up between me and Paul. He didn't bother to introduce us, which was more than fine by me. But, inevitably, we crossed paths in the bathroom as women do. She complimented my lipstick. Revlon, velvet red. And for a moment, I almost felt guilty... almost.

It's obvious Kelly's been crying by the pink swell around her eyes. As the four of them amble into the line of people waiting to gawk at the poster board scrapbook of Tammy's life, she reaches into her purse and pulls out a pack of tissues. God, the two of us could not be more different.

—

An onslaught of curse words is the only self-talk I can muster as my thighs fight the resistance. Heavy, thick, stodgy—like I'm crawling through quicksand. Every push and pull on the pedals reminds me of the cardio torture chamber I'm locked into by the clips of my cycling shoes.

"Fuck, some days I really hate this place," I pant breathlessly to Kate. She doesn't hear me. Or, if she does, she doesn't acknowledge it. Kate's fully in the zone as usual—eyes shut, head nodding along to the deep bass of the club music pumping through the speakers, perfectly synced with the flashing colored DJ lights. Our instructor, who is all of four-foot-nine, shouts harshly at us like a tiny drill sergeant who starts every morning with a shaker of pre-workout and a few lines in the bathroom. After three minutes that feel like three hours, the instructor's voice lowers about twenty decibels, signaling completion of the final rolling hill. I release my grip from the sweat-covered handles and sit up straight on the bike, using the towel from my neck to sop up the bodily fluids dripping down my arms and face. Kate remains annoyingly in-zone as we go through the cool-down stretch, not turning her attention to me until the lights of the studio come up.

"Wow, that one was a killer," Kate says as we walk—or, more accurately for me, wobble—toward the locker room. Even when she says it was killer, I'm never quite sure if she means it or if she's just trying to make me feel better about how absolutely gassed I look. Kate hardly ever misses a class. The same obviously can't be said for me.

After a quick rinse in the shower, we pit stop at the studio's in-house smoothie bar. It's one of those trendy cafes designed specifically to look good in social media photos. All white everything, flooded with natural light and a vibrant green succulent in every corner. I grab a table by the window while Kate goes to the counter and orders us two Green Machine smoothies from the paid-to-be-flirty HIIT instructor slash barista whose muscles threaten to rip right through the sleeves of his Baby Gap-sized t-shirt. I glance up at the menu behind him on the wall, a depressing reminder of what my life has been reduced to—kale, spinach, hemp seeds, pea protein. Long gone are the days of crushing deliciously greasy sausage mcmuffins and hash browns for breakfast without the fear of cottage cheese thighs.

"Here you are, Ms. Showrunner," Kate slides the smoothie to me as she takes a seat across the table.

"*Co*-showrunner," I correct her and suck down my first dose of emulsified grass through an already disintegrating paper straw. As it turns out, a lot of things taste as good as skinny feels.

"Oh, stop. I think it's going to be great, actually. Assuming you two can get along," she says with a tone that's as doubtful as her eyebrow raise.

"That's the million-dollar question, isn't it?" I spin the smoothie absentmindedly in my hand. It really is though, the same question I've been wondering since Paul told me and Jeremy the news. Don't get me wrong, I wanted to be showrunner more than anything—but not like this. *Shared* with Jeremy? What a cop-out. And despite the hunky-dory Boy Scout act, I know, deep down, Jeremy feels the same. How could he not? Paul's been grooming him for this all season. Why the network decided to split the responsibility between us, I'm still not entirely sure. The only thing I can think is, given what the crew has already been through, they'd rather keep things copasetic than have Paul light an atom bomb on his way out. Lord knows my ass would have been out the door so fast if they only promoted Jeremy. I'd be running NTV by now and, based on our meet-up last Sunday, Paul knows it.

Got five minutes to chat? A text from Paul flashes across my phone screen, as if his ears were burning.

Sure, give me five. I shoot back.

"I've got to run," I say to Kate and abruptly stand up from the table. "I'll see you at the villa."

—

"Shouldn't you be off on a golf course somewhere?" I ask as I settle into the driver's seat, the audio switching from my phone to the car speakers.

"Hey, Whit." He steamrolls over my playful sarcasm. "Sorry for the early call. I have a favor to ask."

"Oh yeah?" I ask with a hint of arrogance, my ego flaring up.

"Jeremy's on, too," Paul immediately douses it.

"Morning, Whit," Jeremy pipes in, proving nothing is sacred in this professional ménage à trois I now find myself in.

"I'm sorry to do this over the phone. I would have preferred in person but, after such an emotional week, Kel thought it'd be good for us to spend the week together out at Big Bear." I bite the inside of my cheek at the thought of his perfect little family and their perfect little getaway. Must be nice to have a seven-million-dollar lake home to escape to while the rest of us attempt to salvage not only the season but the future of the franchise as a whole.

"As you both know, the state's investigation ruled Tammy's accident to be just that—an accident. But, unfortunately, it's not quite closed as far as her family is concerned. A gentleman introduced himself to me at the service yesterday, a private investigator. He asked for permission to access the villa."

"I'm sorry—*what?*" I ask.

"*Why?*" Jeremy echoes my confusion.

"I don't really think it's anything to worry about," Paul attempts to reassure us. "The Bergs are a little backwoods, to put it bluntly. Mistrust of the government and all that."

"Can't we just say no?" I respond.

"Technically, yes, but I'm asking for your permission on this as a favor to the family—a favor to Tammy." Paul replies in a way that tells us it's more of a command than a request. God, I hate when he does this. I didn't owe that woman any favors in life, but somehow she's managing to force one out of me from beyond the grave.

"Of course," Jeremy says, his voice dripping in a nauseating sympathy. "I can't even imagine what they're going through."

"Thank you, Jeremy. We can certainly limit access. He understands we're in the middle of filming so it won't just be open season on the property or the contestants," Paul continues. "You and the crew have a job to do, and he knows he is not to interfere with that."

"Totally," Jeremy is quick to fall in line as usual, but I keep my mouth shut. I never trust an outsider. We're dealing with enough as it is without some wildcard threatening to upend the entire system.

"You two just focus on keeping up the great work," Paul says before a momentary pause. "We're still in control of the narrative."

Whether that's true or not, we're certainly about to find out.

Patrick: Week Six, Monday

"Thank you," I mutter sheepishly, nothing but a towel around my waist as a fresh-faced wardrobe assistant passes me a black garment bag. I grab it by the hanger and close the door of my suite. As I carry it to the closet, I take notice of the bag's heavier weight—likely a suit, meaning tonight's date is bound to be more formal. Wardrobe is typically my only indication of what's to come. I hang it from the hook on the back of the door and pull down the zipper. A jet-black James Bond tuxedo confirms my suspicion and then some. Dive bars and hot wings certainly aren't in my future with this get-up.

Tonight is the first double date of the season and my nerves are high. Olivia *and* Reagan. Two drastically different women, but my focus is only on one. And as I swap my towel for the monkey suit and run a hand through my hair, all I can think is "Man, I hope she likes it."

I'm finishing with the silver cufflinks when the door swings open with enough force that it bangs loudly against the wall. I know it's Isaiah without even looking. No one else would barge in on me like that.

"What happened to knocking?" I shout into the hall, picking a small piece of lint from my sleeve.

"Wow-ee! That's a sharp-dressed man!" His voice booms as he appears behind me in the mirror.

"Here, make yourself useful," I hand him the bow tie and he

laughs as he ties it loosely around his own neck before handing it back to me. I'd like to think I would eventually figure it out myself but, after five years on this show, Isaiah's far faster at it than I could ever be.

"Ride just pulled up. You ready for this?"

"I'm ready for this," I say, the suit almost giving me enough confidence to actually believe it. I follow him out to the driveway where two stretch limos are waiting, an upgrade from the standard SUVs. Isaiah opens the door to the first and I duck down to slide in, no sight of the women as ours pulls away. Isaiah pulls two water bottles out of the limo's mini fridge and tosses one to me across the aisle. I peel at the label as we wind down the hillside and head north, unexpectedly away from the city, a direction I've never been. The uncertainty has me as on-edge as the limo, weaving corner after corner, closer to the unknown.

A half hour and another peeled water bottle later, the limo slows to a stop seemingly out of nowhere. We're still very much along the narrow and craggy hillside and, if not for the four WBN vans snugged up tightly to the rock wall, I'd have thought we were lost. I squint through the window, scanning for any indication of what lies ahead. Isaiah opens the limo door and slides out.

"Where the hell are we?" I ask as I follow him, stepping onto the red gravel, moving deliberately slow so as not to kick dust up onto my black pants. He doesn't answer, stepping to the right behind the line of vans, walking the narrow path between them and the wall. From here, I can see that we're heading toward an opening in the rock, about a doorway's width—the vans had obscured it from my previous vantage point. We take a left at the opening, a six-foot walkway leading to a copper-red metal door built directly into the rock. Isaiah puts his hand to the handle and abruptly stops.

"Ah, almost forgot... one more thing." He releases the handle and reaches into his backpack, pulling out an intricately decorated white mask. I take it from him with hesitation, but still he says nothing—only nods at me with a sly smirk. I slowly secure the strap around my head. The mask covers the top half of my face, the bottom falling just above the tip of my nose.

"Welcome to the ball, Cinderella," Isaiah pushes open the door and my senses immediately go into overdrive as we step into a hollowed-out cave. I attempt to get my bearings, blue-green lights reflecting every which way off gemstones set into the cave walls, the dramatic sliding of string instruments flooding my ears with classical waltz music. Above our heads, long thin stalactites extend down from the ceiling, swordlike, like they could break off at any moment and pierce me dead.

"Holy shit... what is this place?" I push my mask up to my forehead for an even better look. The entire cave is about the size of a basketball court, the varying heights of its ceiling lending intimacy to its four corners, creating an illusion of separation. In one is the string quartet—the cello and trio of violins echoing out into the larger space. In another corner, a fully masked bartender jostles a cocktail shaker behind a bar that's been carved out of the rock itself.

"This, my friend, is Sapphire Cave. LA's trendiest new event space," Jeremy crosses the room to greet me. He's wearing a mask of his own, similar style to mine, but deep navy blue to match his suit coat.

"Jeez. Can only imagine the killing they'll make on weddings," I reply. With so many of my friends settling down, wedding planning has become an exhaustingly recurring topic of conversation. And venues like these are all the rage. The kind of diamond-in-the-rough spot you can sweep the cobwebs out of, install a sound system and charge a small fortune to rent. Every time I'm in a place like this, I kick myself for not having had the foresight to think of it first.

"Play your cards right and they could make a killing on yours. Network foots the bill if you agree to televise, you know," Jeremy nudges me playfully with his elbow. It's an element of this process that I'm well aware of, but not entirely sold on. There's just something that feels gross about selling out your love to an audience of millions. I mean, aside from saving some money, does the couple actually enjoy it? Or is it merely a ploy to keep the network's money-making machine churning? Call me crazy, but I don't think it's worth it. I think I'd prefer my wedding to be more intimate. Simple venue, close family and friends, nothing too extravagant. And if I pick right, that's what my future wife will want too.

While I wait for a crew member to finish threading a microphone up through my shirt, I notice a strange-looking elderly woman emerge from the restrooms. She's dressed gypsy-like, with a dark purple turban covering thin gray hair and a long matching shawl that drags across the concrete floor behind her. She takes a seat along the flat side of a half-moon table. The sign draped above her on the cave wall reads "Palm Reading" in elegant hand-written script. I flip over my hand and give a quick look at its lines, scoffing in disbelief that so many people can be scammed into believing they're anything more than meaningless creases. When it comes to cons, I'd put palm reading right up there with tarot cards and astrology.

A crew member shouts that Olivia and Reagan are pulling up, and the director calls everyone to their places. Isaiah ushers me to my mark and mimes a reminder for me to pull my mask back down. I oblige despite the silliness of the request, as if my identity instantly becomes a mystery just because I've got three inches of fabric covering my eyes.

"So we're actually going to have you face away from the door." Isaiah puts two hands on my shoulders and spins me around. "Your cue to turn around is when Olivia and Reagan each touch on your shoulder." Ah, yes, I should have known—the classic double date surprise. Nothing around here can ever be simple.

I take a deep breath as the director starts the countdown. He hits zero and I listen closely to the swinging of metal door hinges above the sound of the string quartet. Next comes the overlapping clack of four heels on hard concrete, advancing alongside my rising heart rate. Olivia and Reagan's hands are in perfect sync as they softly touch my shoulder. I've got a split second to try to recognize Olivia's, determined to see her first when I turn.

As is my lot in life, I guess wrong. Reagan immediately wraps her arms around my neck and I do my best to conceal my disappointment as I hold her loosely around the waist of her sequined gold dress. But when I see Olivia beside us, everything else fades. The air catches in my lungs as I release Reagan and turn to her, soft doe eyes beckoning to me from beneath her silver mask. I pull her in close, feeling the curve of her hips beneath the buttery smooth satin of her long black dress. We're surrounded by cameras, the crew and Reagan's blinding dress but, in this moment, holding Olivia as tightly as I can, the smell of her perfume intoxicating my brain, it's like we're the only two people in the world. At last, I've found a woman who quite literally takes my breath away.

"Well, aren't you three just a vision?" Reg weasels his way out from behind the cameras. He's dressed in a burgundy red suit with a black shirt and tie. His matching red mask is the most elaborate of them all, curving up at the corners like two budding horns. I remind myself to ask Isaiah later if it was intentional or coincidence that he's dressed as Satan incarnate.

"Well," he theatrically brandies an arm out, "What do we think of Sapphire Cave?" The question is directed to the women, bait for the contractual awestruck soundbite that covers the "free" venue rental.

"Almost as good-looking as this handsome stud," Reagan hams it up, draping a hand flirtatiously across my chest.

"Hard to argue with that," Reg quips back. I laugh anxiously and run a hand through my hair, keeping Olivia in the corner of my eye.

"But the ambiance isn't the only thing drawing us to this stunning venue tonight. With only so much time left on this journey to love, every moment is precious. Tonight, we're giving you all an opportunity to be open and honest. To *unmask* anything you've been holding back." Reg dramatically waves a hand toward all of our covered faces. "Welcome, ladies and Patrick, to the bachelor's ball."

I feel my palms begin to sweat as I look to Olivia, searching her face for any hint of reassurance—a smile, a wink, even a quick glance. She gives me nothing, stoic as her focus remains on Reg.

"I'd like to open our evening by introducing you all to tonight's special guest, Mademoiselle Mirage." The cameras remain close as Reg walks us toward the strange woman taking up residence in the corner of the cave. I get a closer look as we approach. The mask she's wearing is thin and cat-like. It covers a small stripe of her rounded wrinkled face, which is caked in thick blotchy makeup that does little to conceal an Orion's belt of warts along her sagging jawline. It's an appearance that can only be described as unsettling, almost to the point of being grotesque.

We take our seats and Mademoiselle Mirage wastes no time before aggressively grabbing Reagan's wrists and pulling them toward the middle of the table, flipping them over to study her palms.

"Hmm, yes. These, my dear, are easy to define," Mademoiselle Mirage speaks with a thick Russian accent, very matter-of-fact. "Long palms, short fingers. Fire hands, they are called. An indicator of passion, confidence and industriousness. These palms know who they are, and what they want. Though sometimes at the expense of tact and empathy."

"Yeah, that checks out," I remark, leaning playfully into Reagan's shoulder as she pulls her hands back and gives a know-it-all shrug. It's a shameless ploy to bait Olivia's attention, an admittedly cheap attempt to make her jealous, to bring her back into the room. But still she remains distant, staring through Reagan's hands, completely indecipherable.

"Your palms, please?" Mademoiselle Mirage's request snaps Olivia from her trance, an embarrassed smile the first semblance of emotion as she offers up her wrists to the aging woman. Mademoiselle Mirage runs her fingers gently over Olivia's palm. "Ah, your heart line, it's…" she hesitates. "Well, see how it begins here? Directly below the middle finger? Most are not like this, most heart lines will be more offset. Like this…" Mademoiselle Mirage shows her own palm, tracing the diagonal line that begins between her wrinkled pointer and middle finger.

"What does that mean?" I interject cautiously. Olivia's eyes quiver in my direction, but remain down at the table.

"Well, my dear, a heart line pertains to just that—matters of the heart. It can signify many things. This particular placement here," Mademoiselle Mirage pauses and taps gently on Olivia's palm, "typically indicates a restlessness. Some type of disturbance, a state of unease."

Olivia leans back in her seat with hesitation, pulling her hands away slowly with a twisted expression of skepticism.

"Yes, well, moving on then," Mademoiselle Mirage turns to me and I extend sweaty hands, nerves amplifying with every incremental second of silence. She squeezes them firmly and begins massaging the pads with her thumbs. "Hmm... another interesting heart line." I glance to Olivia, hoping a similar diagnosis might bridge the peculiarly widening void between us. But still, she expresses nothing.

"This break here," Mademoiselle Mirage taps on a split below my ring finger, "It tells me a significant change lies ahead for you. Something life-altering."

"Well, yeah," I laugh nervously, nodding my head in the direction of Olivia and Reagan. "Good life-altering, I hope?"

Mademoiselle Mirage murmurs as she continues to manipulate my palm with her long bony fingers, gaudy jewelry dangling, cool against my skin.

"I'm sorry, my dear, that I cannot tell," she finally says, perplexed. "What I do I know for certain... you must be very careful with a line like this."

Hannah: Week Six, Tuesday

DASH DINER NOTIFICATION: Sorry, Hannah, your delivery has been delayed. Updated drop-off time: 12:32 p.m.

I groan and shift my feet impatiently as I wait outside the front doors of the villa. It's not the first time this has happened with the crew lunch order, nor is it the first time I've felt guilt over something completely out of my control.

I spot Patrick's unmistakable wave of blonde hair on the opposite side of the driveway fountain and shrink back against the stucco, obscuring my face behind the tall greenery of the nearby planter box. He and Isaiah are dressed for a run, alternating between quad and hamstring stretches. As with everything, running reminds me of Ellie. She loved to run. Loved it so much that, before I moved out here, our friends arranged a memorial 5K in her honor. Thought it would be "therapeutic" for all of us to be together doing one of her favorite things. The only thing therapeutic about it for me was taking a match to the flyer and watching it burn. I guess that was the anger stage in the grief cycle, if you subscribe to that sort of thing. For me, everything ebbed and flowed. All besides the one constant, the one that's not even a stage at all. *Sick.*

The curse in question rears its ugly head as Patrick twists, stretching in my direction. My stomach was already sinking when I saw him before, but it's only intensified following the nightmare funhouse encounter of my subconscious. It's been difficult to face pretty much anyone, truthfully. Patrick, Whitney, Olivia. Everywhere I turn, I'm haunted by undead ghosts.

A truck I've never seen pulls into the driveway and I step slightly forward, squinting my eyes to see if it's my long-awaited sandwich order. I let out a groan of disappointment when it stops before reaching me. I watch closely as a man steps out. He's older, early seventies maybe? Average height with the slight slouch that comes with age. He still looks strong despite it. Notably broad shoulders, like he could have been a football player in his younger years. I squint again to get a better look at his face but his black baseball hat is pulled down low over his aviator sunglasses, jaw covered in a thick greying beard. He's dressed pretty ordinarily, blue jeans and a gray polo shirt covered by an olive green utility jacket. The only thing decidedly not ordinary is the pistol holstered along his right hip. I glance to Patrick and Isaiah, who are also observing the armed visitor, mumbling to each other with a similar look of confusion.

The front door pushes open from behind and startles me into a jump. Jeremy bursts past without noticing me, giving a quick and cordial wave to Patrick and Isaiah as he heads toward the bearded man. Jeremy shakes his hand with an exaggerated vigor, as men tend to do. He's got a big smile on his face, seemingly indicating that it's a welcome interaction.

I'm so distracted by the situation I don't notice Patrick walking toward me. His head remains down, gaze locked on the driveway in front of him.

"Thought you were going for a run?" Whitney's sarcasm triggers the startle this time as she appears from the door behind me next.

"Changed my mind. Something going on with my hamstring," Patrick replies curtly in passing. He reaches to catch the door before it closes and glances my way for all of a split second—an unsettling flash of recognition in his eyes just before he sneaks through.

Whitney, conversely, offers zero sign of acknowledgment as she continues on to join Jeremy and the man from the truck. They also shake hands, though Whitney's greeting lacks any of

Jeremy's enthusiasm—conveying her boredom with a flat smile and a loose grip.

DASH DINER NOTIFICATION: Who's ready to eat?! Your dash diner is arriving now.

Thirty seconds later, a rusted white Toyota Corolla clunks into the driveway, brakes squeaking irritably as it pulls through to the front. I meet the driver at the back passenger door and he unloads four big brown bags onto the ground. He issues no apology or explanation, only a grunt.

"Tip is on the card." I smile, not rudely enough to come across passive-aggressive, though I'm certainly wishing I'd waited until after drop-off to decide whether I wanted to reward this guy. I bend over to pick up the bags as the car rolls away and am startled for what's now the third time when I stand up, finding myself face-to-face with the bearded man.

"Hannah Baker?" He asks, removing his sunglasses and tucking them into the collar of his polo. His eyes are striking, a penetrating icy blue with wrinkles sprouting out from the corners. I nod hesitantly but do not yet speak.

"I'm sorry, where are my manners? I'm Detective Russ Stephens." He sticks his hand out with confident energy. "Private investigator. Retired FBI. I was called to do a little research on Tammy Berg's accident. I'm sure you're well aware." My mind starts to reel as I cautiously grab his thick calloused hand. How does he know my name? Did Jeremy and Whitney tell him? What could a private investigator possibly want with me?

"Ah, it's nice to meet you." My vocal box finally unfreezes. "I'm sorry, I'm not sure I'll be of much help to you. I'm only a first-year production assistant. I hardly even knew Tammy."

"Actually," he says, "That's exactly why I wanted to speak with you. Thought you might be able to give some valuable insight as a new addition to the crew. Folks are typically more apt to pick up on things that are unusual when they haven't been on staff for fifteen years."

"I'd really appreciate the chance to talk to you, if you're willing." Detective Stephens spins the gold wedding band on his left ring finger. There's a kindness to his voice, which makes his request come across neither demanding nor expectant. Though I'm still thankful to be holding four brown bag excuses to get me out of it.

"I'm sorry, I really can't right now," I lift the bags up in reference. "Lunch is already behind."

"Of course, understood," he nods. "What time are you done working for the day?"

"Oh, I, uh, I don't really get off at any consistent time. It's usually pretty late."

"That's quite alright. My wife has book club tonight, so she won't be around to monitor my curfew." Detective Stephens smiles endearingly, flashing a duo of slightly crooked front teeth. "Do you know Mick's? It's a divey little spot, but they've got the best wings in town." I start to protest, but he rolls right through. "I'll be there at 6:30. No rush at all, just come when you're able. I've got plenty of work to keep me busy while I wait." He reaches into his pocket and pulls out a worn brown leather wallet that cracks slightly when he opens it. A teenage girl's school photo smiles at me through its clear plastic window as he sifts through cash and receipts. "Ah, here we go." Detective Stephens pulls out a small white card. I accept it apprehensively, gently flexing the edges between my thumb and pointer finger. He bids a polite goodbye and I stuff the card into my back pocket as he disappears down the drive.

—

"Is there anything else that needs to be done?"

"There's always something that needs to be done, but the rest can wait until tomorrow," Seth replies without looking up, too busy hammering away on his laptop to humor me with eye contact.

"Okay." I pause, anxiously tapping my heel up and down. "Are you sure?"

"Yes. Go home, Hannah."

I glance at my watch. 8:58. Too late to meet Detective Stephens, surely. After more than two hours of waiting, he has to have given up and gone home by now.

I walk to the crew parking lot alone, the path dimly lit by the glow of the in-ground lighting that borders it. A rustling in the bushes spooks me and I jump back as a squirrel bolts across in front of me. I take a deep breath to reset and reprimand myself for not being more aware of my surroundings. Clearly, the day's events have me more on edge than I thought.

The parking lot is eerily silent save for the soft scraping of my tennis shoes on the pavement. I wedge my ignition key firmly between my knuckles and quicken my pace, eyes locked on my vehicle until I'm safely in the front seat. I exhale the breath I'd been holding as the doors click locked. I lean toward the wheel and awkwardly finagle my phone out of my back pocket. Detective Stephens' card tumbles out with it. I should push it down, allow it to become lost forever in the black hole between the seat and the console. But I feel a pang in my stomach. It's different than usual, it's lighter. More of a guilt than a gremlin.

I click on the overhead light and flip the card over, running my thumb across the seal in the upper left corner. It's a familiar governmental crest. An eagle with wings spread wide, holding arrows and an olive branch.

Detective Russ Stephens
Member of the U.S. Private Investigators Union
r.stephens@RSPI.com
805-836-7550

I toss the card into my cup holder and punch Mick's Bar into the maps application on my phone. Four miles, eight minutes, right off the freeway and, as fate would have it, almost directly on my way home. My foot taps anxiously on the floorboard as I weigh my options. It's well after 9 p.m. now. And what was it Seth said? "Go home, Hannah." He's right, "Go home, Hannah," I instruct myself out loud.

I swipe out of the application and toss my phone precariously, sending it bouncing on the upholstery of the passenger seat. As I pull out of the lot, I think of my only other experience with a private investigator—the one Ellie's family hired. The skeletal rat-faced man from the "Association of Christian Investigators", whatever that means. He sure didn't seem very Christian-like to me, the way he stalked around, following me to work, home and everywhere in between, putting me in a constant state of unrest. Another on the long list of things during that time that nurtured the gremlin in its formative period.

I reach the freeway and a billboard for the network zips through my peripheral. Seeing it brings Uncle Craig to mind, and I wonder what he would think of all this. If he would be disappointed in me for blowing off Detective Stephens. I can't unhear the hurt in his voice when I called him after Tammy's death.

Before I fully realize what I'm doing, I'm cutting across two lanes and taking the exit.

Mick's Bar is immediately off the exit, the name glowing atop a tall pylon sign shared by the neighboring gas station. The type of two-for-one stop that's popular with truckers, if I had to guess. There are only a handful of cars scattered throughout the parking lot and I choose the spot closest to the door, another subconscious female defense mechanism. The exterior of the building is barren—a one-story rectangle with a flat roof and a single front door. There are a handful of small square windows, exterior lights either burnt out or about to be. Amidst the flickering, it's hard to tell if the building is tan or just dirty. I take a deep breath and rap my fingers on the wheel, wondering if I'm making a mistake. It's hardly welcoming, and this is only the outside.

Three minutes of second-guessing my better judgment later, I'm opening the door to a place that looks pretty much exactly as I expected. Sticky floor, cracked white ceiling tiles, buzzing neon beer signs clouding the place in a multi-colored haze. There's a long and worn wood bar on the left, stools occupied by a smattering of gruff-looking men in well-worn t-shirts. Thankfully they're all minding their own business, attention set on the Dodgers game playing on the small TV mounted behind the bar. At the far end, a young drunk couple is falling all over each other, sticking out like sore thumbs in their expensive designer athletic wear. They strike me as the type to stop in a place like this more out of irony than of interest, oblivious to the fact that they're one wrong comment away from getting thrown out of here on their asses. And that's if they're lucky to not get it worse.

Off to the back right is a standard dive bar rec area. Pool table, couple dart boards. It's empty, and I scan the rest of the room to little avail. But just as I'm starting to feel relief that Detective Stephens might already be gone, I spot him. Head down, tucked into the very back corner booth just outside the bathrooms. His seat selection is an interesting choice in a mostly empty bar, and I instantly judge him as one of those men who insists on a vantage point that lets him survey every person in the place. Dad is like that. Or at least he claims to be. If push came to shove, he'd prove all bark and no bite. Based on the gun holstered along his hip, I don't expect the same applies to Detective Stephens.

His head remains down as I approach, buried in whatever he's reading, papers strewn about the table along with an empty bottle of Coors Light and a plastic basket filled with barbecue sauce-stained wet naps.

"Detective Stephens?" I reluctantly announce my presence. No turning back now.

"Hannah! Hello!" He scrambles, haphazardly gathering everything into one messy pile. "I wasn't sure if you'd come. Thank you, I really appreciate it."

"I'm sorry it's so late." I slide into the leather booth opposite him, feeling the ridges of tattered leather beneath my jeans.

"Oh no, don't worry about that. If anyone should apologize, it's me. Seeing you here now, I realize this probably isn't the most appealing spot for a young lady such as yourself," Detective Stephens sheepishly replies, cheeks flushing pink beneath his dazzling blue eyes.

"I'm no stranger to dive bars." I give a reassuring smile, attempting to look comfortable all the while anxiously running my hands up and down my thighs beneath the table.

"Can I get you anything, hun?" The bartender appears, running double duty as the waitress. She's sort of pretty, one of those faces that takes every year like it's five. You could tell me she was my age or fifteen years older and I'd believe you either way. She's got a hard look to her, tattooed arms on full display under a faded Harley Davidson tank top and jeans that have seen slimmer fitting days.

"Um, gin and tonic. Please." Unlike Detective Stephens, I'm going to need something stronger than light beer to get through this.

"Any preference?"

"Rail's fine," I reply, well aware that rail is probably more basement than bottom shelf. It's a small price to pay to avoid looking like I think I'm too good to be here.

"Another one for you?" She looks to Detective Stephen. He smiles and waves a no with his hand.

"I'm a one-and-doner these days," he says to me as the bartender steps away. "Had a little run-in with pancreatitis five years back. Wife turned the whole house dry. I still like to sip one when I'm working, more for the ritual than the buzz." I smile politely, unsure how to respond. "Anyway, enough about me. Imagine you'd rather be anywhere else than wasting time in a dingy bar with an old fogey like me. I'll do my best to make this as quick and painless as possible." The gremlin awakens as the bartender returns with my drink. I spin it anxiously, the cool condensation of the glass wetting my fingertips.

"You know, I actually followed your case a bit. Hobby of mine, keeping an eye on what's going on in our country's judicial system. Just can't seem to give it up. Drives Mary—that's my wife—crazy. Most people retire and spend the morning fishing. I keep tabs on peculiar trials like yours." I attempt to distract myself as the gremlin salivates, putting the glass to my lips and taking a big swig. "Ah, I'm sorry. I'm sure you'd rather not talk about it. But, for what it's worth, I just wanted you to know that I'm very sorry that happened to you. Folks sure can be awful."

"Thank you," I reply shortly, gripping the glass so tightly in my hand I'm not convinced it won't shatter right here on the table.

"Funny coincidence, you and Patrick both ending up here.

You two know each other at all back in Minnesota?"

Another surge, a stiffer grip, my bicep and abdomen flexing in unison to contain the glass and my stomach.

"No, not really," I say. Detective Stephens nods but issues no response, presumably anticipating the follow-up that I have no intention of giving.

"Ah, okay. Moving on, then. I'm sure you're wondering what the hell I'm doing poking around a closed case. Which is an incredibly fair question. Police declared it an accident. Cause of death: blunt force head trauma. Should be the end of it, very common in a wreck like that." Detective Stephens speaks clearly, making a point to maintain eye contact while I do my best to avoid it.

"Now, thing is, this isn't just a case for me. Tammy was a very dear friend of mine. Her brother Joe and I served together in Vietnam," his confidence trails off with each sentence. Almost as if he's just now accepting that she's gone.

"I'm very sorry for your loss, Detective," I reply sympathetically and look up from my glass.

"Thank you, Hannah. Guess that's life though, isn't it? And, please, call me Russ," Detective Stephens regroups as quickly as he dropped off. "Point is, the Bergs are like a second family to me. Her brother John contacted me as soon as her body was discovered. Horrible tragedy, how could this happen, really inconsolable about the whole thing. And understandably so. Tammy was careful to a fault. To have an accident like that, so reckless, it just didn't make sense."

I continue to take sips of my drink as he speaks, the carbonation of the tonic working tirelessly to settle the surge.

"Now, you could argue it was never my place to have an opinion in the first place, but I never much liked this world for Tammy. These people, these shallow LA types, she was too good for them. Too pure. Yet season after season, she kept going back. And then that poor young girl, Sarah O'Brien, dies right on set? I should have said something. Really tried to pull her out of there this time... I've got to live with that now. I guess this is just my way of trying to sleep at night... And, as another quote-unquote outsider to all of this, I'm hoping you can help me."

I'm fighting the gremlin so hard now that I want to scream. I didn't ask for this, and I don't want it. Someone else can help, keeping all of these unsolicited secrets is making me sick enough as it is.

"Now, I may look like it in my old age but I'm no slouch. I've been in this business far too long to get swept up in tabloid rumors and conspiracies. I'm not here because of those, Hannah," Detective Stephens continues. "I'm here because of a gun. A 9-millimeter Smith & Wesson... *Tammy's* 9-millimeter Smith & Wesson. The one she kept securely stowed in a case beneath her passenger seat. A case that was never turned in to the police for evidence... because it was never found."

Whitney: Week Seven, Thursday

Never thought I'd see this dump in the daylight.

My tires snap over an empty can as I pull into the parking lot, my BMW far and above the nicest car here. I try to remember whether the spaces were ever lined or if management just gave up on repainting them. Then again, there's not a lot I do remember about this place. I was usually blitzed out of my mind by the time we got to Mick's. Too drunk to care that my shoes stuck to the floor and the toilet seat was hanging on by one hinge.

You know that feeling of dread when you're walking into the gynecologist, about to be stretched open from the inside with the cold metal beak of hell? I have that same feeling right now. Worse, maybe, if you can believe it. I kept deflecting this meeting with Detective Stephens, but the bastard just wouldn't quit. What with all his fucking endearing self-awareness. Everyone else might not see through the nice guy act, but I do. That's the only reason I finally caved on this. The sooner I get his face off my set, the better.

The faint smell of cigarettes tickles my nose as I push open the door. It hasn't been legal to smoke in bars since the nineties but, here, the nicotine is engrained in the fucking walls. It's 1:00 p.m. on a Thursday, but that doesn't stop a disgustingly drunk barfly from muttering something about my ass when I walk by. I flip him the bird instinctively and keep moving.

"Wow, look what the cat dragged in," the trashy bartender quips and I respond with a thin smile. Her wardrobe has changed as little as the bar has. It's oddly gratifying to take in her poor attempt at fitting the same tight clothes over her no longer tight body. She never much liked me, and the feeling remains mutual.

"Not a Mick's first timer," Detective Stephens laughs as I approach. He's sitting alone in the back corner, half-drank iced tea on the table in front of him.

"Another life," I say with all the disinterest I can muster as I take a seat opposite him, crossing my arms in defiance.

"Jeremy told me you two used to come here quite often." Of course. I should have known Jeremy would have already cozied up to Detective Stephens. So eager to show Paul just how cooperative he can be. "I think it's neat you two have worked together so long," he continues. "After so many years, you must be close."

"Very," I say, following up with an equally sarcastic smile. "So, what else did Jeremy tell you?"

"I try to keep what's shared in these meetings confidential," Detective Stephens replies, crossing his hands on the table. "Since you two are so close, I'm sure he'd be happy to share our conversation with you." I flash another mock smile and wiggle a menu out from the condiment rack on the table's edge, cringing at the sticky film that comes with it. I scan it for anything that doesn't come deep-fried or slathered in butter. There is a side salad, but just the thought of floppy wet iceberg lettuce is enough to depress me so, when the bartender crawls out to take our order, I settle for vegetable beef instead.

"That Reagan sure is a spitfire," Detective Stephens says casually once she leaves us. "Thought for sure Patrick would send her home last night. Suppose she's good for the ratings."

"You watch?" I reply with indifference, actively ignoring his passive-aggressive ratings comment. Manipulating eliminations might not be ethical, but it sure as hell isn't a crime.

"Oh you know, just doing my homework. Though, admittedly, it's not the first time I've tuned in. My granddaughter is a big fan. Tammy actually set her up with a villa tour a few years back. I guess that means even she's seen more of the place than I have." Detective Stephens says with a sly grin, a jab at the mandate I was more than happy to put in place for his investigation. Only allowed access to the villa while contestants aren't present—which, to this point, has been never. Only a matter of time until he gets tired of conducting meetings in this shithole and lets us finish the season in peace.

"Sorry, Detective. Rules are rules." Jeremy might have humored him with this little game of Hardy Boys but, make no mistake, I'm still in control. And no bargain-brand PI is going to change that.

"I know, I know, I understand. I'd probably do the same if I were you," Detective Stephens relents. "On that note, I'd love to learn a little more about you. Not the stuff I can dig up online… who *is* Whitney Erickson really?"

"You'll have to wait for the autobiography, same as everyone else." Detective Stephens lets out a chuckle at my response as I look indifferently at my hand, tilting it back and forth to let the bar lights reflect off my freshly manicured hot pink nails.

"You're a tough cookie. I like that." I look up from my nails as he leans back into the torn leather booth, crossing his arms. I respond by doing the same, a regular Mexican standoff. Studying him in full now, broad-chested with those steely blue eyes, I can't decide if I want to stab him with a fork or ask him to take me home—an internal conflict that tells me, assuredly, that I have daddy issues.

"You know, Detective, if I wanted to be watched while I ate my lunch, I'd have sat next to the cockroaches at the bar." I flip my phone over from the table to check the time, a calculated move that both conveys my boredom and lets me know how many minutes I've already wasted on this conversation. Wasted on, what was it he called it? Oh, yes. My *continued patience* with the investigation.

"Well, if you're not going to tell me anything about you, perhaps you can speak a little more to your relationships with your colleagues. With, say, Paul Thomas, in particular." My body tenses at the mention of Paul, irritation flaring for allowing myself to be caught off guard.

"Cup of soup and a basket of wings," the bartender slides our lunches onto the table. It's the first time I've ever been relieved to see her—grateful for a momentary distraction, a buying of time.

"Thank you, Angie. Looks delicious as always," Detective Stephens says with blue eyes still on me, taunting me with his bearded grin.

It's enough to make me question if I'm in control after all.

Patrick: Week Seven, Monday

Not thirty seconds after I hit the snooze button, I'm disrupted by a loud knock at the door. Isaiah has an uncanny way of appearing at the exact moments I want to see him least. I decide to ignore him, desperately needing the extra rest. I haven't been sleeping well these past few days. Way too much on my mind with Olivia. It's like a switch flipped in her on that double date at Sapphire Cave. I was convinced I'd lost her, all signs pointing to rejection going into the elimination ceremony, preparing myself to have the rug ripped out from under me on live TV. But despite the distance growing between us, something made her stay.

Another knock sounds and there's a brief moment of silence before it turns to full-on banging. Loud, repetitive, urgent. I let out a dramatic exhale for no one but myself and push my body up, grabbing yesterday's t-shirt off the ottoman at the foot of the bed. "Yep, coming." I open the door and am immediately taken aback to find myself face-to-face with Reagan, Kate and three members of the camera crew. "Hey, ahh, everyone?" My hand goes habitually through my hair before scratching the back of my head, questioning if I'm still asleep, if the cavalry in front of me is all part of a strange dream.

"Hi. Can we talk?" Reagan asks, but I see it isn't really a question when she pushes past me into the suite, a fiery five-foot torpedo missiling straight into my morning. The cameras follow close behind her. I mouth "What the hell?" to Kate and she brushes me off with a shrug that implies "it is what it is."

"Sorry, can you just give me a second?" I direct the question to Kate, signaling downward to the fact that I'm still in my boxers. Really I'm just hoping to buy a few moments to prepare for the impending drama. It's no secret that camera ambushes don't typically accompany good news in this place. Pair that with Reagan's propensity for theatrics and there's really no limit to the chaos that could be coming my way.

"Mmm," Kate contemplates momentarily as the camera crew begins deploying their equipment. "You know what, sure. We'll roll in three." I smile in appreciation and close the door to my bedroom behind me. I head for the bathroom, crank on the faucet and splash cold water all over my face. I hastily dry it with the nearest hand towel and glance in the mirror. From the disheveled hair to the unwashed t-shirt, everything about me screams unprepared. Which, given the nature of the interruption, is probably exactly the reaction that production wants. I return to the bedroom, slip on a pair of shorts and throw my purple Minnesota Vikings hat on backward to hide my hair, sarcastically muttering "Skol" as I ready myself for whatever awaits me outside the door.

"Sorry about that," I say as I return. The crew is now fully in place, bright lights casting a sickly glow on Reagan as she sits atop the tan suede couch. I take a seat beside her and offer up a smile. The pajamas she's wearing say just rolled out of bed, but her airbrushed face says she spent an hour in the makeup trailer. Clearly this is only spontaneous for one of us.

Kate gives a nod to the cameras which, apparently, is also Reagan's cue to lay it on thick—shifting her solemn gaze downward to her anxiously wringing hands. Kate gestures silently for me to reach over and hold them. Not enough caffeine in me to be defiant, I reluctantly oblige.

"What's up, Reagan?" I ask, my fingers wrapped as loosely as possible around hers.

She looks up at me briefly before dramatically turning away. "There's something I need to tell you. Something that's been weighing on me."

"Okay. What is it?"

"Ugh, I don't know if I should say."

"Okay…" I repeat, waiting her out. We wouldn't be going through this whole charade if she wasn't eventually going to share what was on her mind. Though honestly, I'm not sure I even care at this point. Reagan's fun, but I'm getting pretty tired of the bit. I was ready to send her home last week before Whitney essentially forced me to keep her. A damn fool I was to ever believe my personal feelings would take precedence over the ratings.

"I don't want to sound like I'm throwing the other women under the bus…"

The apathy switch flips off in my brain as soon as "other women" leaves her mouth. There are only two remaining besides her—Kya and Olivia. I pull my hand away from Reagan's, suddenly feeling as though I'm going to be sick. "Reagan, whatever it is, I would very much appreciate if you would tell me."

"It's just… one of the other women said some things that made me question her feelings for you. And you know, I care about you so much, Patrick. And I don't want to see you ge-"

"Who?" I cut her off, heart pounding hard, willing her not to say the name I fear most. "Who are you talking about, Reagan?"

"Olivia."

Her name hits like a sucker punch.

"What did she say?" I'm fighting back more than one rapidly rising emotion now. Confusion, anger, heartbreak. *Stay calm, Pat. Don't let them see you like this.*

"She said things were moving so fast. *Too* fast. Like it was a bad thing. I don't know if you were coming on too strong or what, but just seemed like she wasn't into it anymore." The lights go from bright to blinding as I process Reagan's words. The hum of the camera gets louder and louder until all I hear is a horrible feedback, like when a microphone is too close to a speaker.

I stand up from the couch, trying to find my footing in a

spinning room. The crew scrambles to their feet and a cameraman hustles to position himself between me and the door. I thrust my hand in front of the lens and push past him.

"Patrick, wait!" Reagan calls out from behind me, but I'm already throwing open the door to the hallway. I will my unsteady legs to quicken their pace as the walls blur around me, knowing the circus won't be far behind. Just as I'm about to pass in front of the crew room, Isaiah bursts out in front of me.

"Woah there, easy big fella." Isaiah puts his hands cautiously out in front of him, as if I'm some rabid dog. I spin my head around and see the camera crew closing in on us. Grabbing Isaiah by the arm, I pull him into the crew room, slam the door and twist the lock.

"Jesus, Pat, relax."

"Where's Olivia?" I demand, Isaiah's facial features blending in front of me until it's almost as though I'm looking straight through him.

"Just take a deep breath." His hands go to my shoulders but I immediately shove them off.

"I need to see Olivia. Now."

Hannah: Week Seven, Monday

I was mid-bite on a granola bar when Patrick and Isaiah burst into the crew room. It's sitting there now, suspended in mouth purgatory, afraid that even the tiniest crunch will call attention to my presence. I tilt my head toward the floor, attempting to make myself invisible. Isaiah could easily see me from where he stands but Patrick's back is to me, very obviously upset based on the tempo at which his shoulders are rising and falling. Feels like it's going to take a lot more than the deep breath Isaiah is recommending to calm him down.

"I can't let you see her right now, Pat. You know that's not how this works. I promise you will get a chance to talk to her. In the meantime, do me a favor and cool down a bit," Isaiah's words come out clear and slow, without condescension. Like he's attempting to connect the right wires to diffuse the ticking time bomb in front of him.

"I'm sure I will get a chance to talk to her. And I'm sure all of America will get a goddamn front-row seat." As Patrick's anger continues to rise, I, conversely, sink down more and more in my chair—desperately wishing I was anywhere but here, witnessing this other version of him. It's another secret my cursed conscience can't afford to keep.

"You signed up for this, remember?" Isaiah posits what seems like an incredibly fair, albeit rhetorical, question. Judging by the stiff tension of Patrick's back, I don't think it's going to resonate.

"Fuck what I signed up for." Patrick makes a move for the door and Isaiah grabs his arm. He tries to tug it free, looking more and more like a toddler throwing a temper tantrum by the second. "You know how much I care about her. I've been on edge about this all week, and now this? Like, is she just trying to fuck with me?" I've sunk about as low as I can go now without being completely under the table. I take the momentary chaos as an opportunity to swallow down the granola, now nothing but mush.

"Patrick. Look at me." Isaiah maintains a strong hold while Patrick gives one more pull toward the door before ultimately relenting with an exasperated exhale. Isaiah releases him and moves a hand gently to his shoulder. "We will work through this. But this right here, this overreaction, it's got to stop. You're acting crazy."

—

"You're acting crazy."

The words hit me straight in the stomach.

The evening had started uneventfully, no different than any other Tuesday. I got home from work around 5:30 and Ellie followed soon after, neither of us wasting any time swapping uncomfortable businesswear for leggings and athletic tees. We shared the bench in the entryway, hip to hip as we tied our tennis shoes for our nightly walk, chatting about how nice the weather had been that day. The warmth in the air was unseasonable but not unprecedented. In Minnesota, fall is always a toss-up. Nineties one week, fifties the next. You learn quickly when growing up to be prepared for either.

One of the things we loved most about our new house was its proximity to a great local park, only a half-mile away. Far different than the grid-locked apartment building we moved from downtown. As we walked the path around the park's small lake, we exchanged the usual monotonous workday details, Ellie getting frustrated for me over yet another story about my needy and ungrateful clients. I would respond by telling her it was all part of the job, she would respond by telling me to give the agency the middle finger and go work for my

Dad instead. Familiar neighbors walking dogs and pushing strollers would greet us as we passed. We were thrilled to have finally found a community that felt both friendly and safe. A perfect place to raise kids someday.

I made dinner when we returned home from our walk. Chicken breast and riced cauliflower—trying to keep our diet on the straight and narrow as we counted down the days to the wedding. Ellie decompressed on the couch while I cooked, glass of wine in one hand and a palmful of potato chips in the other. She would probably tell you I made a snarky comment about spoiling her dinner and, as always, that's not quite how I'd remember it.

It wasn't until halfway through dinner that Ellie nonchalantly lit the fuse.

"I talked to my mom today," she said the words casually, as if it were a daily occurrence. As if her mother wasn't Satan incarnate.

"What?" I stopped mid-bite, the clink of my fork dropping into the bowl ringing through the kitchen. "Why?"

Ellie's eyes averted mine, gaze sheepishly down as she pushed the tiny cubes of cauliflower around in her bowl.

"Yeah... She called me."

"And you answered?" I have the patience to put up with a lot of things, probably too many, but Ellie's family had ceased to be one of them. Every time they came up, I could literally feel my blood pressure start to rise. It was as unstoppable as the gremlin is now, only instead of nausea it was a red heat sprouting itself up inside me from the tip of my toes all the way to my brain.

"Hannah... she's my mom." Ellie laid her most forlorn expression on thick, but her effort was in vain. She knew by then she wasn't going to get any sympathy from me.

"What did she want?" I crossed my arms tightly across my chest, fingertips gripping at the sides of my shirt.

"They want me to come home, just for the weekend. They're throwing a party for Gia's golden birthday." Gia is, or, was, Ellie's younger sister. An eight-year gap between them, I found her to be a total brat—something Ellie brushed off with the usual "baby of the family" excuse. Granted I only interacted with Gia twice in as many years, the stories I'd been told were more than enough to deduce that she took after her mother.

"Hmm," I nodded a curt acknowledgment and returned to my dinner. I didn't have to ask to know the invitation had not been extended to me.

"Anyway, I think I'm going to go," Ellie continued.

"Very funny," I replied, rolling my eyes while taking a bite of chicken.

"I'm serious, I thought about it a lot today. She's my baby sister and it's her eighteenth birthday. I really think I should be there."

I swallowed hard and pushed my bowl away from me. It nearly rolled on its edge, the sound of ceramic wobbling as it balanced back out. "I'm sorry, did you forget what they said about you? What they said about us?"

"No. I didn't forget, not at all. But they're still my family, Hannah. I can talk to them. With the wedding coming up so soon, maybe they'll come around."

"They won't," I replied flatly and abruptly stood up from the table. "You done eating?" Ellie nodded silently and I carried both dishes to the sink. I angrily scrubbed the bowls longer and harder than needed before carelessly tossing them into the drying rack.

"Okay, Jesus, Hannah, relax. I get it. You don't want me to go." It was obvious by the quiver in her voice that she was on the verge of crying but, in that moment, I didn't even care. If she wanted to, let her. This was on her now. Those people didn't deserve my tears.

"Do you get it, Ellie? Do you?" I turned to face her, the heat of my blood nearing a full boil. "We're getting fucking married and your parents still refuse to acknowledge our relationship. She called me a dyke, Ellie. Treated me like some fucking pervert trying to steal away their precious little girl for sport. So, yes, forgive me for not being thrilled at the idea of you spending the weekend with these people." I stormed past her just as her tears started to flow, an onslaught of uncontrollable sniffling coming from her nose. I yanked on my shoes, still tied from our walk.

"Where are you going?" Ellie asked, tears wetting her cheeks.

"Out," I replied, void of all emotion as I swung open the door.

"Hannah, stop! Please!" She caught it just before it slammed shut, but I was already halfway down the driveway. She stepped onto the front step and shouted after me with desperation in her voice. "Stop, Hannah! You're acting crazy!"

But I didn't turn around. I didn't stop. Just took a right onto the street and kept walking. Away from the house. Away from her. Forever.

—

The memory is suffocating. So consumed in it that I didn't even notice Patrick and Isaiah had left the room. Crippling regret gurgles aggressively in my stomach, a guilt that never quite vacates. And I deserve it. Ellie was right. I was acting crazy. Ellie needed me and, rather than comforting her in a moment of vulnerability, I walked away. Selfish. Angry. Blinded.

And now, with the gremlin, cursed.

I stand up from the table, the regret rising higher and higher. This time, I know I'm not going to be able to fight it down. I step into the hallway and see Taylor and Seth heading right toward me. I force an anxious smile from a distance and turn on my heels, walking with purpose in the opposite direction so they think I've already been tasked with something. It's then I realize the nearest bathroom is the other way.

Desperate as vomit crawls its way up my throat, I duck out the first available door—the one that leads to the courtyard. There are a handful of crew members milling around and I hold my breath, shuffling quickly to the side gate. I'm trapped between needing fresh air in my lungs and knowing a strong inhale would be enough to trigger everything I'm holding inside. I push through the gate just in time to spew the contents of my stomach into a gap between two tall hedges. I brace myself against the fence and close my eyes, taking long slow breaths. No matter how many times this happens, it never fails to take the wind out of me. The squeak of the gate opening alerts me and I stand up stiff-straight, turning as I come face to face with the last person I want to see.

Whitney: Week Seven, Monday

Hannah stares back at me like a deer in headlights, a wretched chunk of vomit dribbling down her chin.

"Sorry, I'm going to have to call you back." I abruptly hang up my phone call and look her up and down. "Um, you've got a little…" I make a brushing motion across my chin. Her cheeks turn bright red as she relocates the chunk to her jeans. It isn't much better, but at least now I don't have to make direct eye contact with it.

"Thanks," Hannah says with her eyes down, anxiously shifting her weight.

"You good?" I ask. I don't really care but, given the circumstances in which I stumbled upon her, it would be weirder not to acknowledge that she just desecrated our pristinely trimmed hedges.

"I'm fine, thanks," Hannah replies hurriedly, eager to end the embarrassment as quickly as possible. I stare at her blankly, eager to prolong it. Watching people squirm always fascinates me. The lack of confidence it must take to allow another person to make you feel visibly uncomfortable.

"Must have been something I ate," Hannah finally breaks the silence. Something she ate—or guilt eating her? I typically wouldn't waste a second thought on finding a crew member in a compromising scenario, but my conversations with Detective Stephens have me on high alert. Someone here is squealing secrets big time. And I'll be damned if I don't slaughter the little piggy myself.

"Mmm, bummer." I reply, still giving her nothing. I look at my phone to check the time. "You really should get that cleaned up before scrum. Supposed to hit ninety degrees this afternoon. Last thing we need is hot vomit stinking up the courtyard."

—

Hannah isn't looking much better when I see her again fifteen minutes later in the crew room. I can only hope she's at least washed her hands.

We're two hours behind our usual schedule, delayed by that fun little ambush with Reagan at Patrick's room this morning. I notice Isaiah missing from the room, so I assume he's still doing damage control. Spontaneous opportunities like that can be a goldmine. Kate activated quickly, again proving why she deserves to be handling the best contestants. A lot of folks in this room would have sat back on it. Twiddled their thumbs while waiting to bring it forward in the next scrum. Kate's a professional. She understands how critical intel like that in a confessional is. The minute you hear it, you're on emergency response—snapping on the emotional surgical gloves to prevent a flatline. Female contestants are always a higher risk. Only takes one second of hesitation for them to overthink and change their minds.

The fireworks couldn't have come at a better time, really. Reagan's been fantastic for viewership but, with the finale next week, we can't force Patrick to keep her around any longer. Might as well milk her for all she's worth before we put her out to pasture.

Jeremy joins me at the front of the room, looking absolutely hunky-dory for another co-led scrum. These morning powwows are my least favorite part of the promotion. More days than not, an all-team check-in is incredibly unnecessary. Everyone already knows what they need to be doing. If they don't, they shouldn't work here. Most of them will spend the entire time half-paying attention—checking emails, online shopping, literally anything else. And I don't blame them, it's exactly what I used to do when I was in their shoes.

"Alright, let's get this going so you all can get back to your Monday," I speak first, projecting loudly over all the small talk.

"Yes, we'll keep this brief," Jeremy tacks on unnecessarily, like an annoying little brother desperate to prove to Mommy that he's also in the room. "First and foremost, thank you to Kate and everyone else who pulled together this morning's scene with Reagan so quickly and cleanly."

"Yes." I tug the proverbial rope back over to my side. "Should really give us a boost in the ratings. And it's great teaser content for the finale, so post team, let's make sure we get that footage running as soon as possible." The head of our post-production team gives me a thumbs up from the back of the room and a hand goes up beside her—one of the junior story editors.

"Yes, Ashley, question?" Jeremy jumps all over it.

"When are we going to film Patrick's conversation with Olivia? He seemed pretty upset."

"Well-" I begin.

"Isaiah and Kate are working through timing on that," Jeremy cuts me off. "Conversations like this can be very delicate. We want to be sure we're maximizing it in a way that's going to garner the most attention going into finale week. Given the inevitable departure of Reagan on Wednesday night, we're going to need the drama. Ah, which reminds me, are we all set to film with CD on Thursday?" He hardly takes a breath before jumping topics to CD—also known as Charles Diamond, LA's premier celebrity jeweler and a staple of the *Heaven's Match* franchise. He comps the hundred-thousand-dollar finale rings, we comp the exposure to millions of viewers. Everybody wins.

"All good, boss," Seth replies. The way he refers to Jeremy as "boss" grates my ears.

"Great. If you're not on the CD crew with me, Whit will need all hands on deck here. There's quite a bit that still needs to be done in prep for Napa. Including reminding Isaiah that we leave on Friday." Jeremy makes a playfully dull and Paul-like jab, a reference to Isaiah nearly missing last year's finale flight to Cabo. The entire crew laughs and I force out a smile so as not to look too obviously like a petty bitch.

"Any other questions?" I cut off the residual chatter, demanding the group back into focus.

"Yeah, uh, what's the deal with the cop?" An unidentifiable crew voice chimes up from the back.

"He's not a cop. He's a contracted investigator. And he's assured me he will be wrapping up his investigation soon," I reply quickly and directly before Jeremy gets the chance.

"Yes, please, there's enough going on here that we do need to worry ourselves with Detective Stephens' work," Jeremy fights for the last word. "I am staying very close with him and he is finding exactly what we thought he would... which is absolutely nothing. But if anyone still has concerns, please reach out and I'd be happy to do what I can to dissipate them. My door is always open."

"As is mine," I tack on. Jeremy turns and gives me a literal fucking salute. I return it with a sarcastic smile as everyone gets up and begins to move toward the door. I follow, eager to be done with the charade. I mean, Christ. I figured Jeremy would find another ass to kiss with Paul gone, I just didn't think it would be the entire fucking crew.

A build-up at the door slows my exit, leaving me impatiently stalled behind a pocket of field producers. "I feel bad saying this, but I hardly even miss Paul," one says to the other, oblivious to the fact that I'm directly behind them. I try not to concern myself much with anyone's opinion either way, but it is nice to have the reassurance—even if the showrunning duties are unwillingly shared.

"Dude, I know. Jeremy is crushing it. I hope they promote him beyond interim next season." My ears register the reply and my vision shrouds in red. I've suddenly got the urge to grab this scrawny little shit by the collar, throw him to the ground and rip his throat out right here on the break room floor.

I brazenly push my way through the queue. After all I do, how hard I work, the insane number of hours I put in while the rest of these snowflakes clock out for the sake of "mental health" and "work-life balance." But what would this ungrateful, untalented lot of swine know about that?

Forget the Detective Stephen's snitch, fuck every one of them at this point. See how they fare without me. My hands shake as I make my way to the front entry, scroll through my phone and dial Lisa Sanchez's number.

Patrick: Week Seven, Wednesday

"It's just been such a crazy week, you know. I feel like all of my emotions are on overdrive. Worrying about you and everything that must be going through your head."

I smile softly with uncertainty, pulling her in tighter next to me, my fingertips drawing circles on her shoulder. I put my khaki suit coat around her because she was shivering, neither of us quite accustomed to the fall temperature drops that have started to affect evenings in the courtyard.

"I know," I reply, anxiously shifting on the sofa. I take a deep breath and push back my hair with my free hand, the one that isn't around her. Tonight is the last elimination ceremony. Only three women left—Olivia, Kya and Reagan. After this, we fly to Napa Valley to film the finale, where I'll be faced with the biggest decision of my life. I'm not just feeling the pressure, it's crushing me like a truckload of bricks.

"Honestly, there is a lot going through my head," I continue, the fear of making a mistake loading every word. She nods with understanding, but doesn't reply. "All week, I've been wanting to talk to you. To ask you something... in particular." Her brow knits in genuine concern, her eyes maintaining their warmth. I take it as a go-ahead to proceed.

"Reagan came to my room a few days ago... Unexpectedly. She brought up that there was some questioning of feelings going on. It's hard to know what to believe, especially with

Reagan. But, of all people, the relationship we have, I trust you to be upfront and honest with me if something like that was happening. So, I guess I just wanted to ask you, straight up. Have you heard Olivia say anything like that?"

Kya's body stiffens. She remains motionless for a moment before shifting out from beneath my arm. Any shred of concern is overtaken by a look of annoyed offense, almost a disgust. And it's in that moment that I realize the severity of my mistake.

—

The absence of somewhere to wipe my sweat is only making the situation worse. Tonight of all nights, my dumbass just had to let them put me in khaki. I feel it dripping everywhere—my neck to my back, my back to my waist, down the inseam of my pant legs, armpits to my palms. I resist the instinct to wipe it through my hair and, as the director begins the countdown, a wardrobe assistant springs out from behind the cameras and passes me a handkerchief. I wipe my brow quickly and sop up my hands before stuffing it into my back pocket.

When I envisioned this elimination in my head a week ago, everything was simple. Send Reagan home, head to Napa with Olivia and Kya—the two women I've imagined there with me since week five. Man did all of that blow up in a hurry. The weird distance from Olivia all week, the surprise visit from Reagan. And now, my colossal screw-up with Kya tonight. I must be the dumbest man on earth, using my limited time with one woman to ask her about another. And now I can't help but shake the feeling that I won't have anyone to bring to Napa at all.

"Good evening, ladies, Patrick," Reg speaks from beside me, a dreaded indication that we've officially gone live. My heart pumps against my sternum as I imagine being dually rejected by Olivia and Kya. In a few short minutes, I could be standing alone, America's most eligible bachelor turned America's biggest loser.

"Welcome to the final villa elimination. After tonight, only two women will remain. Two women, two futures, one life-changing decision." Reg pauses for dramatic effect and it's like I can literally feel the weight of his words on my shoulders. Smug asshole, I'm sure the entire predicament has him on cloud nine.

"But getting to finale week won't be without heartbreak. For one of you, this seven-week journey is about to come to an end... Patrick, whenever you're ready."

I take a deep breath and close my eyes, letting myself live for a moment in the black, wondering how I ever ended up here, wondering if the sweat from my armpits is starting to show through my coat.

"Patrick?" Reg asks again and I open my eyes, looking up from my shoes to face the three women in front of me. Olivia in black, Kya in purple, Reagan in red. All beautiful in their own way. All terrifying in their own way.

I pause for what feels like hours, failing to decode their indecipherable expressions. And then, suddenly, in a flash, it hits me. I know what I have to do.

"Reagan."

Her name leaves my mouth slowly and clearly. Reagan smirks as she walks toward me. I glance behind her at Olivia and Kya, their faces twisting in confusion. I hold Reagan's hands gently, with care, the same as I've done with each woman week after week.

"Reagan, from the moment I met you, you've kept me on my toes. You truly are one of a kind." She gives a playful shrug in response, as if she's urging me to tell her something she doesn't already know. "And, Reagan... the right man will be so lucky to have you. But I'm sorry to tell you that that man is not me."

Reagan's brow furrows with offense as she pulls back, dropping her left hand from mine. It's not too dissimilar from the face Kya gave me earlier when I asked about Olivia. Reagan raises her free hand and I brace myself, preparing to be physically assaulted by a five-foot blonde on national TV.

Instead, she lightly pats me on the cheek. "Oh Patrick, my sweet, sweet gentle Patrick. You are so right. You will *never* be man enough to handle all of this. And you'll only spend every day of your sad pitiful life wishing you were." She releases my other hand and I make a move to escort her. "I'll walk myself out," she stops me with a raise of her hand, heels snapping hard across the stone as she exits out the side of the courtyard. A cameraman follows close behind, soaking up every last second as I stand there, eyes wide, immobilized with bewilderment.

Reg laughs boisterously and returns to his mark beside me. "In like a lion, out like a lion."

I sneak a glance off-camera at the crew as I regroup. The producers won't be happy with me for breaking protocol again. On my life, I didn't come into tonight planning to do that. But seeing all three of them standing there, what with all the uncertainty I was feeling, it overwhelmed me with empathy. I might not be able to save myself the heartbreaking embarrassment of being left alone in the courtyard tonight, but at least I could do it for Reagan.

"Anyway, shall we continue? In the proper way?" Reg asks with a snarky eyebrow raise.

"Yes, please, sorry." I pause and smile sheepishly at Olivia and Kya, hoping my good deed hasn't gone unnoticed. My heart sinks as both women return stares as blank as my future, now completely in their hands.

"Kya."

Kya remains stone-faced as her heels clack toward me.

"I'm so sorry," I whisper softly in her ear as I pull her in for a hug.

"Kya," I say as I step back, maintaining hold of her hands. "Will you please continue this journey with me?"

She purses her lips together and ever so slightly softens her expression. There's an empathy in her dazzling green eyes, an unspoken forgiveness.

"I will."

I exhale a stupid smile of relief. "Thank you," I say with both my words and my eyes as she steps past me toward the villa.

One down, but that was the easy one. Now, there is only Olivia. The woman I'm losing sleep over. The woman I'm falling in love with.

I look to Olivia with longing, desperately searching her face for any form of reassurance. She continues to give me nothing.

"Olivia," her name drops from my mouth, a silent prayer dropping with it.

She puts her head down before stepping slowly in my direction, back hem of her dress floating gracefully across the stone. When she reaches me, I pull her in tight and throw up a proverbial Hail Mary by rapping my fingers three times along the small of her back—our own special sign. My breath suspends as she steps back and places her hands hesitantly into mine, heart thudding so strongly inside my chest that I hear it reverberating in my ears.

"Olivia, will you please continue this journey with me?"

Her eyes drift from mine. First off to the side and then down at our hands. I close mine and wait. Three seconds, but it might as well be a lifetime. A lifetime that flashes before my eyes. *Our* lifetime. Me on one knee, a happy marriage, a house filled with kids. And then, I feel it. Ever so gently along my thumbs. Three clear taps.

"I will."

My relief when Kya said the words came in a wave, but this is the whole damn ocean—flooding through my head, heart, stomach and toes. Olivia says nothing else before walking inside, leaving me standing there, grinning like an idiot from ear to ear. It's amazing, all of my anxiety washed away in three little taps. It's in this moment that I realize. I'm no longer just falling, I have completely fell. Assuredly, hopelessly, completely.

I am in love with that girl.

Hannah: Week Eight, Thursday

"Sitting here this morning, I can confidently say it. I am falling in love with Patrick Olsen." Olivia blushes from atop the confessional interview stool. She's rocking her signature look— effortlessly cute in a grey v-neck shirt and dark wash jeans, the remnants of last night's curls loosely falling to her shoulders. There was a completely different air about her when she came into the room, greeting both Kate and me with an enthusiastic hug, a complete one-eighty from the introspective version of her we experienced last week. The intimacy of the contact took me off guard and I'm still reeling now from her warm but unexpected gesture.

"Wow, that's huge!" Kate revels equally in Olivia's newfound confession. The magic four-letter word the producers spend weeks waiting to hear. "Especially considering the last two weeks. I mean, up until last night's elimination, it seemed you weren't so sure?"

"I think I just got trapped in my own head. I've gotten so used to being careful and guarded in relationships, to taking things slow—and, well, this experience is so not that. The reason I applied to begin with was to push that comfort zone. But as soon as things started progressing more quickly, I found it harder to break the habit. I started questioning everything I was feeling. Like, there was no way I could actually be ready to commit my whole heart to someone I'd only known for eight weeks. I just panicked."

"So what happened last night to change that?"

"Ugh, last night. This is going to sound crazy I'm sure, but it all hit me in this one divine moment. I was trying to play it cool, to act tough, but, standing there next to Kya and Reagan, I found myself wanting him to say my name so badly. Like, if he didn't say it, my heart would shatter right then and there. And that was when I knew. Like, 'Wow, it's him. This is the guy I've been waiting for."

"I don't think that sounds crazy at all," Kate replies with a genuine smile. "After all that, I imagine you're pretty excited to get to Napa?"

"Definitely! Excited, nervous, all the feelings. I just really can't wait to see him and be with him, enjoying the last week as we continue to grow our relationship into something even stronger than it is now." The more Olivia gushes about Patrick, the more my stomach pangs. That feeling, being swept up in the early stages of really falling in love. The infectious giddiness, energy buzzing inside of you as someone begins to consume your every thought. Hanging on their every word, relishing even a momentary touch...

"Well, I'm sure I speak for all of America when I say the rest of us can't wait to watch," Kate says before leaning in. "Now, obviously the overnight dates are a big part of that. No cameras, no producers. What does getting that alone time mean for you?"

"Oh gosh, it means everything. Getting to spend uninterrupted time together, just the two of us," Olivia replies with more excitement. "It's going to be really special."

"And do you think the two of you will... solidify your relationship?" Kate asks and I cringe as another pang hits over her indiscretion. I watch with intense focus as Olivia shifts anxiously in her seat. It feels wrong to insert ourselves into such a deeply personal experience. Wrong to contemplate what their first time together is going to be like.

Wrong to wonder what it's like to be alone with Olivia.

—

"This should be the last one." I heave the final box off the dolly and into the back of the U-Haul. Taylor bends down, arms wobbling as she attempts to pick it up. She groans in failure and stands up straight, resigning instead to slowly scoot the box to the back corner with her foot. Exhausted in physicality but never in spirit, she cheerily plops down, letting her legs dangle loosely off the back of the truck.

"I can't believe we're going to Napa tomorrow! My roommates and I have been absolutely dying to do a girls trip there. Which you're totally invited to join if we do, obvi." I smile politely at the offer, doing my best to remind myself that what Taylor lacks in self-awareness, she makes up for in genuinity. I wipe the sweat off my forehead with the back of my hand, still not quite believing that a few days of filming necessitates bringing all of this stuff. And that Taylor and I get the unique privilege to drive it seven hours north tomorrow while everyone else hops on a chartered flight.

With the way the universe has been conspiring against me lately, it shouldn't surprise me this is the year they chose Napa Valley. Of all the places they've filmed finales before—Cabo, Coronado, Santa Barbara—it just had to be Napa.

I still have the voicemail saved on my phone. I tortured myself listening to it every day this week, reminding myself of her and what we had. The pure joy in Ellie's voice as she called to tell me she booked the tickets. A honeymoon in wine country wasn't my first choice, but it was her dream. Happy wife, happy life, right? I kept joking that she was more excited for Napa than she was to marry me and she'd laugh it off with "damn straight I am!" Tomorrow, ten months and nineteen days to our scheduled arrival, I'll finally be there. Without her.

My stomach lets out a loud grumble of hunger, distinct from the kind that precedes one of my usual episodes. Not that I'd have anything to upend even if it was—it's going on two o'clock and I haven't had a thing to eat all day. Taylor and I ordered the crew lunch, but opted to skip it so we could keep powering through on packing. It's a decision I'm certainly feeling now.

Taylor talks my ear off about Napa Valley as we walk to the crew room in search of leftovers. I open the fridge door to one measly salad. "Shoot!" Taylor exclaims. "We can split it?"

"No, that's okay, you take it. I think I've got a granola bar somewhere in my bag." She takes the salad without hesitation, hardly getting to a table before she rips open the lid and dives in. I find my backpack where I ditched it in the corner this morning and hastily yank on the front pocket zipper. Much to my frustration, it snags. I bring the zipper back up and pull down more gently this time, revealing the culprit—a small white envelope corner jamming its teeth. I freeze with confusion, certain it was not there this morning. Crouched over, I twist my head slowly around to Taylor. Having devoured the salad, she's now scrolling zombie-like through videos on her phone, paying me no mind. I turn back to the envelope. Completely blank, no address. I wedge my pointer finger into the seal and very delicately slide open the top.

As I pull the card out, a black Labrador retriever puppy pleads to me with an unrealistically photoshopped frown and sympathetic eyes. "Sorry you've been feeling ruff" is printed in cartoonish blue letters across the bottom. I open it to find a similarly confusing "Get Well Soon!" message printed across the inside.

But at the bottom of the card, a decidedly different sentiment awaits. Scrawled in red pen, it causes my hands to shake and the gremlin to lurch.

... And keep your mouth shut if you want to stay that way.

Whitney: Week Eight, Thursday

It's amazing how a few short days have made me unequivocally hate this place. I pull a cigarette out of my purse and light it, taking a long drag as I lean my back against the villa's cool stucco exterior. I haven't soberly ripped a dart since high school, but this week gave me no choice but to walk into that 7-Eleven and buy a pack.

I'm sorry, Whitney. Given everything going on behind the scenes over there, I don't think it's going to work out anymore. Maybe in a few years, if things ever settle down.

Lisa Sanchez's text burns a hole in my phone. A month ago, NTV was offering me the world on a silver platter. Now they won't even answer my calls.

No one to blame but yourself.

This time it's Mom in my head when I suck in, letting the smoke infiltrate my lungs. Funny how my negative self-talk always seems to sound just like her. And, this time, she's right. Somehow, someway, I let a man ruin my life.

It all started with that stupid fucking Christmas party. Back when we were allowed to call them that. Before the pencil pushers in human resources canceled the open bar and renamed it a "holiday" party—a feeble effort at diversity and inclusion considering the network is run by a strong contingent of card-carrying WASPS.

I'd been with WBN for just under a year at that point, having finally ascended to network ranks after years of putting up with frumpy housewives on a low-budget cable makeover show called *Second Act*. *Heaven's Match* was big league—and Paul Thomas, well, he was the pinnacle. Showrunner on America's most watched reality show. We'd had our share of brief run-ins on set, but mostly I'd just admired his commanding leadership from afar. Paul Thomas was talented, he was captivating. The type of man who had a way of making everyone feel like the most important person in the room—even though we all knew that he was. I was hungry for what he had, and I was willing to do anything to get it.

His wife Kelly was at home that night, which wasn't at all out of the ordinary from what I'd experienced thus far in the entertainment industry. Lots of big wigs rolled stag. The novelty of tagging along wears off after enough late nights of incessant schmoozing—and a trophy wife only shines for so long. Anyway, I can't remember quite how our conversation started but, somewhere between martini one and four, Paul Thomas' attention had turned entirely on me. And you can bet I wasn't going to waste a second of it, reveling in the residual power that came from being even remotely near his orbit. We closed down In-N-Out Burger that night after the party, just the two of us, drunkenly laughing our asses off like stupid high school kids. But we woke up in our own beds that next morning, having shared nothing more than a container of greasy french fries.

Of course, it didn't take long for that to change. Back then, being Paul still felt like a pipe dream—so I guess I just settled for being with him instead. This whole thing is a bit ironic, really. Throughout our entire relationship, I always felt in control of the situation. I made a point of it to never let my emotions interfere with my career, to never give him the upper hand. But here I am, despite all my efforts, so damn close to achieving what I've always wanted and Paul is the very thing that's holding me back. So, yes, mother, I suppose you're right. I do have no one to blame but myself.

God, if I end up having to report to Jeremy, I'll literally off myself. Three deaths in one season, how's that for drama? Stunt like that, they might even name me showrunner posthumously. At this point, it might be my best bet to avoid plunging forever into WBN obscurity.

"Morning, Ms. Erickson." I look up from the cigarette at my side to see Detective Stephens. Why fucking not, right? He's dressed in a black hat, faded jeans and navy windbreaker. As innocent as if he's about to load the grandkids into the station wagon and bring them to a ballgame instead of fan the flames on my raging dumpster fire of a career.

"Detective Stephens, always a pleasure." I bring the cigarette to my lips and take a long drag, exhaling a cloud of smoke carelessly in his direction. I wait for him to fake cough or make a fatherly remark about secondhand smoke, but he stands his ground—not so much as flinching as the nicotine swirls around his eyes and nose. "Who's on your list to harass today?"

"No intention of harassment, Ms. Erickson," he replies, neither matching nor acknowledging my sharpness. "I'm actually here to see you."

"Wow, must be my lucky day," I scoff, kicking a stiletto up onto the wall behind me, feeling the smooth stucco beneath my heel. I've yet to confirm the identity of Detective Stephen's gossipy informant, but I've got a strong premonition that I'm pretty damn close.

"I've been told you'll all be heading offsite tomorrow. Wine country, is it? Beautiful spot for the finale. Took my wife up there for our twenty-fifth anniversary."

"Jeremy tell you we're leaving, I assume?" I say before taking another long drag.

"He did, actually. But that's neither here nor there. Given the absence of all cast and crew, I was hoping to get your permission to access the villa."

"Considering you already spoke with Jeremy, my permission seems like a moot point, Detective. Sounds like you have all the clearance you need."

"Ms. Erickson, please... I know you don't much care for me and that's fine. I've been in this business long enough to know it comes with the territory. But that feeling is not mutual. I have a great deal of respect for you and your wishes, which is why I have not pressed the issue until this point. Just know that the sooner I can get inside, the sooner I will be off your set and out of your hair." Detective Stephens speaks with a softness and understanding. It infuriates me, because I know I'm about to give him what he wants.

"Fine, fuck it. After we leave tomorrow, security will be the only ones on the premises. Under their supervision, you can go in and play Sherlock Holmes. Though I'm not sure what you think you're going to find."

Detective Stephens smiles like it's the best news ever gotten in his life, which is depressing in itself. "Just doing my due diligence. Thank you, Ms. Erickson. I can't tell you how much I appreciate it."

He can tell me how much he appreciates it by keeping his nose out of my business and my name out of his mouth.

Patrick: Week Eight, Thursday

"Holy shit."

My eyes go wide as I step through the grand entry of the Charles Diamond jewelry showroom, contemplating if I should take off my sneakers so as not to trace any middle class onto the pristine ivory carpet. If I had to describe it in one word, it'd be regal. Intricately molded white wall panels rise up to meet a vaulted ceiling adorned with four-foot crystal chandeliers. To my left, floor-to-ceiling windows flood the entire room with natural light—casting a heavenly glow on the long and narrow glass display case in the center of the room.

I find myself moving toward the case, as if my feet are being pulled by some magnetic force. I shove my hands in my pockets as I lean over so as not to be the dumbass that smudges the glass. Inside are extravagant bracelets, rings and necklaces studded with blinding diamonds and rare gemstones. All uniformly aligned, none a single degree out of line from the rest.

"Pretty insane, huh?" Isaiah steps beside me, putting a hand on my shoulder.

"I feel like I'm in a heist movie. Can you even imagine what all of this is worth?" I ask, attempting to process the sheer amount of sparkle illuminating through the case.

"More than all of our lives," Jeremy chimes in. I'd been so distracted I hadn't even noticed he was here, posted up on the side of the room running logistics with today's camera crew.

"Welcome, gentlemen!" A voice booms through the doorway at the back of the showroom and Charles Diamond emerges boisterously with it. He looks so exact to how I've seen him on TV that I almost wonder if he's a hologram. Deep navy suit over a white shirt, top button undone with no tie, receding silver crew cut, tan skin tinged with just enough orange to know it didn't come naturally from the sun. He reminds me of Reg, a personality frozen in time.

"Ah, there he is... The man, the myth, the legend!" Jeremy exclaims.

"You exalt me, dear Jeremy. I am but a mere mortal. And, today, your humble servant." Charles Diamond bows dramatically. Even in my head, I can't bring myself not to refer to him in full.

"CD, you know Isaiah. And this, of course, is Patrick." Jeremy makes the introduction and I step across the room to meet him.

"It's an absolute pleasure," Charles Diamond reaches out his hand and I shake it. His grip is strong but his palms are anything but. Baby soft, no calluses. Suppose you don't build a multi-million dollar jewelry empire by roughing up the goods.

"Alright, modus operandi here," Jeremy nods to the director. "The usual shopping montage and then we can send you guys on your way."

"That's when the real magic happens," Charles Diamond leans over and gives me an exaggerated wink before twirling flamboyantly toward the cameras. "Just say the word, Mr. DeMille, I'm ready for my close-up."

Isaiah holds open the front entry door. "Alright, Pat, from the top. Hit us with more of that childlike wonder." I eye roll at the oddity of the ask. Having to enter again, just for the cameras, pretending like I'm seeing the showroom for the first time. Isaiah ushers me out and I expect him to follow but, with an unexpected show of trust, he remains inside. The door clicks shut and the warm LA sun hits me along with the realization that, if only for a moment, I'm back in the real world. Alone. No cameras, no babysitters, no invisible fence to shock me if I stray too far. If not for the crew van parked out front, I might not know we were filming at all. My face twists into a stupid smile, pathetically amused at the free world in front of me.

The Charles Diamond store is only one in a long stretch of fancy brand-name boutiques. Louis Vuitton, Dolce & Gabbana, Versace. Leisurely shoppers leisurely file in and out of them, bags stuffed with expensive designer purchases. I step aside as a young family approaches. A tow-headed little boy, not unlike myself at that age, sits perched on his Dad's shoulders, giggling as they bob along. The mom walks beside them, pushing a stroller holding a wispy white-haired baby girl. I smile and wave at the boy as they pass. He laughs and playfully sticks his tongue out in response. Observing them feels like looking into the future. Olivia and me, five years down the road. She laughed in disbelief when I told her I wanted to have at least four kids. Apparently, she's more on the two train. Said she didn't see herself budging on that, but I'm holding out hope that I can persuade her to compromise with three. Gosh, look at me, getting ahead of myself again. One step at a time, Pat. Have to get this ring on her finger first.

I turn back to the window, messing with my hair in the reflection. Isaiah steps toward it and loops his finger impatiently at me while mouthing "let's go." I take a deep breath and pull open the door handle, doing my best to exaggerate my reaction from twenty minutes ago. Eyes wide, jaw drop, the whole shebang. Charles Diamond stretches his arms out wide to greet me as I step further inside. Cue the firm handshake and we're right into the made-for-TV song and dance. Charles Diamond is a pro, waltzing me around the room, taking out different rings and dropping every "like your love, diamonds are forever" cliché under the sun. The charade lasts about fifteen minutes, shooting the same scene from multiple angles to be sure the cameras catch the sparkle of the rings just right. Should be more than enough to stitch together the highlight reel that pays for the outrageously expensive ring Charles Diamond is about to comp us.

"Now for the real fun," Charles Diamond says suggestively with a wink as Jeremy dismisses the director and camera crew.

"If you thought those rings were impressive, wait until you see this," Isaiah nudges me as Charles Diamond leads us toward the back. We step out of the showroom into a narrow hallway, stopping outside the first door on the left. Interestingly enough, the selection of the actual engagement ring is one of the very few untelevised phases in this process. It's got this weird don't-ask-don't-tell energy about it. As if they're dealing in blood diamonds.

"Excuse me one moment, gents. Just need to grab the key." He pushes the door open and I catch a glimpse inside his office. Like a high-profile steakhouse, every surface is covered with gold-framed autographed photos of Charles Diamond posing with big-time celebrities. Madonna, Harrison Ford, Denzel Washington, Jennifer Lopez. I keep an eye on him as he removes a small key from his pocket and unlocks the top desk drawer. From the drawer, he removes yet another key. He holds it precariously as he rejoins us, shutting the office door behind him. We follow him to a door at the very end of the hallway, where he inserts the key carefully into the lock. With a solid click, it opens, revealing a dark windowless room. My eyes adjust as Charles Diamond snaps the knob on a small wall sconce, illuminating the rich mahogany wood walls in a dim gold haze. It's intimately small, only about ten feet long and eight feet wide—a striking contrast to the natural light and spaciousness of the main showroom. A large wood desk sits in the center of this room, two sturdy burgundy leather chairs tucked into either side. Along the wall behind the desk is a black metal safe sitting intimidatingly atop an ornate wood table.

"Have a seat, Patrick," Charles Diamond gestures to the chair. I look hesitantly at Isaiah, who returns a nod of encouragement. The chair is as heavy as it looks, and the thick legs slide slowly and loudly across the hardwood floor. I get halfway seated and awkwardly inch myself forward. Flushed but settled, I feel Isaiah's hands heavy on my shoulders as he massages down on them from his perch behind me.

Charles Diamond's back is to us now as he hovers above the safe. The lock dial whizzes softly and then abruptly stops, the thick metal door swinging open with a loud click. Through the crook in his arm, I spot three shelves, each holding a long rectangular jewelry box. He lingers momentarily, lording over them before removing the bottom box and shutting the safe with another resounding click. I'm painfully aware of how swiftly my heart rate is rising as he sets it down carefully on the desk in front of me. Isaiah remains unusually silent, and I find myself desperately wishing he'd make one of his stupid comments to relieve the nervous energy buzzing in my brain. Charles Diamond sits down, flips the latches open and spins the box to face me.

—

"Oh, what a wonderful afternoon it's been!" Charles Diamond's voice breaks through the fog in my brain. We're back out in the main showroom and I'm experiencing a spinning sensation similar to lying down at the end of a borderline blackout drunken night. And, honestly, I might as well be. The last two hours were a whirlwind. Carats and cuts, clarities and colors.

"Yes, thank you," I stammer. "The ring is beautiful."

"Beautiful and then some. I assure you, she will not be disappointed," he winks, still putting on a show though the cameras are long gone.

"And I'll see you next week…" Charles Diamond not-so-subtly turns to Jeremy who forces a smile as his cheeks flush red. "I've got some real good stuff picked out just for you."

"Woah, woah, woah. Next week?" Isaiah practically shouts across the showroom. If the moment had any discretion to begin with, it's certainly lost now. "Jeremy, you dog!"

Jeremy lets out an uncomfortable laugh. "No, no, nothing like that. Birthday gift… for my mom."

"Yeah, okay, like we're going to believe that," Isaiah replies through a laugh of his own. "Don't worry, my man. Your secret is safe with us."

PART FOUR

Hannah: Week Eight, Friday

5:30 a.m. arrives painfully slow. I spent all night tossing and turning over the veiled threat of the anonymous *Get Well Soon* card, terrified at the prospect of spending the next week trapped in a resort with the person who delivered it.

A myriad of faces haunt my consciousness as I stand at the bathroom sink and attempt to scrub the circles out from under my eyes. I know Detective Stephens is just trying to do his job, but it seems all his job does so far is put mine at risk.

Having gotten up restlessly to pack my bag around 2 a.m., I brush my teeth and get out the door in record time—putting me right on schedule to pick up Taylor at 6 a.m. sharp. I pull the U-Haul up to her apartment and open up a text to let her know I'm there, just now realizing I completely forgot to respond to her message last night asking if I wanted anything from Starbucks this morning. Not seconds after I hit send, Taylor comes bouncing out of the lobby, a walking stereotype pulling a lavender hard-shelled suitcase with one hand and balancing a drink carrier with two whipped-cream-topped cups in the other.

"Road trip!" Taylor squeals as she slings her backpack into the front seat and nestles the drinks into the cup holder. "I figured you were asleep by the time I texted you, so I just got two of what I usually get. Iced caramel macchiato, extra whip." I pick one up and twist it around to examine it as she loads her suitcase into the back. The sugar will probably wreck me, but my sleepless night has me desperate for whatever trace amount of caffeine this milkshake contains. It's cold through the straw as I take a long sip. I want to hate it, but it's too damn delicious.

"Isn't that so good?" Taylor says, catching me in the embarrassing act of spooning whipped cream into my mouth with the end of my straw. "I'd save so much money if I just made coffee myself but, the way I see it, if God didn't want me to treat myself, he wouldn't have put a Starbucks inside the lobby of my apartment.

"Oh! And I also made muffins!" She opens up her backpack and pulls out a plastic bag. Condensation wets the inside—still warm, fresh out of the oven. I don't even want to know how early she woke up to make them. Taylor unzips the bag and hands one to me, the scent of baked banana and cinnamon filling the front seat. "Bite-sized so they're easy to eat on the go!" I barely finish chewing the first by the time I'm asking for another.

I'm weighing our drive time against the minutes of small talk I owe Taylor in gratitude for the morning's treats when she makes the relieving suggestion that we spend the drive catching up on the latest *Heaven's Match* podcasts. While there are about fifty in existence, only two are worth their weight in followers. Both aptly named, *Heaven Sent* is run by two super fans who recap episodes in earnest while *Hell's Match*, conversely, built a cult fandom on satire and cynicism. Taylor's told me on multiple occasions that she prefers *Heaven Sent*. I haven't dared to tell her I'm partial to the latter.

Taylor takes diligent notes on her laptop as we drive along, hammering on the keys to make record of any particularly interesting segments or fan theories discussed by the podcast hosts. The topics are all over the place leading into this week's finale. Are Patrick and Olivia the real deal? Is Kya a shoo-in to be the next lead? What should fans make of Paul Thomas' departure? Does it signal the end of *Heaven's Match* as we know it? And then, of course, there are the murder conspiracies. Both of the shows have exhausted most of the Sarah O'Brien narrative by now, but it doesn't stop the gremlin from perking up at each mention.

Around hour three, my phone buzzes. I quickly snatch it from the console and turn it over cautiously to avoid Taylor's ever-wandering eyes.

The split second I see *Detective Russell Stephens,* I hit ignore.

"Ugh, I'm so sick of spam calls," I deflect Taylor's attention before it starts. Moments later, my phone buzzes again.

"Geez, persistent!" Taylor looks over from her laptop screen as I ignore it again. My stomach is really brewing now, a sickly feeling that comes and goes in waves for the next several hours as we make our way north. I do my best to discreetly combat it with intermittent breath holds as we battle traffic through the Bay Area before finally arriving in downtown Napa right around 2:30. Despite Taylor's protestations, we don't have time to stop and get out in the town itself—the resort still another half hour north in the St. Helena area. It really is beautiful, though. Picturesque Victorian architecture tucked cozily along the river. Smiling visitors moving in and out of charming little restaurants and shops. I wish Ellie was here to see it. I bet it's even better than she imagined.

"I read in *People Magazine* that Meryl Streep's niece got married at our resort!" Taylor rattles off another pointless fun fact, distracting from what would otherwise be a peaceful drive as we wind past countless vineyards, their massive green expanses rolling out for miles on the horizon.

Reaching our destination is the only thing that finally puts Taylor at a loss for words. The sprawling French-inspired Auberge de Lux Resort emerges like a beacon of luxury, nestled into the hillside as though it's as native to the landscape as the lush olive trees surrounding it. I bring the U-Haul to a stop in front of the main lobby and am suddenly very aware of the truck's every creak and rattle. As if it's announcing to the entire valley how much we don't belong here. Taylor clearly does not share the sentiment, enthusiastically hopping out of the front seat and shamelessly marveling at everything around her, wide-eyed as a five-year-old at Disney World.

A young valet approaches, but I wave him away. He doesn't

skip a beat, moving immediately on to the shimmering silver Aston Martin that just pulled in behind us. Seth steps through the lobby's tall French double doors next, a smattering of field producers and camera crew following closely at his heels. Even in a place as spectacular as this, he manages to look painfully unenthused.

"This is amazing," I address him first, an attempt at polite conversation.

"Mm," he nods his usual. "Drive was okay?" He doesn't wait to hear my answer before twisting the back latch and loudly sliding the truck door up. The crew descends upon it like a swarm of bees, tossing boxes to each other in assembly line form. Their efficiency reminds me of my place. It wouldn't have been asking much for even one of them to help Taylor and me with the load out that took hours yesterday.

Seth reaches into his pocket and hands us two key cards. The sleeve on mine reads 317. I peek over at Taylor's which says the same. Sharing a room, just another indication of our status in the *Heaven's Match* pecking order.

"Scrum is in the main level conference room in twenty minutes," Seth speaks flatly. "Go drop your stuff. We'll take care of getting the rest unloaded."

We pull our suitcases through the massive French doors into the lobby, cueing an aggressively smiling concierge to step out from behind the gold-accented front desk. "Bonjour, madames! Welcome to Auberge de Lux. We're thrilled to have you here." His French accent is thick and he is, objectively, attractive. Curly mop of black hair, thick eyebrows, trim physique evident beneath his perfectly tailored black suit. In the tall-dark-handsome trifecta, he's only missing the first—standing just a fraction taller than me, five-foot-eight if you could even give him that.

"Please, can I help you to your room?" He asks and I glance to Taylor who might as well have hearts where her eyes should be. She stares but remains silent, tongue-tied for the second time since arriving at Auberge de Lux.

"Oh, thank you, but that won't be necessary. I think we can

figure it out. Room 317?" I turn my key sleeve toward him, hoping to make our escape before Taylor loses all composure entirely.

"Yes, you and your colleagues are staying at the far end of the east wing. Out the courtyard to the left, very last building on the grounds. Third floor for 317, take a right out of the elevator and you will find it." His eyes linger on Taylor for a moment, observing her inquisitively as she fumbles with the handle of her suitcase. "My name is Gabriel. If there's anything I can do for you, please do not hesitate to ask."

"Thank you, Gabriel," I reply while Taylor bobbleheads beside me. I usher her through the back doors and she releases her breath.

"I've never seen anyone so beautiful in my entire life," she says with a gasp.

Any response I might have had escapes me as we step out of the lobby and into the courtyard. Its crowning feature, a massive sapphire blue infinity pool, stretches the length of the lawn. Surrounding the pool are luxurious cabanas, elegant outdoor dining tables, extravagant fountains and vibrant overflowing floral arrangements. Beyond it, the resort's lush vineyard rolls out as far as the eye can see. It's enough to stop both of us in our tracks.

"We better get to the room," I say following a few moments of stunned silence.

"Totally," Taylor nods, still in a stupor from the combination of Gabriel and the resort itself.

We begin our trek to the far end of the resort, taking about five minutes to reach the secluded east wing. It feels like a clear attempt to segregate our filming from the regular guests—and vice versa. Exactly as Gabriel promised, we find our room in the back corner of the third floor, opposite side of the hall from the more illustrious vineyard view suites. I turn the key and push open the door, surprised to find a room that's actually pretty normal, all things considered. Two queen beds, a mini fridge and a microwave. There's a small patio off the back, but it's a bit claustrophobic given how the resort was wedged into the hillside—foliage from the trees crowding into its already limited space. I choose the bed closest to it and throw my backpack down before collapsing next to it. I raise my watch above my face and drop my arm in exasperation. Seven minutes to spare. As Taylor pulls out her toiletries and heads for the bathroom, my phone begins to buzz. I grab it from beside me and see Detective Stephens' name once again flashing demandingly across the screen. I sit up and tiptoe out onto the patio, slowly sliding the glass door shut behind me.

"Hello?" I answer quietly.

"Hi, Hannah. Detective Stephens… I apologize for all the calls today, but I really wanted to reach you before you got to Napa." The urgency in his voice triggers an immediate shot of nausea. I don't bother to tell him he's too late. "I searched the villa today. Got in the moment the last crew van left. I was hoping I might be able to find Tammy's gun."

"Okay," I pause, forcing myself to take a deep breath in anticipation of the impending sickness.

"Either it's not here and never was… Or someone brought it with them."

Whitney: Week Eight, Friday

"What the fuck do you mean? We literally just got here." I'm staring at Kate, trying to comprehend the asinine sentence that just came out of her mouth. We're standing outside the resort conference room, the entire crew waiting for us inside. Kate's just broken the news to me that, right now, two months into this thing, six days until the finale with only one other woman left, Kya wants to go home. I've half a mind to bust down her door, put my hand to her throat and squeeze until she comes to her senses.

"Yeah... it's not ideal," Kate says, defeated. Not ideal is an understatement and she knows it. This is fucking catastrophic.

"I'll talk to her," I state, refusing to accept it. I'm sick and goddamn tired of these people thinking they've earned all this autonomy. It's a direct result of the bullshit Patrick's been pulling all season, acting like he's above the rules of this contract. Someone has to remind Kya that this isn't the way things work around here.

"I don't know, Whit. Sounds like her mind is pretty made up."

"So we private chartered her ass all the way up here just for her to tell us she wants to pack it up?" I ask, absolutely dumbfounded at the idiocy of it all.

"Apparently."

"Jesus Christ. Who else knows?"

"No one, just me."

"Not even Patrick?"

"Not even Patrick."

"Okay. Give me a few hours after scrum to figure this out. In the meantime, don't tell anyone. Not even Jeremy. The less headless chickens running around this place, the better." Kate nods with slight hesitation. She's been pretty loyal to me, but God knows where the crew's allegiances lie at this point. Everyone's got their own agenda. Kate could very well be kissing Jeremy's ass behind my back in case he gets the authority to promote her to executive producer next season, smiling through her teeth while she comes for my job.

"I'll tell you one thing," I hush my voice as Kate moves to open the conference room door. "If that little bitch thinks we're footing the bill for her return flight, she's got another thing coming."

—

Scrum concludes quickly, a single person none the wiser about the shitstorm brewing with Kya. I let the crew know I'd be unavailable for a few hours, shutting down any would-be spontaneous requests that might otherwise come my way. If Jeremy raised an eyebrow, I didn't stick around long enough to see it—heading straight from the conference room to the privacy of my suite.

Once inside, I waste no time untwisting the cap off a single-serve wine bottle, one of many included in the overflowing "Welcome WBN" basket that greeted me in the kitchenette upon my arrival. It goes down easy in a single slug. I drop the empty bottle onto the counter as the reality of the situation continues to stress into my veins. A finale with one contestant? How novel that would be. Sur-fucking-prise, America.

I pull my phone out and scroll until I reach Paul's number. My thumb threatens up and down over the "call" button for a few seconds but my resolve ultimately prevails as I flip it face down onto the counter. Fuck Paul. I untwist the cap on another mini bottle and head out to the terrace.

The resort's general manager has assured me that I, not Jeremy, have the largest suite of the entire WNB team. The terrace itself is nearly double the size of my first studio apartment in Encino—a rags-to-riches comparison that's not lost on me as I gaze out at the valley. Everything I've ever wanted is right here in front of me. The power that was mine for the taking, slipping through my fingers with every passing whisper. I down the second bottle and toss it over the ledge. Boy did Kya picked the wrong time to mess with me.

Fifteen minutes and another fun-sized wine later, I'm at the door of her suite, face-to-face with the latest addition to my hit list.

"I told Kate I didn't want to talk to anyone else..." Kya protests as I push past her into the room, not waiting for an invitation.

"Good thing I'm not anyone else." I head straight for the kitchen. Her suite has the same general layout as mine, but it's smaller, of course. By the time she catches up to me, I'm already clutching two of her mini bottles. I effortlessly spin the cap off one and toss the other in her direction.

"I'm good, thanks." She catches it without missing a beat and sets it back down on the counter.

"Suit yourself." I tip my head back, open my throat and dump another down the hatch. Kya just stands there, arms crossed defiantly, no doubt judging me with her perfect mid-twenties body and her perfect mid-twenties face and her bullshit ungrateful mid-twenties attitude.

"Have I not been good to you, Kya?" The alcohol in my brain starts to take over and I make a conscious decision not to fight it.

"It's not like that at all, Whitney," she replies, maintaining an obnoxiously self-righteous sense of calm. "I'm incredibly grateful to have had this experience, but I know how it ends. Some women might be naive enough to stick around, but I can't do it anymore. I've played second fiddle all season and I'm tired of looking like a fool."

"Second fiddle?" I scoff. "So Patrick doesn't want you, boo fucking hoo. You know who does? Every other man in America." A small burp of wine bubbles up my throat and I release it without restraint. "So, yeah, you're welcome."

"I never asked for that. I didn't come on the show wanting to be the next lead. I came here to explore a relationship with Patrick. And based on how much further along his relationship is with Olivia, that exploration has clearly run its course."

"Oh spare me the bullshit, Kya. Being the next lead is what you all want. The whole desperate lot of you. But that's beside the point. You signed a contract. You belong to us."

"I know what the contract says," Kya's tone sharpens. "But your drunken threats don't scare me, Whitney. And I highly doubt Jeremy and the network will take too kindly to hearing about them."

My feet lurch forward and I put a hand on the counter to steady myself, Kya's body doubling as my vision blurs. *Jeremy and the network.* As if it's already his fucking show.

"I think you should go now." Kya walks back to the door and holds it open. "Before you embarrass yourself further."

I cash what's left in the bottle and drop it. The cheap plastic bounces across the white tile in hollow thunks, a trail of red splattering in its wake.

Hannah: Week Eight, Friday

It's nearly midnight when Seth finally grants me a reprieve to turn in for the night. The crew may have helped us unload the U-Haul when we got here, but they conveniently disappeared once it was time to unpack and organize. To make matters worse, it was a one-woman job, with Taylor still busy with her task of categorizing every social media mention the show received over the past forty-eight hours.

I scan the key card to our room, the satisfying click of the door unlocking followed by a not-so-satisfying grumble from my stomach. The thought of what Taylor might uncover online kept the gremlin on high alert all day so, out of precaution, I didn't dare eat a single thing. It's becoming a horrible habit. And considering I was already too thin when I arrived, it's weight I can't really afford to lose.

The grumble is louder this time, more of a demand than a suggestion, my body fighting my mind for its own survival. I could order something to the room, but I don't really want to risk being awake when Taylor gets back. I take inventory of the minibar—nuts, chips, candy, booze. Peanuts seem like the most substantial option to get me through until morning. I rip open the bag and dump half of it into my mouth, prioritizing efficiency over enjoyment. I chew them into a peanut buttery paste and swallow hard before downing the other half while en route to the bathroom. I brush the remnants out of my teeth and expedite my face wash routine with a quick splash and pat of the towel. As I finish up, a text from Taylor flashes onto my phone.

*OMG. Just finished but Gabriel asked if I wanted to walk the vineyard with him. Don't wait up for me :**

Sounds good, be safe. I fire back, the handsome concierge harmless enough not to flag any legitimate concern. Quite frankly, if anyone's safety is to be worried about with Taylor, it's probably his.

Relieved to go to bed in peace, I decode the room's various switches and knobs until all the lights are turned off. I use the flashlight on my phone to navigate through the darkness to the bed, pulling back the tightly made sheets and sliding myself beneath them. They're crisp and cool after spending all day with the air conditioning on full blast. I prop my neck unnaturally onto the pillow to be able to see my phone and the nightly social media scrolling ritual begins. Photos and videos of friends, babies, dogs. I get hit with the usual twinge of guilt from watching other people's lives progress through a screen. I've all but completely detached from everyone back home. And it only makes me feel worse to admit that it's actually been kind of nice. Home in Minnesota, I couldn't go a day without a call or text from someone checking in. Spontaneous drop-ins to see how I was feeling, stocking my freezer with another casserole when I wasn't even halfway through the last one. I discovered quickly that even the most genuine intentions can drain you. It was just so constant, I couldn't escape it. How could anyone possibly expect me to move on when it was all they ever wanted to talk about? Anxious as I am to get away from what I've stumbled into here, I'm not ready to go back to that hell yet either. But then again, where else would I even go? Trouble seems to follow me everywhere.

Maybe there's no place for me.

Maybe it's better if I cease to exist entirely.

I zip past two more newborn baby photos when, suddenly, Ellie's face stops me in my tracks. I know the photo well, taken a few years back at a friend's cabin on the Fourth of July. She's wearing a red USA tank top over a royal blue bikini, arm slung loosely around Jenna—her college roommate, the one who posted the photo. I can't help but smile looking at it. She's making that damn goofy face. Eyes crossed, tongue sticking out. The one she always made when someone shoved a camera at her. But even with the absolutely idiotic expression, she's still so damn beautiful. God, I miss her. Tears well in my eyes as I scan to the caption.

Happy 30th birthday, my sweet silly angel. I miss you every day.

My stomach drops in panic as I check the date underneath. Posted eight hours ago? No, it can't be, Jenna's wrong. I click out of it frantically to check the date on my calendar app. August 26. My pulse races, heart thudding loudly in my ears. No, fuck. This can't be happening. I rush to the bathroom and barely get there in time, spewing peanuts and bile into the toilet. I stand up too quickly and the blood rushes to my head, dizzying my vision. I grab hold of the counter to steady myself before I fall over.

I search desperately for my toiletry bag beside the sink as my eyes recalibrate, tearing the zipper open as soon as I spot it. I recklessly toss its contents onto the floor—makeup, toothpaste, face wash. I find the orange vial I'm looking for and twist open the cap, pouring two white pills into my shaking hand. I hold them there momentarily, staring at them, hating the way they make me feel, the things they make me see. Most of all, hating myself for being so reliant on them. The gremlin grumbles with hunger and I raise them into my mouth, swallowing dry, feeling the two little lumps scrape their way down my throat. If I want to make it through this night, to forget what I forgot, there's no other way.

I fumble back to the bed and pull the covers all the way up to my eyes, starting the countdown from one hundred while I plead for sleep to overtake me. I reach twenty-four and a sharp noise startles me out of rhythm. I focus my ears. It's laughter, I think, coming from outside the patio door. I peel back the covers and carefully push myself out of bed—legs shaky as I step unsteadily to the glass patio door. I pause to stabilize myself on the handle before sliding it open. I squint through darkness and overgrown trees, spotting the figure of a woman three patios down. Her back is leaned against the railing, gaze facing toward the room. She laughs again, unrecognizable to me. A branch rustles in the wind behind me and I audibly gasp. She turns toward me and her eyes lock with mine.

Patrick: Week Eight, Saturday

"Sorry, can you repeat the question?"

It's my first confessional interview since we got to Napa and I'm having a hard time focusing, probably something to do with the large brown and white falcon perched above us on the ledge of the third-story terrace—peering down at me like I'm it's next meal. If I was one to put stock in these things, I would say it's a bad omen.

"I asked how you're feeling about the overnight dates," Isaiah repeats from the other side of the camera. We're filming in a quiet corner of the resort, the million-dollar view of the vineyards at my back. A view I'd much rather be enjoying than answering all these questions. And judging by Isaiah's tone, I can tell he's losing patience with my inattentiveness. It's a reminder that, in many ways, our friendship will always be contingent on the quality of the soundbites I give him.

"Oh, yeah, overnights. I'm excited, of course." I run a hand through my hair. "I'm really looking forward to spending time with the women away from the cameras... No offense." As short as Isaiah's wick is becoming with me, mine is equally if not more with the process. I mean, seriously, what a stupidly obvious question. In what world would I not be excited to spend time with Olivia and Kya without a camera shoved in my face?

"Hah, hey man, we get it. No offense taken," Isaiah replies and the camera guy nods knowingly in agreement. "But seriously, you know, overnights have historically been pretty pivotal for couples on this show… An opportunity to take things to another level both emotionally *and* physically."

My hand goes to my hair again, a defense tick against my own awkwardness. It's cooler up here than in LA, but it doesn't prevent my face from flushing and my palms from clamming up. I'm 15 years old all over again, cringing in the passenger seat of my Dad's suburban, desperately wishing he would stop our "man-to-man" conversation about the "nice young woman" cheering me on during my junior varsity baseball game. Only this time, I'm twenty-nine and the conversation is going to be publicized on national TV.

Attempting to dodge it, I let the silence linger uncomfortably. Isaiah technically didn't ask a question so, technically, there's nothing for me to answer. The way he shakes his head and raises an eyebrow at me indicates otherwise.

"Yeah, I mean, obviously that thought has crossed my mind. Connecting in, erm, uh, both ways," I reply, fumbling over each sentence.

"In both ways with both women?" Isaiah fires point blank, evidently fed up with my skirting of the issue.

"Jeez, man," I say, attempting to back him off. I glance up again at the ledge above. The falcon is still leering down, laser-focused, threateningly shifting back and forth on its claws. "I'm trying not to go into either date with expectations. I care a lot about Olivia and Kya and I'm open to wherever each night takes me. Let's just leave it at that."

Isaiah sighs at another of my non-answer answers. If only he understood that the only thing worse than a non-answer is the truth. The producers are upset enough with my antics as it is. Even I'm smart enough to know I can't admit, on camera, that I have no intention of sleeping with Kya. I can't spoil the finale by revealing to all of America that my heart, my mind and my body race only for Olivia. On the flight here, I came up with every excuse I could think of to get up from my seat just for a second of eye contact, a flash of her smile. There's not a man in America who would willingly turn down a night with Kya, but there's also not a man in America as hopelessly in love as I am with Olivia.

"You really should consider a career in politics," Isaiah says flatly as he gives the cut signal to the camera guy. "You're lucky I'm starving. Otherwise I might have kept you here for another hour."

I slap my hands upon my thighs and stand, sighing in relief to have the interrogation over and done. I look up at the ledge where the falcon still lurks, eyeing me with a tilt of its head. A dryness catches in my throat and I cough to clear it. The falcon pushes itself off at the sound—sprawling wings casting a shadow as it disappears into the sky.

The breakfast buffet at the resort is what dreams are made of. Made-to-order omelets, thick-cut bacon, cinnamon swirl french toast, towers of fresh-baked pastries. After starting the day with that confessional interview, it's taking everything in me not to wreck my maintained-for-TV body by going full Denny's Grand Slam on the situation. Begrudgingly, I settle for a scoop of scrambled egg whites, yogurt with fruit and a black coffee. As God is my witness, as soon as we're done filming, I'm getting a Big Mac.

I carry my sad little breakfast to one of the tables that overlooks the pool and vineyard. Isaiah joins soon after and I instantly salivate at the sight and smell of his plate, piled high with pancakes, eggs benedict and every kind of meat under the sun.

"You're killing me, man." I shake my head and take a sip of coffee.

"Wait until you see what I've got planned for the second course," he laughs, tortuously bringing a breakfast sausage to his mouth and snapping it with his teeth. "Oh God, and it's *maple*." I roll my eyes as I poke clumps of egg around with my fork. Isaiah takes a loud gulp of fresh-squeezed orange juice and begins to scroll through his phone.

"Oh shit," he abruptly blurts out.

"What?"

"Ah, nothing. Minor change of schedule."

"What's the change?" I ask, not buying the brush off.

"Nothing for you to worry about... You just focus on resting up. You're going to need your energy tomorrow night," he deflects again with a smug grin. "I gotta run." Isaiah stands, leaving his half-eaten breakfast on the table in front of him. Unsure how long I can resist the temptation to clean his plate, I shovel in what's left of my eggs and carry my coffee back to the suite.

I push open the door and am immediately startled to find that I'm not alone. Out the sliding glass door on the patio—waiting, watching, hunting... my frightening falcon friend.

Whitney: Week Eight, Saturday

"Large red eye—actually, make it a black." God knows I'm going to need the extra espresso to get through the rest of this fucking day.

Kya left in the dead of night. Car picked her up at 2:30 a.m. Much as I'd like to credit my pettiness for her untimely departure, it's all procedural. The guests at the resort signed an NDA upon check-in, but you can never be too careful. To further mitigate the risk, Kya will spend the next three days sequestered at a nearby hotel, waiting for the live finale to air. When the final credits roll, we'll green-light her to return to her stupid miserable life.

"Two shots, you got it. Anything else?" The young resort cafe barista asks, bright-eyed and bushy-tailed with impossibly white teeth beaming at me. The kind of teeth I'd like to punch.

"Can I get just, like, dry toast?" I ask. I've got one of those special hangovers today, the type that no amount of greasy eggs and bacon can fix. Even walking by the breakfast buffet this morning made me want to hurl.

"Absolutely! What kind of toast would you like? We've got white, sourdough, cran-"

"White's fine," I interrupt the barista's well-rehearsed gluten spiel. "Or, no, wheat. Whatever, actually. I don't care."

"Wheat it is! Are you sure you don't want any whipped butter or fresh jam? All of our preserves are grown right here on

Auberge's grounds!"

I stare back at her blankly, unsure what about my current demeanor is possibly inviting the excess of conversation. "No, just dry. Charge it to the room… Erickson, 36."

"My pleasure! I'll get that started for you right away, Ms. Erickson." She pops a slice of bread into the toaster and fires up the espresso machine. It whirrs loudly over the sound of her exhaustingly cheerful humming. "Here you are, have a splendid day!" She practically sings as she hands me my order. I manage a half smile and reluctantly make my way to one of the resort's meeting rooms.

"Mornin', Whit," Jeremy greets me when I enter, not bothering to look up from his phone. Kate and Isaiah sit beside him equally engulfed in their own devices. "How's that head feeling?"

"Never better." I pull the chair out hard enough that it clanks into the wall. It's claustrophobically small in here, a table and four chairs jammed in with a massive watercolor painting of the vineyard looming over us on the wall. I'm close enough to Jeremy to get high on his shitty cologne.

"So, last night obviously got a little dicey," Jeremy says, flipping his phone face down on the table. "We're all aware of the stress this job puts on us. The situation between Whit and Kya was unfortunate, but it easily could have happened to any of us."

My eyes roll so far into my head that I momentarily lose vision. There you have it, WBN. There's your fearless leader. Executive kitty soft paws, unable to shoot anything straight. As if I can't handle the truth.

"I checked in with Kya this morning to clear things up," he continues. "She's a little miffed, understandably, but she's assured me she won't be going public with it. She just wants to get through these next few days and be left alone." I bite the inside of my cheek to stifle my laughter. Honestly, his righteousness is comical. Jeremy Rowe—the hero we need, but not the one we deserve. Give me a fucking break.

"Well, that solves half of our problem," Isaiah sits back

defiantly, crossing his arms. "Pat deserves to know about this."

"If you knew how to handle your lead, we wouldn't be in this mess to begin with." The words escape my mouth with little regard for any hurt they might cause. I like Isaiah enough, but he's always been too lax when it comes to contestants. You can't succeed in this business and be everyone's friend. When push comes to shove, you've got to put the job first. We've been telling him to get a lid on the Olivia obsession for weeks. And, clearly, based on Kya's reaction to Patrick's lovesick puppy routine, he's been failing miserably to get the message across.

"Hey, same team here, remember?" Jeremy presses his hands down in a calming gesture. I look to Kate for backup and she averts her eyes. She's conveniently quiet even considering all the spin class vent sessions we've shared on this very topic. I'll say it again—everybody's got an agenda.

"All we can do at this point is move forward with what we've got," Jeremy continues. "I think our best plan right now is to keep Patrick excited for his date tomorrow with Olivia, which shouldn't be too difficult, all things considered. That buys us another twenty-four hours to figure out how we're going to break the news to him about Kya."

"What if we don't tell him at all?" I offer nonchalantly and take an audibly crunchy bite of room-temperature toast, molars fighting against the dry crust before it scrapes its way down my esophagus.

"Very funny," Isaiah scoffs.

"Hang on, no idea's a bad idea," Jeremy chimes in. I glare at his response as I crunch down loudly on another bite. I don't need his advocacy. Even nursing the world's most brutal hangover, I've still got better ideas than any of the hacks in this room.

"Think about it... Not once in the history of this show has a contestant ghosted the lead on finale night. With what we're seeing on the social media feeds, America already knows he's going to pick Olivia—and we all know nothing bombs ratings like predictable reality TV. Why not throw Kya's disappearance in the teaser and give people a reason to tune in anyway?"

"Hmm," Jeremy replies, rapping his fingers annoyingly along his cheek, worthlessly contemplating it in his little brain. Meanwhile, I'm Rumpelstiltskin over here spinning straw into fucking gold. "I don't hate it. What do you guys think?" He looks to Isaiah and Kate.

"I like it," Kate speaks up, finally. Better late than never.

Isaiah sits back and melodramatically blows a raspberry with his lips while throwing his hands into the air. "Whatever, not like my opinion matters here anyway."

"That's that, then. We can update the crew at tomorrow morning's scrum." Jeremy states matter-of-factly, grabbing his phone and standing up from the table. Meeting's over, I guess. He holds the door open for Kate and Isaiah as they walk out.

"She's done it again," he turns back to me with a smile and a wink. "Really great work, Whit."

"Fuck off, Jeremy."

Hannah: Week Eight, Saturday

Hi Hannah. Sorry to bug you, know you're busy. Give me a call when you're able, please. Promise it's important.

The text from Detective Stephens came hours ago and I've just now found time to sneak away to the room. Busy work is usually a welcome distraction, but I'm finding it harder and harder to escape today's particularly harrowing doom spiral. The hallucination on the balcony last night was the most vivid yet. A crystal clear vision of her—of Ellie, throwing her head back and laughing, blurring the line so severely between reality and fantasy that I woke up questioning if she actually died or if I've been living in some twisted yearlong simulation.

The room is empty as I expected. Taylor's moonlight stroll through the vineyard with Gabriel last night went well enough I suppose, considering every free moment she's got today has been spent trying to occupy his time. I sit down rigidly at the end of the bed and read Detective Stephens' text one more time.

Promise it's important.

My thumb mirrors the anxious tapping of my foot, shaking up and down over the dial button as I debate whether I'd be better off not knowing what lies on the other end of this phone call. I'm only being a little facetious when I say that more information at this point feels like it might actually kill me.

I'm about to hit delete on the message when my phone rings.

"Hannah, hi!" Detective Stephens' voice comes through before

I get a chance to say hello. "How are you?" The question is as rushed as the greeting, more habitual pleasantry than genuine concern.

"Fine, busy. Been pretty nonstop since we got here," I reply, trying to obscure the quiver in my throat.

"Yes, I imagine so," Detective Stephens says. "Listen, I apologize for the brevity. Was hoping to catch you earlier, but I actually just pulled into the parking lot at LAPD... Hannah, I'm here to ask them to reopen the investigation."

"What?" My heart immediately begins to pound. I stand and walk toward the bathroom as the gremlin clamors uncomfortably in my gut.

"I'm sorry to tell you this way, so abruptly. It's just that, for the last day or so, hard as I try, I can't reconcile that damn gun. It doesn't add up." I can tell Detective Stephens is doing his best not to alarm me, but his voice is dripping in concern. It's unsettlingly unfamiliar for a man who is usually so composed.

"Do you think they'll actually reopen it?" I shut the toilet seat and sit atop it, leaning my wobbling elbows onto my knees. "How long will that take?"

"Depends how strong they believe my case is. Could be hours, days, weeks. Impossible to say."

"Wow." The single word is all I can muster as the discomfort sprouts outward from my core, sending restless prickles into my legs and arms. I can feel my heart beating in my ears as I reach a shaky hand for my toiletry bag. I pull it onto my lap and remove the vial, ahead of schedule for today's visit with my two-faced orange friend.

"I don't think you're in any immediate danger, but I do want you to be careful." Detective Stephens pauses and takes an unmistakable deep breath, the pills settling momentarily on my tongue as I wait for him to resume. "You're the only one I've told, Hannah. If there is foul play here... the worst thing we could do is give someone time to cover it up."

———

The salt from my tears stings the dry skin of my cheeks as I lift my head up off rigid hands, coarse as the cement church steps beneath my thin black dress. A gust of wind rustles through the pines and whisks away the cardstock program I was loosely holding between my bare knees. It's bitterly cold—well, from what people have told me, at least. I haven't noticed. It's no match for my heartbreak, no match for my pain. No match for the pure hatred inside of me.

She should be here.

"Hannah?" A voice calls out. I turn back to the massive church doors. They're wide open, but no one is there.

"Hannah," the voice repeats again, closer and louder. It's familiar, but I can't quite make it out.

"Hannah." A hand gently shakes my shoulder. "Wake up, Hannah."

I will my eyes to open and Taylor's blonde hair gradually comes into focus. Awakening again with the sickly feeling that accompanies another nightmare. This time, Ellie's service. The service she didn't even get to be at, her family refusing to grant us her body, hoarding her casket for the "official" funeral being held at the Catholic Church in her hometown. In my rotation of pill-induced bad dreams, it's one of the most frequently recurring.

"And I thought my Dad was a heavy sleeper!" Taylor laughs far too loudly for the weight of my head on my neck. "It's almost 7:15, so I'm heading down! Can't believe we're finally to overnights, eek!" Taylor cheerily slings her backpack over her shoulder. She's wearing an excessive amount of makeup for 7 a.m., no doubt an effort to impress Gabriel. What I wouldn't do to trade places with her today. To move through the hours blissfully unaware of anything besides a crush on the handsome French concierge.

It takes nearly all my strength to push myself up and swing my legs around until my feet touch the floor. I focus my weight on my heels and stand, pinpointing a spot on the wall to maintain my balance as the blood rushes to my head. I steady myself enough to make it to the bathroom, where I run a washcloth under cold water and hold it tightly to my face until my nerve endings come to. From there, I'm on autopilot. Brush my teeth, pull my hair up into a messy bun, a quick wand of mascara on each eye. I throw on yesterday's black jeans with a black v-neck tee and I'm out the door with five minutes to spare.

I step into the hallway and hear the heavy twisting of the handle from a door a few rooms away. I slow my pace as Jeremy steps out from it. He doesn't seem to notice me as he casually slips the "do not disturb" sign around the handle. I linger back for a moment, waiting for the ding of the elevator and the subsequent closing of its doors. I've had very limited interaction with Jeremy and I'm not exactly in a state to add more right now.

"Psst." The sound makes me jump, heart racing as I snap my neck around in an attempt to identify the source. I see no one and shake it off in embarrassment, suspecting the pills may still be wearing off.

"Psst, hey!" I turn again and see Patrick's blonde hair jutting out from a side corridor—the stunted little hallway that holds the ice maker, vending machine and housekeeping closet. He beckons me closer with a wave of his hand before disappearing back around the corner. I step reluctantly around it. The door to the housekeeping closet is open, Patrick waiting inside. There's a nervous energy to him as he smiles and anxiously runs a hand through his hair. I'm close enough now that I can smell the sweat dampening the collar and armpits of his maroon Minnesota t-shirt.

He pulls me inside and shuts the door behind us.

Patrick: Week Eight, Sunday

Red.
Black.
Red.
Black.
Red.
Black.

My eyes shift back and forth between the two pairs of boxer briefs I'm holding out in front of my face. I would normally just grab whatever is on top of the drawer but, tonight, every little detail matters. I finally decide on black, a safer choice, and now it's onto shirts. The suite's walk-in closet is massive, just a handful of my button-down shirts and suit coats taking up a fraction of the space on the shiny gold rod. I reach for the hanger that holds the light blue waffled henley long-sleeve I wore during week two. The wardrobe department pushed to bring in an entire closet of new designer clothes for finale week, but I politely declined. I can only imagine how much they'll cringe when they see me show up again in this. Outfit repeating on TV is a cardinal sin. But, what can I say? Olivia gushed over me the first time I wore this. Said it made my eyes—and my muscles—pop. I might be an outfit repeater, but I'm an outfit repeater in love.

Only a few more hours now. I pause at the doorway between the closet and the bedroom. Seven more hours until Olivia will be here. With me. In this room, in this bed, just the two of us. Finally alone.

I didn't know it was possible for me to think about her more than I already was but, somehow, since Isaiah told me she'd be getting the first overnight date, Olivia has all but consumed me entirely. Her infectious laughter, how it brings out that elusively adorable little dimple on her right cheek—the one she didn't even realize she had until I told her. The faint freckles on her forearms, the fresh-baked cookie warmth of her smile. The way her brown eyes look almost hazel when the sunlight hits them just right. I see all of her. Everything, everywhere. Every waking moment and every sleeping dream. I had no idea someone could make me feel like this. This complete and utter free-falling, out-of-my-head love. It's a feeling I'd rather die than lose.

The bedroom looks straight out of a magazine. I've been doing my best not to touch anything after housekeeping made it immaculate this morning. It's hard not to look at the expensive oil paintings and abstract tabletop sculptures without wondering what Olivia will think when she sees the autographed Randy Moss jersey hanging in my one-bedroom apartment. The apartment that could fit inside this suite three times over.

That said, I don't imagine I'll be living there long. Olivia loves Seattle, and there isn't much anchoring me to Chicago. Maybe I'll try the Pac Northwest for a while. At least until we have kids. Little William or Gus, Harper or Ivy. By then, I'd like to be back in Minnesota, close to my family. It's pretty insane to think I found the woman I want to spend my life with and the most important people in it haven't even met her yet. Soon enough, though. And I have no doubt they'll love her just as much as I do.

I break from my daydream and get back to the task at hand, pulling a slim pair of khaki chinos out from the heavy mahogany drawer. I fold the pants neatly across a hanger and place them off to the side next to the blue henley shirt. Shoes are my easiest choice. I've got to go with my all-time favorites—

Nike low-tops, white with navy. Simple but classic. I spin them around and give a quick spit to any scuffs, wiping them away with the hem of my college t-shirt.

Satisfied with my decisions, I make my way to the corner of the closet and click open the cabinet that contains the safe. I punch in the passcode with the pad of my pointer finger. 9207. My birth year and my baseball number—inspired by Joe Mauer, my favorite hometown player. My mom still hasn't taken the poster of him off the door of my childhood bedroom. The safe beeps twice and swings open. Inside is a black cardboard box with a golden "CD" script stamped on the exterior. I remove it and pop off the top lid. The first box is just a formality, the second one is made for the close-up. It's smooth and cool in my palm—ebony, so dark it almost looks black. Charles Diamond told me they specially imported the wood from Africa with the diamonds themselves. I delicately flip the sturdy clamshell open with my thumb, rotating the gold ring so that its 3.5-carat emerald-cut diamond reflects light onto the ceiling like a disco ball.

Won't be long now.

Whitney: Week Eight, Sunday

"Should we feel bad that everyone in America is going to know about this before Patrick does?"

"Feel bad all you want. It's still going in the teaser," I reply to the nameless girl in the back of the conference room, ear to ear as I lean over the shoulder of our lead post-production producer, Chelsey. I've quite literally been breathing down the necks of her team all morning. If we're going to do this, we've got to do it right.

I keep my eyes locked on the screen as Chelsey plays the spot again. Standard thirty seconds, it opens with Patrick standing on the terrace of his suite, looking longingly out over the vineyards. It's classic b-roll footage, taken with a handful of other scenes when we first arrived at the resort. One of those stereotypical shots you know you'll inevitably use for something or another.

"Two women, one proposal," Reg voices over the next cut of Patrick meticulously comparing rings in the Charles Diamond showroom. "But if you think you know what happens next, think again..." The line cues a quickly flashing montage of tense Olivia and Kya scenes captured at various points throughout the season.

"I don't know if I can do this." We hear Olivia first, a soundbite pulled from a confessional a few weeks back.

"Everything about this is insane." Kya's voice comes next. It's a line Chelsey's team has expertly manipulated, originally spoken in the context of the zip lining group date. Cut then to a black SUV door dramatically closing and the vehicle pulling away from the resort grounds.

"It's a *Heaven's Match* finale like you've never seen before," Reg's voice returns, closing out the spot as Wednesday, 8/7 Central flashes across the screen.

"Hell. Yes. Great work team, I say let 'er rip!" Jeremy speaks from behind my right shoulder. I was so dialed in on the teaser that I hadn't even noticed him slither in.

"Whit?" Chelsey turns to me for final approval.

"Yeah, think we finally nailed it. Send it over ASAP. The sooner we start running it, the better," I instruct. With only two days until the finale, we've got to maximize every second of promo that we've got. Especially when it's as juicy as this one.

"See? Everything's coming together," Jeremy says with a smile. "You have a few minutes, Whit?"

I laugh right in his face, in slightly better spirits now that the teaser is ready to go. "No one has a few minutes, Jeremy. It's finale week."

"Touché," Jeremy responds with a chuckle of his own. "I think you're going to want to hear this, though."

"Okay, shoot," I say flatly, reacting to the serious shift of his tone.

"Ah, not here," he hesitates, nodding at the post-production team around us. "Want to walk the vineyard? I haven't had the chance to get out there yet."

"Um, sure." It's an odd time to suggest a leisurely promenade, my to-do list and suspicion growing in tandem while Jeremy talks overnight date logistics on our walk from the courtyard down to the vineyard. We reach the end of the paved path and the grounds open up into rows of trodden paths, purple-blue Cabernet Sauvignon grapes hanging down in thick bundles from tall vines that stretch above our heads. My heel sticks almost immediately in the soil and I pause to remove my shoes, better to go barefoot. Jeremy offers a supporting shoulder but I brush him off. Didn't think I'd be taking a fucking mid-morning nature hike when I put on stilettos this morning.

The small talk subsides as we advance further, immersing ourselves deep in the vines. My mind flashes to that scene in *The Shining*, you know the one. When a crazed Jack Nicholson hunts down his family in a hedge maze. The thought of it brings a smirk to my face. The two of us. Alone. No witnesses.

"You drag me all the way out here to kill me?" I ask, deflecting my own sinister impulses, becoming more and more impatient with every email notification that buzzes through the pocket of my blazer.

Jeremy slows to a stop and I turn back to face him. He sighs, conflicted. "Rosalie Foster called me this morning. She was looking for a quote on a piece the Post is running."

"A piece about the show?" I ask with distrust. No rest for the wicked Queen of Hollywood slander.

Jeremy clears his throat. "About you and Paul."

"Jesus fucking Christ," I say it as nonchalantly as I can considering the heat rising inside me, determined not to let Jeremy see me falter. "Did she say who her sources were?"

"She wouldn't tell me. I'm doing what I can do to kill it, but I might have used up all my favors with her," his reply drips in feigned sympathy. *Used up all his favors*. Isn't that fucking convenient? Exposing an affair between Paul and me would be the single greatest thing for Jeremy's career—and the final nail in the coffin on mine. No YTN, no showrunning gigs. Hell, probably no more TV industry at all. Just another woman who shamelessly slept her way to the top. I'd be lucky to be relegated to the bowels of public access.

"I'm sure you have your questions," he continues, "But I think it's best for the show if you just let me handle it. We don't need another Kya situation on our hands."

The internal struggle against my own rage grows more with every bullshit word that comes out of Jeremy's mouth. The mouth attached to that stupid fucking "everyone loves me" face. Typically able to control myself, the red haze I'm feeling now is unlike any I've experienced before. It swells down from my brain, through my chest and into my legs, turning me on my heels and carrying me away from Jeremy, a defense mechanism against my own self-destruction.

"Whit, stop," he calls out from behind me as I stride purposefully back toward the resort. "What are you going to do?"

I'm going to handle my fucking self, Jeremy.

Patrick: Week Eight, Sunday

I pick an errant thread off my pants and flick it onto the closet floor. Sizing up my own reflection in the mirror, I find myself transported back to night one. Sweating bullets in that blue suit, self-conscious about something as trivial as a floral tie, wondering how in the hell a guy like me was ever going to pull this off.

To a viewer, I'm sure fathoming everything we've been through since then is impossible. But I understand now, finally, that it all happened for a reason. That every step along the way has brought me to this very moment. About to go on my last date with Olivia, my girlfriend. Soon to be Olivia, my fiancé. And then, at last, Olivia, my wife. My kind-hearted, down-to-earth, ridiculously out of my league wife. Somebody pinch me. I'm the luckiest bastard in the world if I pull this off.

That first week crosses my mind less and less these days. There was a while when I couldn't go more than a few minutes without thinking about it, it seemed. Without thinking about *her* —about *Sarah*—about what *I* did to her. But then, gradually, the guilt began to subside. I started to believe it when people told me I couldn't take the blame for what happened. Sarah chose to come on the show. Everything that happened after was of her own volition. I've found that's about the only thing that makes it possible to live with.

I buzz the suite one last time, obsessively straightening the bouquet of roses on the kitchenette counter for the fifth time this afternoon. The set designer advocated for more. More roses, more candles, chocolate-dipped strawberries, flower petals all over the bed. But much like when wardrobe wanted to bring in an entirely new closet, I denied it all. All of that just isn't me. It isn't us.

Us. God, I love how that sounds.

I pause and put my hand on the door handle, turning back for a final check.

Tonight, all of this will be ours.

And all of Olivia will be mine.

PART FIVE

Whitney: Week Eight, Monday

Patrick Olsen's life was over at 10:47 p.m. One bullet. Straight through the heart. A loud bang followed by a bloodcurdling scream echoing down the corridor and an aggressive pounding on each and every one of our doors.

My phone toppled to the floor as I jumped from the couch and ran to the hallway, stepping out just in time to see Olivia collapse into Isaiah's arms. Her wrists and neck were bruised, still-warm blood staining her white floral dress. I was quick on Jeremy's heels as he rushed into Patrick's suite. And that's exactly where we found him—his lifeless body slumped on the bed, a thick red pool of his blood seeping through the white sheets to the mattress. A gun was strewn on the floor beside him. A gun the police just told us was registered to a one Tamara E. Berg.

It took Olivia nearly three hours to calm down enough to coherently recount what happened, all of us waiting in panicked limbo as her brain processed the fresh trauma. Everything had been going so well. Perfect really, as overnights go. They'd nauseatingly gushed over each other while sipping resort wine, giggling like a couple of teenagers as Olivia lobbed grapes into Patrick's mouth, both absolutely gobsmacked when we surprised them with a private acoustic performance by one of Nashville's up-and-coming country music stars. They held each other tight as they slow danced, overlooking the sprawling vineyard, gifting us an excess of sticky sweet shots we could use in their inevitable engagement montage. With how seamlessly everything was going, it was no surprise when Olivia instantly accepted the invitation to stay with Patrick overnight. Their excitement was boiling over as they closed the door on the cameras. The two of them, for the first time, completely alone.

Olivia described what happened next as an "eruption." Pent-up desire unleashed as they kissed their way from the door to the bedroom, hands roaming all over each other, knocking into the walls along the way. But then, abruptly, he stopped. She opened her eyes in confusion and was overwhelmed to see a collection of all her favorite things laid out on his bed. Pink Starburst, mini Snickers bars, a stuffed animal meant to look like her dog back home. Patrick walked to the nightstand and proceeded to click play on a 2000s-era CD player. Through it came the voice of Tim McGraw—her first love, as she had jokingly told Patrick many dates before. In Olivia's words, her heart "completely melted" that he had pulled together such a thoughtful surprise.

Now, this next part of her story is what really put me onto the floor. If all of that wasn't already enough, the rat bastard got down on one knee and proposed, right then and there. The *grandest* of romantic gestures. Kya, the network and his contract be damned. He explained that he wouldn't feel right spending the night with her unless she knew, one hundred percent in her heart of hearts, that she was the only one for him. In there somewhere is a very dark irony about chivalry not being dead.

Anyway, in what turned out to be a literally life-changing plot twist, she hesitated. Not because she didn't love him but, because unlike our stupid piece of shit lead, she actually read her fucking contract. He promised her no one would know. It could be their secret to reenact on finale night. But she wasn't quite sold. And the more she wavered, the more his desperation turned to anger. To the point where she finally suggested it might be best they end the night early and talk about it with clearer heads tomorrow.

And that's when he completely fucking lost it.

He yelled at her for lying to him about her feelings, for leading him on in front of millions of people. She begged and pleaded for him to calm down, told him he was really scaring her.

When she made a move to leave, he grabbed her by the wrist and dragged her toward the bed. She said it was like his eyes "went black", the man she had fallen in love with transforming into a monster before her. With Patrick's free hand, he clumsily yanked the drawer open and removed the gun. Patrick pushed Olivia to the mattress and forced his body on top of hers—all the while saying he was sorry and he loved her. The sick fuck. But God bless this girl, she fought back. Had it in her to wrestle against him until she got in the right position to knee the mother fucker hard, right in the balls. The blow debilitated him just long enough to allow her to grasp hold of the gun and turn it on him. When he grabbed for the chamber and tried to spin it back, it went off. One bullet. Straight through the heart.

Dead man aside, what my producer brain is stuck on is how the hell he pulled it all together without anyone on the crew flagging it. We're supposed to have secret-service-level surveillance on this guy. Isaiah went hand-on-bible to maintain he had zero knowledge of Patrick's intention to propose in secret. He needs to go hand-on-bible to maintain he's absolute shit at his job, also being at fault for regularly allowing Patrick to stray from the villa, running him right into the scene of Tammy's accident—and her gun.

But figuring all that out is someone else's problem now. I'm not taking the blame in the slightest. I warned them all season about this, and you better believe anyone who didn't think it was a big deal before sure will now. This is exactly the type of thing that can happen when you let these people believe they've got free will.

My phone rings for the eighth time in as many minutes. There's a half-drunk bottle of wine on the table next to me as I sit back, feet casually kicked up on the terrace railing. I could let the call go to voicemail again but, this time, I chuck my phone right over the edge.

I take a long drag on the Marlboro I bummed from a police officer, sucking the smoke into my lungs, taking in the spectacular view one last time.

Yes, Patrick Olsen's life was over at 10:47 p.m.

And as of 8:03 a.m. when the Hollywood Post released their expose on my affair with Paul, so was mine.

Hannah: Week Eight, Monday

No amount of showers can wash the disgust from my body—from my soul. The scent of vomit seems resolved to linger permanently in the back of my nose, the taste sticky in the walls of my throat. I'm curled up in the fetal position on the cold tile of the bathroom floor, door locked shut, fan on to obscure the sounds of my retching.

I'm due for questioning in a half hour and it'll be a miracle if I make it through without another episode. I'll have to tell the police all of it. That I knew Patrick before the show—mutual friends shared in a past life. That I didn't acknowledge it all season, didn't tell a soul out of fear that it would drudge up the troubled backstory I was desperate to keep under wraps. I'll have to tell them that, in spite of my best efforts, he knew all along. I'll have to tell them that I allowed him to take advantage of me because of it. When he pulled me into the storage closet and convinced me to help him sneak in some of Olivia's favorite things, a special surprise I promised I wouldn't tell anyone else on the crew about. I'll have to tell them that because I'm selfish and weak, I complied with hardly any convincing at all—afraid less of the professional consequences than what Patrick might reveal about me if I told him no. I mean, how can I possibly explain my thought process when I can't reconcile it myself? I've been absolutely out of my head since arriving here. And here was Patrick, coming to me "friend to friend" like the nice boy in class who needed help with his homework. He seemed so earnest, so unassuming. No warning signs of the psychopath that lurked underneath.

I'll have to tell the police all of it because, if I don't, they'll find out anyway. As soon as they talk to Gabriel, the concierge, who helped me bring everything in. I asked him for his discretion and he gave it. He didn't know any better, had no idea it was against show policy—but I did.

And that isn't even the worst of it. All of those conversations with Detective Stephens, the threatening card I received. I mean, how will it look when they find out everything I was already hiding? I had plenty of opportunities to come forward, to raise a flag over what was going on behind closed doors. But no, I could never do that. I had to keep everything hidden. Trapped in the shadows. Too much of a coward to create a scene, a selfish fear over what it might expose about me. If only I had the backbone to say one thing, maybe, just maybe, things would have turned out differently.

The gremlin murmurs, as if to remind me, "Stupid Hannah. Things will never be different."

After Ellie passed and I started taking the pills, I believed the gremlin was a curse, a necessary evil endured to survive long nights without her. Day by day, I was learning to live with it, to adjust to the feeling, aware that I could cut it off at any time if I had the resolve.

But now, I know that the curse doesn't just live in me.

The curse is me.

PART SIX

Olivia

The studio audience's applause tapers into the commercial break and I readjust my posture in the white leather lounge chair, carefully crossing one leg over the other so as not to flash my underwear beneath my curve-hugging navy dress. Monica Curt, Queen of daytime TV, sits opposite me. She laughs and playfully swats me on the knee, recalling a witty remark I made during the previous segment about adjusting to Los Angeles traffic.

I've gotten pretty good at this whole thing by now. The bright stage lights, the banter. It's hardly my first talk show interview —I've probably sat through upwards of forty in a year's time— but it is the first since WBN announced me as the newest *Heaven's Match* lead.

Yeah, you could say my life has definitely changed.

It really is nonstop, one appearance to the next. I quit my job as a nurse and hired an agent just to manage all the requests. My face has been plastered over TV screens and magazine racks. Primetime news, celebrity podcasts, syndicated radio shows. WBN even invited me to present an award at the Emmys— which happened just shortly after I was named one of People Magazine's *Women of the Year*. I've currently got an email in my inbox about an ongoing book deal negotiation. *Match Made in Hell*, or something clever like that. It seems everyone and anyone wants a piece of the girl at the center of the entertainment industry's biggest scandal.

I glance off stage at Jeremy, standing close by in pressed navy pants and a crisp white shirt, top button casually undone. He's flashing his million-dollar smile, charming a group of young bright-eyed production assistants. We've been through so much together, the two of us. And all of it led us here. The network firing Whitney for the affair and promoting him to sole showrunner. Me being named the most highly anticipated lead in reality television history.

Looks like we both got exactly what we wanted.

—

I hardly even knew *Heaven's Match* existed until season three. My conservative Christian parents weren't much for television as it is, much less "brain-rotting reality TV." As a result, everything I knew about the show came from school. All of the cool girls would get together every Wednesday at Sadie Starkey's house to watch it. The morning after, it was all anyone talked about. When I finally proved myself worthy of an invite, I begged my parents to let me go, citing its absolute criticality on my status as a St. John's middle schooler. Not wanting their daughter to become a social pariah, they relented. And the moment that episode started, the course of my life changed forever.

Kaitlyn Jensen was the lead that season. Your standard issue platinum blonde bombshell with questionably natural double Ds. I was as enamored by her as the male contestants were. It was absolutely fascinating to watch fourteen adult men desperately claw over one another for mere seconds of her attention. As badly as the contestants wanted her, I wanted to *be* her. Not for the romantic love story like all the other gushy girls at school, I wanted to be her for the power. The spotlight. The control. The magical ability to make a man break down and admit deeply personal feelings—the type of things the boys in my classes wouldn't be caught dead saying to a girl. Needless to say, I was hooked.

From that point forward, *Heaven's Match* became my secret obsession. One I would carry with me through high school and college, never letting on that I was anything more than a casual fan. Meanwhile, I was watching every episode, analyzing every word. I knew the date clichés and the canned lines, the villa's preferred florist and which designer boutiques women bought their dresses from. There wasn't a behind-the-scenes I hadn't watched or an exclusive interview I hadn't read. I knew it *all*.

Twenty-one is the minimum age to apply but, when that birthday hit, I resisted the urge. I was playing the long game. Statistically speaking, contestants younger than twenty-five didn't stick around past week four—and the few who did were never selected to be the next lead. So I waited... and waited... and waited. Six agonizingly long years I spent biding my time as America leaned more and more into the fandom. The rapid evolution of social media provided round-the-clock access to the lives of their favorite contestants, enabling a higher level of *Heaven's Match* mania than I ever could have dreamed. If this is how crazy they were over these amateurs, just wait until they met me.

Now, I'd done more than enough of my homework not to worry much about whether or not I'd be selected for the show. I knew exactly which boxes to check to make my application stand out. Pediatric nurse, physically fit, heartbreaking sob story about an ex-boyfriend who cheated on me. And I didn't have to lie about any of it, not even the last part. I came home early from work one afternoon and there he was, naked in bed with my roommate. It didn't break my heart though, so I suppose I did lie to the network about that. I simply deleted his number and moved out of the apartment, secretly grateful to the two of them for gifting me a traumatic backstory on a silver platter.

Two months after my twenty-seventh birthday, I received the call that my application had passed through to the next round of screening. The network paid to fly me out to Los Angeles for the weekend to meet with the casting team and my plan was officially in motion.

The first few interviews were even easier than I thought they'd be. I had the low-level casting assistants eating out of the palm of my hand. But the moment Jeremy walked into the room, everything changed.

There was chemistry between us from the very start. Jeremy wasn't like the other hacks I'd interviewed with. He was sharp. Driven. Handsome as all hell. The type of man I might actually be tempted to fall in love with if I didn't have higher sights. Not that it stopped us, though. One insinuation led to another and we ended up spending the entire weekend holed up in his apartment, divulging our deepest darkest ambitions between intense romps in the sheets. My obsession with being the lead, his to become showrunner. It was a bond I'd never experienced before. An inalienable trust built on a mutual understanding of what it's like to want something so badly you'd do anything to achieve it. And I mean, *anything*.

Together, we formulated a new plan. Phase one was to capture more eyeballs. *Heaven's Match* was surviving because of cultish diehards, but casual viewership was waning with repetitive storylines. Secret relationships back home, using love as a front to boost a business or a singing career. America was bored with all the ways contestants could be on the show for the "wrong reasons." Most concerning of all, Jeremy had intel that the show was flirting dangerously with the network's cut list. No, any old scandal wasn't going to be enough. We needed something new, something big. Something never before seen on television.

A death on set was actually Jeremy's idea. Coincidently enough, it was sparked by a story he heard about some programming honcho's niece who just so happened to be joining the show as a production assistant. Sleeping pill suicide. It was common enough. Not as likely to raise a red flag as hardcore drugs like oxycodone or fentanyl. Far less room for error than a staged hanging. Plus, all things considered, it was pretty humane. Just because we were committing a murder didn't mean we had to be monsters about it. A relaxing eternal nap. I mean, really, that's how I'd prefer to go if I had the choice.

Jeremy had already told me about Sarah at this point. He'd been involved enough with her casting interviews to know she was our best candidate. Annoyingly gorgeous, but a lone wolf type. No close friends or family, deadbeat parents who bounced her in and out of foster care. The type of girl you wouldn't be surprised to hear had a history of substance abuse. The type of girl without anyone around to claim foul play.

That week one twist? The one where Patrick was forced to pick a woman on looks alone? Jeremy's idea. He planted the seed to Whitney and waited for her ego to bring it forth to Paul as her own. God were these people predictable. From there, everything fell perfectly into place. Patrick took the bait and saved Sarah. And then the women took their bait too, immediately turning against her. It was their jealousy that gave me the opportunity to swoop in as the one person Sarah could trust. A trust that I took advantage of, letting her cry on my shoulder as we went drink for drink, shot for shot. Simple Sarah never once realized it was her vodka to my water. As the alcohol hit her bloodstream in full force, I suggested she go lie down for a bit. You know, regroup before the elimination ceremony. I planned for this part to take more convincing, but away her little drunk self went, too intoxicated to ask questions when I slipped her the pills. B12 vitamins, I said they were, a go-to hangover prevention trick. I couldn't believe how easy the whole thing was. Surely it should be more difficult to take a life.

The next morning played out just as smoothly. The villa was in a state of utter chaos, allowing Jeremy and I to seamlessly blend in amidst the widespread pandemonium. But we weren't quite in the clear yet. Phase two was contingent on our theory—our faith—that WBN would consider just about anything before pulling the show and all of its advertising revenue. Of course, our faith wasn't totally blind. When the network started grappling with its moral dilemma, Jeremy was armed and ready with the highly calculated mental health angle. Check and mate.

Tammy's hero complex steered us a bit off course. As God is my holy witness, she was never meant to be part of the plan. But, you know what they say, you can't make an omelette without cracking a few eggs. Unfortunately, Tammy was just collateral damage. Jeremy got word from Paul that she had started asking questions about Sarah, raising too much concern at the network's decision to continue filming. Let this be a lesson

—there's a price to be paid for sticking your nose in places it doesn't belong. Luckily we had a disaster preparedness plan that covered virtually every scenario, anticipating we would have little to no opportunity to conspire alone once on set. And with cameras on me at all times, it was pre-determined that Jeremy would have to both orchestrate and execute.

He refused to share much about how he did it. Swift blow to the forehead, rolled the Jeep down the hill. That's all he ever told me. Any time I pressed him for more, he became visibly uncomfortable—squeamish even. It was hard for him, I think he genuinely liked Tammy.

He happened on the gun serendipitously while he was wiping away his prints. It was on his list to acquire one eventually via the black market, but that still came with a major paper trail risk. Stumbling upon Tammy's pistol in the front seat was solid consolation for having to up the body count.

I could waste more time telling you about Detective Stephens but, quite frankly, he isn't worth my breath. Jeremy sussed out almost instantly that he wasn't a serious threat to things. All Jeremy had to do was redirect him toward the scent of the Whitney-Paul affair and the wild goose chase was on. If only he'd been an ounce as good at his job as we were at ours.

All that was left then was Patrick. My poor, sweet, gentle Patrick. As predictable as the rest of them, he fell hard and fast for the girl-next-door fantasy. You should have seen him, down on one knee with that gaudy ring in hand. I knew I had him wrapped around my finger, but a forbidden proposal? I was even better at this than I thought. I said yes instantly, taking advantage of the opportunity to grab him by the collar and pull him to his feet while kissing him hard. The ring box tumbled to the floor as I pushed him animalistically onto the bed. There wasn't a hunger to his kisses, there was a pure starvation. He was so desperate for me—for his *fiancé*—that he didn't even notice when I reached to the nightstand and pulled out the gun Jeremy had planted hours before. I kept my lips tight to his as I deftly maneuvered us, flipping him on top of me and positioning the barrel just right. Patrick immediately tensed up when he felt it, his eyes flooding with confusion at the foreign pressure of cold steel on his chest.

And then, I pulled the trigger.

—

"Knock, knock, sweetheart."

I keep my eyes tightly shut, lingering a moment longer in my daydream—the life that should have been, the fame that almost was.

The knock is followed by all the usual sounds. The heavy metal key twisting in the lock, the creak of the door, the squeaky wheels of the cart.

"I don't have all day."

I sit up and slowly open my eyes. All the usual sights, too. Same four beige walls. Same beefy crew-cut asshole wearing scrubs three sizes too small.

The bottle cap clicks and he spins the top open, pills rattling as he dumps them into a small paper cup.

"Water?" he grunts the question and hands the cup to me. I shake my head no and throw the contents into my mouth. I let the pills sit there on my tongue as I lie back, heavy eyes toward the ceiling. I shut them and listen. The squeaky wheels of the cart, the creak of the door, the heavy metal key twisting in the lock.

I swallow down hard and drift softly into sleep.

Acknowledgments

Typically, this is the part where the author would thank a deluge of editors, agents, publishing teams, managers… the list goes on and on. Maybe it's because I'm impatient or maybe it's because this book isn't that good, you won't find any of that here. But that certainly doesn't mean there aren't *plenty* of folks who deserve my appreciation, so with that…

First, thank you to my family. To Dad, Mom and Joe, who encouraged my love for storytelling from the time I could pick up a pencil. Who, even as time passed and I took a career outside of writing, never stopped telling me not only that I could—but that I should. I would not be half the writer or person I am today without your immeasurable confidence and support.

To all my proof copy readers and my Akimbo Writing In Community peers, specifically George and Ken, who were kind enough to tell me I had something here. I'd like to think I've got a strong enough resolve but, truth is, had but one of you discouraged me, I may have abandoned this crazy idea long ago.

To Al B, creative mentor and motivator, who taught me that nothing cures writer's block faster than a quiet walk through nature. I can't even begin to count all the plot holes that were filled as a result of this advice.

To Westy, for the amazing cover art and all-around hype.

You're a tremendous designer but an even better friend.

To my book club, GAFRI, and to Mal, my most diligent reader. I'd put the collective literary IQ of this group up against any professional, and the thoughtful honest feedback each of you was so willing to share is what ultimately took this book from unpublished draft to finished work.

To Moose and Winnie (yes, I'm thanking the dogs who cannot read). You bring light to every day and I can't imagine a world without you rascals in it.

And last but not least, thank you to Sadie. Over the past two years, you have put up with countless distracted conversations and silent car rides, ever patient with my inattention and incessant keyboard clacking. Through all the long hours of edits and rewrites, I have never doubted your belief that I could finish this. You are not only my home but my foundation, my best friend and my biggest fan. I could not be more lucky to share this life with you.

About the Author

Caroline Ponessa is a professional marketer and an amateur reality television enthusiast. She earned an undergraduate degree from St. Olaf College while, perhaps more impressively, amassing record penalty minutes for the women's hockey team. She currently lives in Roseville, Minnesota with her wife, Sadie, and their two golden retrievers. *Heaven's Match* is her debut novel.